# Vampire Breed
## (Kiera Hudson Series One)
## Book 4

Tim O'Rourke

ISBN:10:147836792X
ISBN-13:978-1478367925

This book is a work of fiction. The names, characters, places, and incidents are products of the writer's imagination or have been used fictitiously and are not to be construed as real. Any resemblance to persons, living or dead, actual events, locales or organisations is entirely coincidental.

**Story Editor**
Lynda O'Rourke
**Book cover designed by:**
Carles Barrios
**Copyright: Carles Barrios 2011**
Carlesbarrios.blogspot.com
**Edited by:**
Carolyn M. Pinard
carolynpinardconsults@gmail.com

*For Joseph, Thomas & Zachary*

# More books by Tim O'Rourke

Vampire Shift (Kiera Hudson Series 1) Book 1
Vampire Wake (Kiera Hudson Series 1) Book 2
Vampire Hunt (Kiera Hudson Series 1) Book 3
Vampire Breed (Kiera Hudson Series 1) Book 4
Wolf House (Kiera Hudson Series 1) Book 4.5
Vampire Hollows (Kiera Hudson Series 1) Book 5
Dead Flesh (Kiera Hudson Series 2) Book 1
Dead Night (Kiera Hudson Series 2) Book 1.5
Dead Angels (Kiera Hudson Series 2) Book 2
Dead Statues (Kiera Hudson Series 2) Book 3
Dead Seth (Kiera Hudson Series 2) Book 4
Dead Wolf (Kiera Hudson Series 2) Book 5
Dead Water (Kiera Hudson Series 2) Book 6
Witch (A Sydney Hart Novel)
Black Hill Farm (Book 1)
Black Hill Farm: Andy's Diary (Book 2)
Doorways (Doorways Trilogy Book 1)
The League of Doorways (Doorways Trilogy Book 2)
Moonlight (Moon Trilogy) Book 1
Moonbeam (Moon Trilogy) Book 2
Vampire Seeker (Samantha Carter Series) Book 1

# Chapter One

There was only silence, darkness, and pain. I eased my eyes open –
just a fraction – not too wide. There was a splinter of white light
and I shut my eyes against its glare. The pain twisted and burned
inside my skull then clawed its way down one of my legs. I wasn't
sure which one – the pain was agonising and it consumed me. The
darkness came again and took the pain away.

The grunting noise woke me. The grunts came in deep, booming
waves, causing my whole body to rattle. I forced my eyelids open
and they felt heavy. Shiny black hair brushed against my cheek and
it felt brittle and coarse. There was a smell too – not the sweet
scent of flowers but the smell of animals and sweat. I was yanked
across a rough stone floor by my ankle and a bolt of pain exploded
inside of me. It felt as if my spine were being twisted out of shape.
I cried out, my throat dry and sore. There were several more grunts
and then the blackness took me again.

My tongue felt swollen and stiff. I ran the tip over my lips and they
were cracked and sore. The need for water was overwhelming. I
opened my eyes and I could see a small silver dish sitting a few
feet away from me on the grey stone floor. Too weak to stand, I
slowly inched my way towards it. There was water in that dish. I
knew it because I could smell it and nothing had ever smelled so
good.

I dug my fingers between the gaps in the floor and dragged
myself towards it. My legs felt heavy and unmoveable. I looked
back at them and they looked fragile and bare. There was a
bandage wrapped around my right calf just below my knee. As I
crawled towards the dish, pain seeped from beneath the bandage
and scampered through my whole body with every inch I covered.

The dish was only millimetres away now and I plucked at it
with the tips of my fingers. I nearly had it – it was within my
grasp. The darkness was coming again. I could feel it.

I made a desperate lurch forward with my hand and took
hold of my prize. But in my haste, I flipped the dish over. The
water poured out and splashed across the stone floor. Tiny little

rivulets snaked away from me and I looked at them longingly. The darkness was nearly upon me again.

I feebly prodded at the upturned dish and as I did, a thin stream of water came running towards me across the filthy floor. I pressed my head flat against the ground and licked up the drops that trickled amongst the grooves and cracks. Those drops of water tasted wonderful, but there was something else – something my body craved for.

Then the blackness took me again.


My whole body felt warm. It was soothing. I looked up and a chink of sunlight was pouring through a square hole in the ceiling above me. The hole was covered with wire mesh. I looked down at my leg. The bandage was grey and filthy-looking. The pain that radiated from it had eased; instead of feeling like someone had submerged my leg into a burning furnace, it just throbbed like a steady heartbeat.

The silver dish still sat upturned and to look at it reminded me of my thirst. I hoisted myself up onto my elbows and looked around. I was in a room made of grey stone. It looked like a prison cell without any windows. Set into one of the walls was a small wooden hatch and I wondered where it led to. On the opposite side of the cell, there was a hole in the floor. From the putrid smell wafting from it, I guessed it was the toilet. In the centre of the wall which faced me was a large black, rusty-looking iron door.

*Where am I?* I wondered. *Am I still in the caves beneath the mountains or have they moved me to a new location?*

*Where was Potter? Where was Luke?*

The only thing that I could be certain of was my name – I knew I was Kiera Hudson and I was thirsty.

# Chapter Two

There was a noise coming from the other side of the rusty, black door. It sounded like somebody was moving around outside. Whoever it was sounded huge and heavy, their feet thundering into the ground, making the whole cell shake.

Then, the booming sound came again and it was similar to howling. The kind of noise that a large dog, no, a wolf would make.

I inched myself away on my elbows, my legs too weak and painful to carry me. There was a rattling and clanking sound as keys were turned in the lock. The door slowly swung open and Phillips came striding in. He looked different in his Vampyrus form.

Phillips stood in the doorway, huge and dominant. He was stripped to the waist, and his torso was ripped with muscle which was covered in fine, silver hair. He stared at me with his dark eyes and puckered his lower lip into a grimace. Then, without warning, he threw his arms into the air and let out a terrifying roar. The sound was deafening and I flinched backwards, sending a bolt of pain up my back and down through my bandaged leg. Brandishing a set of yellow dagger-shaped teeth at me, he slammed his claws together. My cell became filled with a deafening *boom-boom-boom*, and I stared at his giant black wings as he flapped them together. I'd never seen Phillips in his true Vampyrus form before, and he looked even more intimidating than ever. The last time I could remember seeing him, was when he had ripped Murphy's heart from his chest and then set about Luke on the floor of my cell.

I scuttled backwards as fast I could, pressing myself against the far wall. Seeing this, Phillips lowered his arms and sauntered towards me. As a Vampyrus, Phillips looked primitive and savage - like an animal. Covering my head with my hands, I turned away. I knew what Phillips had been capable of in human form - but as a Vampyrus, I knew that anything could be possible. Although I couldn't see him – I dare not look at him – I knew he was right on top of me. The sound of his breathing was deep and menacing and I could feel his breath, hot against my flesh.

6

"What do you want?" I whispered without looking at him.

Suddenly, he grabbed hold of my bandaged leg and yanked me towards him. Although I hadn't drunk anything in God knows how long, I felt my bladder begin to sting as if I desperately needed to pee. Peeking through my fingers at him, I could see that he was now studying my damaged leg. He prodded at the bandage with a hook-shaped finger. Pain exploded in my calf like a firecracker going off. The pain rushed through my veins, and I feared that I was going to lose consciousness again.

*Don't you dare black out!* I screamed inside. *Go to sleep now and you will be defenceless – Phillips' play thing!*

But I was just fooling myself. I knew deep down that awake or asleep he could snap me in half like a twig if he wanted to.

He ripped the bandage free from my leg and I let out an agonising scream. Looking at me, he simply grunted in response to my obvious pain, and turned his back on me. Gripping the soiled bandage in his hand, he ambled back towards the cell door. I pulled my leg against my chest as I rocked back and forth in pain. Tears streamed from my eyes and gathered at the corners of my lips. I poked my aching tongue from my mouth and licked them away.

I looked up and could see him watching me from the doorway.

"I'm thirsty," I whispered, my voice sounding broken and raw.

"Thirsty for what?" he asked, and I could see a smile tugging at the corner of his mouth.

"You know what," I snapped, my throat feeling as if I'd swallowed broken glass.

"Tell me."

"I can't," I whispered, bowing my head in shame.

"There's no shame in wanting what you need," Phillips almost seemed to gloat.

With my body aching with cravings, I screwed my hands into fists and said, "I want blood!"

Looking at me, Phillips seemed to smile as he said, "I'll see what I can do." Then slamming the door behind him, he left me alone in my cell.

# Chapter Three

I pulled myself up onto my elbows and peered down at my leg. There was a deep cut running from my shin to my knee. Although it looked as if it had begun to heal, it didn't look good. A long, black crusty scab had formed over some of the cut, but other parts still looked open and wet. It made me feel sick. It wasn't just how it looked - it was the odour – it smelled *bad*. I desperately fought to remember how it had happened, but I had no real memories of anything after that night I had been taken kicking and screaming from my cell hidden beneath the mountains. But how long ago that had been, I didn't know. My back hurt, too. I didn't want to think about that because when I did my mind was full of the memories of Kayla telling me how Doc Ravenwood had cut those little black bones from her back.

So instead, I looked down at my hands and inspected them. They were covered in dirt, and my fingernails were black. They reminded me of Luke as he had clawed at the cave floor beneath the mountains when Phillips and Sparky had beaten him.

"Whatever had happened to Luke?" I wondered aloud as broken images and memories came flooding back to me. I hadn't seen him since Phillips and Sparky had…but my mother had been there too.

*And what about Potter? Had he escaped?* I prayed that he had. Snapshot images of our last stolen moments together swept across the front of my mind and I pushed them away. Not because I regretted what had happened between us, but it was just too painful to remember them.

Suddenly the hatch in the wall – the one I'd noticed earlier – was forced open. Without thinking, I scuttled backwards again and pressed myself against the wall, wincing at the bolt of pain that flashed up my back. I watched as a bony hand with long misshapen fingers shoved a bowl of food and a fresh dish of water into my cell. With an ear piercing screech, the metal hatch was slammed shut.

With my leg trailing painfully behind me, I crawled over to the food and water. Without even looking at the food, I raised the dish to my mouth and gulped down the water. It was cold and crisp and it tingled in my mouth and down the length of my dry throat. I drank so hard and fast that some of the water oozed from the corners of my mouth and splattered the grubby looking hospital gown I was wearing.

*Hospital gown?* I briefly wondered, but the water was too precious to waste. So turning my thoughts back to that, I slowly pulled the dish from my mouth and placed it back on the floor. I had no idea how long it might be before I had water again, so I decided to drink it sparingly – just small sips when I could no longer stand the thirst.

But it wasn't water that would cure the real thirst - the *thirst* inside of me that made my stomach cramp with pangs of hunger and made my skin burn hot as if I had a fever. It was what lay in the second dish that would do that. I turned towards it and stared at the large slab of meat. It hadn't been cooked. It was raw and blood oozed from it forming a little red lake in the dish. Not able to resist it, my stomach flipping with excitement, I began to wolf the food down in large, succulent handfuls. Tearing it apart with my fingers, I stuffed handfuls of the pink-red meat into my mouth. At first my stomach began to tighten but then welcomed it. Blood streamed from the meat and ran off my chin, splashing the floor of my cell. I ran my tongue across my lips, then sucked the blood from my fingers.

Once my initial hunger – *craving* – had been dealt with, I began to break off smaller pieces and pop them between my splintered lips, savouring every mouthful as if it were some expensive delicacy. There was an overwhelming desire to finish it all at once, to lick the bowl clean of the 'red stuff' as Potter liked to call it, but just like I had with the water, I left enough of the meat to last me until the cravings became unbearable again – whenever that might be.

I pushed the leftovers to the edge of my cell and lay down next to the dish. I wanted to stay close to it, just in case Phillips came back and took it from me. If I did hear those keys in the lock again, I would ram as much of what was left of the bloodied meat and water down me. So curling up on my side next to the two dishes, I lay looking at them, as if protecting them like a junkie protecting the last of their stash.

With my thirst and hunger now at bay, I already felt stronger

and more comfortable. With my eyes open, I lay still and silent –
listening intently for the sound of Phillips' return. I waited and
waited but he never came. As I lay on the stone cold floor, I caught
my reflection in the shiny silver dish. I peered at myself, and like
my hands, my face was covered in dirt and grime. My black hair
was matted together in lumps and sat limply around my shoulders.
Deep shadows hung under my hazel eyes and I was scared to see
that I was starting to look older than my twenty years.

   *What has happened to me?* I wondered, as I closed my eyes
against the reflection. As the day outside grew old, the sunlight
which had spilled in through the square hole finally faded. It was
gradually replaced with darkness. Without even being aware of it,
my own darkness came again and I fell into a deep and troubled
sleep. This was the start of my nightmares.

# Chapter Four

*I could hear screaming. It wasn't the sound of someone in pain – it was fear. The screaming came again in long, terrified bursts. I was in bed and the sounds had woken me. More screaming followed and I listened to their agonising groans. Throwing the bedclothes to one side, I stood up and crossed the darkened room. There wasn't any carpet, just hard, cold sterile tiles.*

*The screaming came again and it was coming from somewhere nearby. I tried to pull open the door but it was locked.*

*There was a small, round window in the door and I pressed my face against it and peered through the glass.*

*More screaming.*

*Whatever lay outside my room was shrouded in darkness and I couldn't see anything, I could only hear the sound of running feet – lots of running feet as they dashed up and down on the other side of the door.*

*Screaming! More Screaming!*

*I twisted the door handle again, but it was locked tight.*

*"What's happening?" I called out.*

*My question was met only by the sound of those feet dashing back and forth.*

*I peered through the round window again, my eyes flickering from left to right. Then suddenly, a face appeared at the window and I recoiled violently, staggering backwards and falling to the floor.*

*A young male pressed his face against the window and stared in at me. His hair looked wet and was plastered in black streaks to his brow. His face glistened with sweat and I could see the wispy tails of steam coiling up from his skin as if he were burning alive with a fever. His face was contorted with pain.*

*The sound of running came again.*

*"Kiera!" the male screamed as he looked in at me lying on the floor. "Help me!" he begged, banging weakly against the window with a set of bony fingers. "We have to get out of here, Kiera!"*

*As he looked into my face, my heart began to race in my chest as I recognised who it was staring back at me.*

*"Isidor!" I screeched.*

*But he was grabbed roughly away by someone or something on the other side of the door and was gone.*

*I clambered to my feet and rushed back to the door. Again I pressed my face against the glass and peered out into the darkness.*

*Someone appeared on the other side of the glass and met my stare with a set of cold, black eyes.*

*"I want to see my friend Isidor!" I shouted, banging my fists against the glass.*

*"Get back from the window!" the face ordered. "Go back to bed, Kiera Hudson!"*

*I stepped away from the door and made my way back to my bed – all the while, that face glaring at me from beyond the glass.*

*All of a sudden I felt incredibly thirsty – my throat felt dry. I desperately needed water.*

*The face at the window continued to watch me.*

*Any thoughts of Isidor faded and I just wanted to tell the face how thirsty I was and that I only wanted a cup of water, but no words would pass over my cracked, blistered tongue.*

*"Go back to bed!" the face screamed.*

*Pulling the blankets over my head I closed my eyes.*

*I forced my fingers between my lips and sucked them, hoping that this would moisten the inside of my mouth. But it wasn't water I wanted, it was something else - warm and sticky that would not only quench my thirst, but sedate my hunger too. It was the red stuff I wanted. So with my fingers in my mouth, I began to chew. Slowly at first, just enough to draw some...*

# Chapter Five

…blood on my tongue and it tasted coppery. I woke suddenly and pulled my fingers from my mouth. The tip of my right forefinger was bleeding from around the edge of the nail. Sucking the blood away, I felt a woozy feeling wash over me, like I'd had too many glasses of wine.

My cell was cool and dark and a beam of blue moonlight shone through the square hole above me. Just like my dream, my throat was dry and sore again and my leg was throbbing, too. I picked up the dish with the water in it. Trembling, I brought it up to my mouth and took a sip.

It was then that I became aware of something or someone moving in the far corner of my cell.

"Who's there?" I croaked.

Silence.

Staring through the darkness, I watched the shape move along the far wall. Whatever it was, it was huge. Carefully placing the dish back on the floor, I shuffled away from the shape.

"What do you want?" I mumbled.

As if in response to my question, the shape made a woofing sound. The noise was deep and throaty and it made me shudder in fear.

It then began to move out of the shadows and come slowly towards me. I pressed myself against the rough stone wall, whining at the stabbing pain in my back and trying to make myself as small as possible.

It moved into the centre of the cell and stepped into the moonlight. It looked at me, its eyes sharp and clear. A huge, pink tongue snaked from its gaping jaws as it licked its own face.

I felt both petrified and in awe at the same time. Although it looked fearsome and deadly – the wolf now standing before me was magnificent. The moonlight shimmered off its fur and glittered in its piercing eyes. But the wolf just stood and stared at me. My heart thumped in my chest and I began to shake uncontrollably as I remembered now that I had seen such wolves before. They had been called the Lycanthrope - a group of serial killers dammed by God to walk the Earth half human/half wolf. Seth! *Jack Seth!* Was he here, too? No, he had escaped the caves and I closed my eyes as I saw Potter racing away from me up a long tunnel - screaming back over his shoulder that he would return for me. But just like Luke, where was Potter now? Why hadn't he come for me?

"Are you cold?" the wolf suddenly asked.

I sat feeling numb, too scared and shocked to reply.

The wolf stepped forward, its paws whispering against the stone floor.

"Are you cold?" the wolf asked me again.

On hearing it speak to me for the second time, I placed my hands over my ears and turned away.

"Why won't you answer me?" The wolf pressed.

"Because you're not really talking to me! I'm imagining it and if I answer you then that means I'm talking to a werewolf – a Lycanthrope – and that would mean the memories that I'm having are all true!" I shouted.

I heard the soft patter of its paws as it closed the gap between us. The wolf was so close to me now that I could smell and feel its breath against my cheek. Its breath smelled of raw meat – just like the meat I had eaten earlier. I didn't want to think about that, not because it made me feel like an animal, but because if I thought about it, I would want more of it.

"But you can *hear* me, right?" the wolf whispered in my ear.

"Okay I can hear you – but you're not really here - I'm imagining you!" I groaned.

Then, I felt something rough but wet run up the side of my face. I quickly turned to see the wolf slipping its pink, fleshy tongue back into its mouth.

"Imagine that, did you?" the wolf teased.

I wiped its spit from my face in disgust.

"Well?" the wolf asked me.

"Well what?" I whispered, reluctantly resigning myself to the possibility that the wolf was really there and *talking* to me.

"Are you cold?" the wolf asked again.

"No."

"Then why are you shaking?"

"Because I'm scared," I said softly.

"Scared of what?"

"Of you!" I told him.

The wolf tilted its head to one side as if genuinely puzzled. "Why are you scared of me?"

"Because you're a Lycanthrope," I said. "A werewolf - a *serial killer*."

"But why would I want to hurt you?"

"Because that's what werewolves do," I said. "I've seen it with my own eyes - I'm starting to remember it." And I was remembering. I could see how the Lycanthrope had deceived my friends and me, leading us into a trap beneath the caves that were hidden behind the Fountain of Souls. "You're not to be trusted." I hissed.

The wolf made a woofing noise as if laughing at me. "If you are worried that I might eat you, then don't."

I dared to meet the wolf's stare and said, confused, "Why not? That's what you do, isn't it?"

"I only eat humans," he purred, "You're only half human - so you don't really count. You taste different."

"How would you know?" I asked.

He glanced down at the wound on my leg, and with a swish of his gigantic tail, he walked away and back into the shadows. I heard the sound of the cell door wail on its hinges as it was pushed open. For a moment there was silence, and then I heard the wolf speak again from the darkness.

"By the way," he said, "I'm Nik. It was good to have met you."

"Where am I?" I asked.

There was no reply, just the sound of the cell door closing on its rusty hinges behind him.

Curling up small, I nestled my head in the crook of my elbow. I closed my eyes and concentrated on the throbbing in my leg and wondered if it had been caused by Nik biting me. But I couldn't remember if he had. The pain in my leg had a rhythm to it - like a heartbeat. *Boom-Boom-Boom* I timed my breathing with the throbbing and then felt myself begin to drift off to sleep. As I did, I wished more than anything that I had my iPod with me so that I could fall asleep listening to The Calling sing *Where ever you will go,* instead of the pain beating in my leg. Humming the tune softly, I drifted...

15

# Chapter Six

*"...out!" someone screeched.*

*I was standing in the middle of my room – the one with the bed and cold, sterile floor. Ignoring the screams, I continued to stand rigid - refusing and unable to move - staring at the little round window in my door.*

*"Please let me out of here!" the voice screamed again.*

*Just like Isidor's voice had, these screams came in thin, shrill cries.*

*"You've got to let me out..." the voice screamed once more, but the screams were cut short – silenced – as if someone had placed their hand over the person's mouth.*

*Now they were quiet.*

*I inched my way back towards the window and dared to peek out. This time there was light and I was peering down a long, white corridor. There were doors which were identical to mine at intervals down the length of each side.*

*Two men dressed in surgical scrubs and masks were struggling with a girl, and I guessed it had been she who had been screaming. The girl was dressed in a white hospital gown.*

*She struggled with them, her arms and legs pin-wheeling as they tried to restrain her. Then suddenly my view of the girl was blocked by a face at my window.*

*Throwing my hands to my face, I screamed and stumbled backwards from the sudden apparition. The lower half of the face was covered with a blue surgical mask, but there was something about the eyes that peered at me from over the top of it. They seemed familiar.*

*"Get back from the door," he said softly. "I promise no harm will come to you."*

*Stepping away from the door, I stole one last glimpse over his shoulder and I could see the girl was still struggling with the men in the surgical scrubs.*

*The man pushed the door open and came inside followed by two others, one female, the other male. All of them wore surgical face masks and long, white lab coats.*

*"What do you want?" I asked, edging away and back towards*

my bed. "Keep away from me!"

"Just calm down," the female said.

"I am calm, I just want to know what's going on here!" I demanded.

Without answering me, the female produced a syringe from behind her back.

I looked at the needle and then at the covered face which looked vaguely familiar.

"You look tired, Kiera, we've got something here that will help you sleep," the familiar-looking man said.

"I'm not tired!" I barked, screwing my fists together as if preparing for a fight.

They came towards me, the female holding the syringe above her head. The second male lunged at me and pushed me onto the bed, taking hold of my wrists.

I kicked out with my feet striking the approaching female in the stomach. She made a burping kind of sound as I knocked the wind from her. The syringe flew from her hand and somersaulted through the air. She spun around and chased after the syringe as it skidded away across the tiled floor.

"Goddammit!" she shouted. "Keep her still!"

Then, both masked males were pinning me down. The male who seemed familiar took hold of my arm and yanked up my sleeve, revealing veins which pulsated green and purple beneath my skin.

The female came back towards the bed with the syringe. When she was only inches from me, she looked at the male who held out my arm and said, "Keep her still, Doctor Hunt!"

Hearing the name Hunt, I glanced up at the masked face, but as I did, I felt a sharp scratch in the crook of my elbow. Looking down, I watched the female sink the needle into my flesh. Immediately, I began to relax and loosen, my eyelids becoming heavy and wanting to close.

Doctor Hunt gently laid my head onto my pillow and stepped away, where he stood looking down at me.

All I wanted to do was close my eyes, but I fought the urge to do so.

I stared past him to the corridor. The girl who'd been struggling with the men wasn't fighting anymore. She lay on her

17

*back – face gleaming with sweat. Her eyes were open and staring at me, but they looked dazed and sleepy and I knew that they had injected her, just like they had me.*

*"Just let yourself sleep, Kiera," Doctor Hunt hushed.*

*I stole one last look back at the girl's face and my heart almost slowed to a stop as I realised that it was Kayla.*

*Unable to fight it any longer, my eyes closed, and before slipping into unconsciousness, I heard a scratching sound – like metal being scrapped across stone and as I...*

# Chapter Seven

...opened my eyes, I was startled to see that huge white paw snaking through the open hatch and dragging the remains of my food and water away.

"No!" I shouted, shaking the sleepiness from my head. "That's my food and I haven't finished with it yet!"

I lurched forward, but with my leg not yet fully healed, I fell and landed in a heap on the floor next to the hatch, which had now been hurriedly closed.

"Give that back! You can't treat me like this!" I yelled. "I'm not an animal!" but all I could really think about was the loss of that red, bleeding meat. The thought of it being taken away from me filled me with panic.

The hatch was forcibly thrown open again and that big white paw shoved two more bowls of fresh food and water into my cell. Once again the food bowl was full of fresh flesh - *meat*. I waited for the paw to disappear and for the hatch to close, and then I took the bowls to the opposite corner of the room and began to eat.

I was so engrossed in ramming chunks of the raw meat into my mouth, that I hadn't been aware of the heavy footfalls outside my cell door. A set of keys jangled in the lock, and I looked up. The door was flung open and Phillips came striding in.

He eyed me with an air of superiority, and then sauntered forwards, his arms swinging loosely by his sides. He stopped only inches from me and I cradled the bowl nervously in my lap, fearing that he might snatch it from me. He glanced back at the doorway and I followed his gaze. On seeing the wolf standing there looking at me, I dropped the bowl from my hands and it clattered onto the stone floor. The wolf trotted towards me and I could see that its coat was a light grey colour with white flecks that made it look as if it were covered in a fine layer of snow. Its muzzle was black and its head was attached to a long, muscular neck.

The wolf stopped beside Phillips and sniffed the air around me.

"Hello, Kiera," the wolf said, releasing a hysterical little laugh that sounded almost human. Hearing that laugh reminded me of the nervous laugh my friend Sparky once had. I looked into the wolf's eyes as it stood on its hind legs and began to twist out of shape. It lurched forward as if in pain, grabbing its stomach and snapping its huge head from side to side. And then it almost seemed to shrink before my eyes. Its arms and legs grew shorter and its snout receded back into its face. The wolf's skin appeared to blister and stretch as its hair began to shed like a moulting dog, revealing human-looking flesh beneath. With the last of the fur falling away, Sparky stood and looked down at me. Just like I'd always remembered him, the skin on his face was flushed with angry-looking spots, his glasses sat skew-wiff on the bridge of his nose and his hair was sleeked back and greasy.

"Where are my friends?" I snapped at him.

Ignoring my question, Phillips grunted and then said, "Show me the leg."

I just sat there. Before I'd the chance to comply, Phillips impatiently grabbed hold of my right leg and pulled it towards him. I flew backwards and smacked my head against the wall behind me.

"Ow! That hurt!" I shouted.

"Silence!" Phillips warned, meeting me with his hard, red stare.

Sparky grinned and loomed over my leg.

As if I wasn't there at all, Phillips said to Sparky, "What do you think? Is the infection clearing up?"

Sparky glanced at me, then turned his attention to the cut that ran down my leg. Dropping to his knees, he jerked his head forward and rubbed his nose into the wound. I cried out in pain and disgust, not believing what I was seeing. He then ran his tongue down the length of the gash and it felt as if it was being cleaned with sandpaper.

"Get off me, you animal!" I roared and kicked him away.

Licking his lips, he looked away, seeming to savour the taste of my leg. "Mmm, I'm not too sure. Maybe we should get Doctor -" Sparky started.

"No! Not him!" Phillips growled. "Lame is no good to me. I need her to be healthy!"

I looked at the both of them as they stood and discussed me.

"Like I was saying," Sparky said, "We should get her to the doc..."

"I don't know if I can trust him," Phillips said.

"But if the infection doesn't clear up, then -" Sparky said.

"Then, what?" I asked, cutting over him.

"Then you will be put down," Phillips barked.

"What do you mean, *put down*?" I asked, but I knew exactly what the Vampyrus meant.

"Destroyed," Phillips replied. "Got rid of, killed…"

"You can't just destroy me because I've got an infected leg!" I protested.

"You're no good to us in this condition," Phillips insisted, as he took hold of my leg again and yanked it from side to side.

"Well it won't bloody get better if you keep prodding and licking it every five minutes!" I snapped.

"Just as feisty as ever," Sparky grinned. "Lame or not, she still has that fighting spirit!"

Phillips grunted thoughtfully again and eyed me carefully as his wings flapped behind him. Then, without warning, he let go of my leg and slammed it into the floor. I shrieked in pain and fought the urge to puke as Sparky yelped in excitement.

"We'll come back in a day or so and I'll make my decision then," Phillips said. Turning away, he headed back towards the door. Sparky grinned at me again then went after Phillips.

"What do you want from me?" I cried out in frustration and anger.

At the door, they both turned to face me.

"You'll find out all in good time," Phillips grunted as his turned-up snout twitched. "Just pray that leg of yours starts to get better."

Sparky looked at my leg then back at me and said, "You're useless to us with an infection and the only way of killing the infection will be by killing you." He then licked his lips slowly and purposefully.

Slamming the cell door closed behind them, they left me alone again in my cell. I guessed that Sparky had once more changed back into a wolf as I sat and listened to the sound of his howling echoing off the stone walls outside. Throwing my hands over my ears, I fought back the tears that burned in the corners of my eyes.

# Chapter Eight

I sat like a statue until the day grew dark outside. My leg still hurt and I continued to wonder where I was and what the Vampyrus and Lycanthrope had planned for me. What would be the point in killing me? Didn't they need me? Wasn't the whole point of this to extract my DNA somehow – for them to find a way of breeding more like me – more like Kayla and Isidor?

And then as if a bright light had been switched on inside my brain, I could see the girl in the room at the monastery – the one who looked like Kayla – the one Isidor had killed. But there had been something wrong with her. The girl in the room hadn't bred properly – there was something missing. Perhaps my DNA was the missing key? But they had me now – they could extract as much as they wanted. In my mind's eye, I could see the unfinished email that I'd read on the computer at the monastery. It had said something about me being delivered dead or alive. But delivered to who, and where?

To think of those things made me think of my friends - Luke and Potter. *Where was Luke now? Was he still alive? And why hadn't Potter come for me? Was he dead too?*

The only way to know for sure would be to get out of the cell and find out for myself.

*But how?*

I looked around my cell in the gloom of the dying light which spilt in through the square hole above me. Somewhere inside me, I knew that I used to be good at seeing things - like really *seeing* things, so I should be able to *see* a way out of my cell. Sitting back against the wall and taking a deep breath, I saw there were only three exits available to me.

Firstly, there was the most obvious – the cell door, but that was always locked. Secondly, there was the hatch that my food and water was pushed through – but the big white paw lived on the other side of it. And finally there was the square hole in the ceiling, but that was covered with wire mesh and well out of reach.

I sat and looked up at it and tried to work out if it were big enough for me to fit through. It was hard to tell from where I was sitting on the floor. It seemed so far away. But even if I could fit through it, there was all that wire mesh that would need to be removed, and I had no cutting tools, nor could I reach it. Even if I could, what would I find on the other side?

My mind see-sawed with a million questions and doubts. The whole escape idea seemed impossible – but what other options did I have? Phillips and Sparky would be back in a few days and I feared that if my leg were not healed, I was going to be in serious trouble. But then again – even if my leg did heal, what was it they had planned for me?

However impossible my escape seemed – I had to try something – I had to get out of my cell.

But if I left my cell – escaped from wherever it was they kept me, what would I do about the…the blood? How would I get more? To think of it again made me want it. So picking up the bowl, I closed my eyes, and put some of the flesh inside my mouth.


It was dark when the cell door creaked open and Nik came trotting in. He stood in the wedge of moonlight that illuminated the middle of the cell, and looked at me.

"I've brought you something," he purred and then quickly turned away and disappeared back into the shadows by the door.

I could hear a scraping sound as he dragged something into my cell. Nik came walking slowly backwards towards me, pulling a chair between his wide jaws. He stepped into the pool of moonlight and let go. The chair tipped over onto its side and the sound of it hitting the stone floor echoed off the walls like cannon fire.

"I thought you might like to sit on this, instead of being on the floor all of the time."

I was momentarily touched by his kindness but then wondered if it was not some sort of a trick.

"Why?" I asked.

"It will be more comfortable," he simply added.

Sensing my unease, Nik backed away from the chair.

I got up slowly and hobbled over to the middle of the room. I righted the chair and sat down on it. The chair wasn't particularly comfortable with four straight aluminium legs, a green plastic seat and cushioned back – but Nik was right, it beat sitting on that hard stone floor.

I looked at him, as he waited on the outskirts of the moonlight.

"Thank you," I said.

There was an uneasy silence between us, as I sat on the cheap plastic chair and he stared at me. I eventually broke the silence.

"You're Lycanthrope, right? A werewolf?"

"Yes," he said, sounding a little confused.

"So why did you struggle in here with that chair between your jaws when you could've simply done it in the form of a man?"

"I've been captured," he said.

"So you're a prisoner like me?" I asked him, shocked at the thought that perhaps there were Lycanthrope imprisoned here.

"Not that kind of *captured*," he started to explain. "I've been captured in the form of a wolf, like frozen – stuck like this."

"How come?" I asked, confused. "If I remember rightly – and to be honest I could be wrong, my memory seems a little fried at the moment - you can change form at will."

"Not me," Nik said, dropping to the floor by my feet and resting his giant head on his paws. "My father is punishing me and until I make amends – I'm stuck as the big-bad-wolf."

"What did you do that was so bad?" I asked him.

"It doesn't matter now," he barked, his tail snaking back and forth across the ground. He licked one of his massive paws and then rubbed it softly over his face. Knowing that he didn't want to talk about what it was he had done to be so cruelly punished, I changed the subject asking, "How did I come to be in this cell?"

"You were brought here with the others," Nik replied, as he licked his paw again and started to wash his huge ears.

"Others?"

"A boy and a girl," Nik said, looking at me from the floor.

"Isidor and Kayla!" I breathed, my heart starting to thump with excitement in my chest. "They're here, you said?"

"Yes," Nik woofed.

"You've got to let me see them!" I told him, getting up from my chair.

"Impossible," Nik said and licked his long black snout.

24

"Why?" I pushed. "You have to let me see them."

"I can't do that," he said.

"Why not?"

"If I were caught in here with you, I'd be...well, I've been punished enough don't you think?" he said, flicking his tail from side to side.

"Are they okay?" I asked him, lowering myself carefully back onto my chair.

"They're very much like you," he said, looking at me with his yellow eyes that glinted in the shaft of moonlight.

"What's that s'posed to mean?"

"They've been operated on."

"Operated on!" I spat, getting up from my seat again and wincing at the pain in my leg and back.

"They've been tested...perhaps *operated* was the wrong word," Nik said.

"But I've seen them in my dreams...nightmares," I told him. "I saw Isidor and Kayla and they were in pain. They were screaming."

"Are you sure they were nightmares?" Nik asked fixing me with his brilliant stare.

"Of course they were nightmares! I was in them. I was locked in a room that was similar to a hospital and I was wearing a hospital..." Then looking down at myself, I whispered, "...gown."

Nik just looked at me, his tail swishing back and forth across the stone floor of my cell.

"Oh, my God!" I breathed deeply. "They're not dreams or nightmares – they're memories! All that stuff has really happened!" Then twisting around on the chair, I reached over my shoulder and touched the space between my shoulder blades. At once, pain exploded across my back and I snapped forward. I waited for the pain to ease but it never truly faded, so I touched my back again. With the tips of my grubby fingers, I could feel those little black bones sticking from my back as they twitched and wriggled like fingers.

Snatching my hand away, I yanked the hospital gown from over my head. Folding my arms over my breasts, I showed my back to the wolf and said, "What have they done to me?"

Nudging the metal bowl across the floor towards me with

his snout, Nik said, "See for yourself."

I crouched down, and picked up the bowl with my trembling fingers. Holding it in the air and slightly behind my left shoulder, I turned my head and peered at the reflection of my back in the shiny surface of the bowl. At once I dropped it, and it clattered to the floor, spilling what was left of the meat.

"No!" I whimpered at the sight of the cuts and gashes that covered my back. But it was the sight of those black bony fingers wriggling from the cuts that frightened me the most. They protruded from wounds that were bruised green and purple where they had been stitched together.

Pulling the hospital gown back over my head, I slumped back onto the chair and wrapped my arms around myself, rocking back and forth.

"Why are they doing this?" I whispered as tears fell onto my cheeks.

Ignoring my question, Nik stood up on his four muscular legs, and said, "Oh, I nearly forgot, I brought you something else." I heard the sound of his paws padding against the floor as he headed back towards the door. He returned moments later pushing a book along the floor with his snout.

"I thought you might want to read this, you know, to relieve the boredom," he said.

Numbly, I glanced down at the floor and at the book he had bought for me. I didn't say anything – I couldn't.

"I thought it might help you," he said, stepping out of the moonlight and heading back towards the cell door.

"Wait a minute…don't go!" I called out to him.

"What?" he woofed, from within the gloom.

"Where am I?" I asked softly. "You can at least tell me that."

"You're in a zoo," his voice floated back out of the darkness.

"A zoo?' I whispered. "What do you mean, *in a zoo*?"

"That's where animals are kept, isn't it?" he asked.

"I guess," I said numbly, not really taking in what he had just told me.

I don't know how long I sat there for, dazed and confused. But when I peered around the cell some time later, the werewolf had gone and my cell door was closed again. My skin had started to itch again and my stomach had started to flip and I knew what I needed to make those feelings go away. Glancing down at my feet, I could see the upturned bowl and the dirty strips of bloodied meat that had fallen from it. I picked it up with my filthy fingers and brushed away the dirt that had stuck to it from the cell floor.

Closing my eyes, I put the meat in my mouth and it tasted bitter and felt gritty against my tongue. Swallowing hard, I forced the raw meat down my throat. I sat on my chair, stinking and dirty with the taste of raw meat in my mouth, I shut my eyes and wondered if Nik hadn't been right after all. Perhaps I was an animal and deserved to be kept in a zoo.

# Chapter Nine

*Doctor Hunt came into my room at the facility - zoo? Again I felt incredibly tired and struggled to keep my eyes open, let alone focus in on him. It was like I was coming around from anaesthesia.*

*He came towards my bed, the lower half of his face covered with a blue surgical mask. There was something about him...perhaps it was his eyes and his jet-black hair that lay across his brow that made me think I had met him before.*

*"Do I know you?" I babbled, my mind feeling groggy and my lips opened and closed as if out of sync with my voice.*

*"I don't think so," he replied softly, picking up a book that he had brought into the room. He began to read.*

*My eyes closed again and I could hear Doctor Hunt reading 'The Wind In The Willows'. My father had read the book to me as I child, and for a moment I could see myself nestled on his lap, my head resting against his chest and listening to the soft beating of his heart. I'd been about six then and I'd loved to hear about the adventures of Ratty, Mole, Badger and Mister Toad. But I was older now – twenty – so why was Doctor Hunt reading this children's book to me?*

*Hunt's voice was soft and soothing, and I couldn't help but let my eyes slide close again. I listened to the story but there was something not quite right. Why hadn't he started reading the story from the beginning? Why had he started the story towards the end, where Mister Toad had been sent to prison and needed to escape?*

*I struggled to open my eyes again, but I managed to look past the doctor who sat beside my bed. He had left the door to my room open, and like Mister Toad, I knew I needed to escape. I raised my arm off the bed and it felt heavy and sluggish as if held down by a thousand weights. Pointing towards the open door, I...*

...tipped forward and fell off the chair onto the hard stone floor. I wailed in pain as I landed awkwardly on my injured leg and back. I rolled onto my side and gripping my shin, I told myself never to fall asleep on the chair again. It was still night and pale blue light continued to slice my cell in two from above.

Looking up at the square hole then at the chair, an idea came to me. So, with the tips of my fingers, I positioned the chair directly under the hole. Using it as a crutch, I hoisted myself up and climbed on. I held the back of the chair and pushed myself into a standing position, gingerly teetering on the foot of my good leg, being mindful not to put any weight on my bad leg.

Balancing like a tightrope walker, I slowly raised one arm above my head and reached up towards the hole. To my amazement and delight, I could reach it. I pushed my fingers through the wire mesh and felt the cool night breeze dance over them. The chair wobbled beneath me and I gripped onto the wire mesh as tightly as I could until I had regained my balance. Hovering on a chair on one leg wasn't easy, but at last I felt that perhaps there was a way out of my cell – some hope. I tugged on the mesh, but it was fixed firmly into the surface of the ceiling. Running my fingers around the inner edge of the hole, I could feel that the wire had been embedded into the plaster and concrete that went to make up the structure of the cell.

I clenched my teeth tightly together and yanked several times on the mesh, hoping it would come away, but however hard I pulled on it, the wire didn't budge. Unless I was mangled through a mincing machine, there was no way I was ever going to fit through the tiny holes that made up the mesh.

With growing frustration, I tugged on the wire one last time but in doing so I lost my footing and cartwheeled through the air, landing on the floor. There was an explosion of pain in my calf and I bit my arm to drown out the sound of my screams.

I lay on my side panting like a wounded animal.

"Let me out of here!" I screamed, in frustration, but my cries just echoed harmlessly off the walls.

I felt cheated and more frustrated than before. As I'd stood on that chair and poked my fingers through the holes, I felt for a moment that perhaps I could escape – perhaps I would be free. But the most infuriating thing about it all was that the only thing separating me from the outside world was a small square of wire mesh.

I pounded my clenched fists onto the floor and screwed up my eyes until I could see white spots dancing around on the inside of my eyelids. *I wouldn't be beaten – not ever!* I told myself. I was

Kiera Hudson – I could *see* things. Wasn't I meant to be good at figuring things out?

*"We've been sent a right little Miss Marple, this time around,"* I heard Potter say inside my head, and it was almost as if he had whispered it in my ear. Hearing his voice like that just frustrated me even more. *Where was he?*

When my hands became numb from the constant banging against the cold, hard floor, I opened my eyes and looked across my cell at the upturned chair. It was then that I saw something; I could *see* my way out. It gleamed at me in the moonlight and I wondered if there could still be yet a glimmer of hope.

I crawled across the room to the upturned chair and inspected its legs. The base of each leg had been fitted with a silver-coloured cap – each one was the size of a £2 coin. I felt around the edge of the caps and found a small grove where each one had been fitted to the legs of the chair. I dug my fingernails into the groove and without too much effort, managed to prise one of the caps free. The inside of the chair leg was hollow.

Holding the cap in the palm of my hand, I could see that one side of it was concaved like a tiny dish. I tossed it up and down in my hand like a coin and looked up at the hole, grinning to myself.

Gritting my teeth against the burning sensation in my leg and the ache in my back, I pulled myself up onto the chair. Balancing again on one foot, I took hold of the wire mesh. With my free hand, I took the metal cap and began to chip away at the grey-coloured plaster that housed the wire.

To my delight, the plaster began to break away in tiny pieces and fall to the floor below. I scratched the cap against the edge of the hole again and more of the plaster began to crumble. It only broke away in minute pieces at a time, but it was something. I wondered how deeply the wire mesh went into the ceiling. If it was only an inch or two then it wouldn't take me too long – but if it went further than that, it could take me days – perhaps weeks - and that was time that I didn't have.

I reasoned that I could probably do with releasing the wire mesh on two sides. Once I had them free, I could bend it to one side and this would give me a big enough gap to climb through.

So without wasting any more time thinking about it, I put my plan of escape into action. For the rest of the night, I teetered to and fro on the chair as I hovered on one leg and chipped away at the ceiling. It took longer than I had originally thought, as I had to keep stopping to rest. It wasn't my leg which caused the problems, it was my arms and back. With one hand, I gripped the wire mesh and with the other I furiously scratched away at the plaster. With both arms constantly held above my head, they began to ache with numbness and tingle with pins and needles. When the pain became too much to bear, I'd carefully climb down and shake my arms.

As soon as I could feel them again, I climbed back onto the chair and started all over again. I worked through the night until I could see the first rays of sunlight fan across the morning sky above me.

*I can't wait to be standing under that sun and feeling totally free!* I thought to myself.

The urge to continue was strong, but it was light now and I might be seen and if I were to be caught now, I may never escape. So reluctantly, I climbed down from the chair and looked up at my handy work.

"Oh, shit!" I gasped.

All along one side of the square hole the plaster was broken and chipped. The wire mesh could now be clearly seen, where once it had been hidden. It would be obvious to anyone what I had been up to, should they glance upwards.

Frantically, I looked around the room and searched for anything I could use to cover the gaps and cracks with.

*Kiera, how could you be such a dumb arse?* I scolded myself.

Then I spotted my bowl of water and had an idea. I hobbled over to it and brought it back to the chair, mindful not to spill any as I only had a little left and I would probably need all of it for my plan. Placing it on the floor next to the chair, I turned to the book that Nik had brought me and froze, my hand hovering over it. Looking down, I could see that the book was *'The Wind in the Willows'*.

This was the book I remembered Doctor Hunt reading to me. But had he? Perhaps I had noticed the book when Nik had brought them into my cell and it had somehow worked its way into my dream. But if Hunt had really read this book to me – why had Nik brought it to me? Had it been by chance or a deliberate act?

I thumbed through the pages and looked at the wonderful

illustrations inside. Running my fingers delicately over the pages, it pained me to carry out what I had planned.

Closing my eyes so I couldn't see those illustrations and the neat rows of printed words, I slowly began to rip out several of the pages. I then tore these into thin strips.

Opening my eyes, I looked down at these torn pieces of paper and cringed. I felt awful for destroying the book, partly because I knew books were precious – but more importantly, I got a feeling deep inside that this book had some significant meaning but I didn't have time to figure out what – it was just a strange feeling that I had.

The toad had escaped from his cell. He'd gained the sympathy of the jailer's daughter and she had disguised him as a washerwoman and helped him escape. But there was no jailer's daughter and definitely no disguises to be had.

So slowly, I gathered up the strips of paper and placed them into the bowl of water.

"Sorry Mister Toad," I whispered.

Once the paper was sodden, I squeezed the strips into several small, mushy pulps and climbed back onto the chair. With my thumb and fingers, I worked and moulded the wet paper into the cracks and holes that I had made during the night. I smoothed the paper over with the palm of my hand and blended it into the ceiling. When I was happy that I had filled in all the gaps, I climbed down off the chair and looked back up at the ceiling. The colour of the paper didn't match perfectly with the colour of the ceiling, but it was close enough. I guessed it would fool the passing glance but perhaps not a careful examination.

As I stood and admired my cunning, I heard the rattling of keys in the lock of my cell door. I quickly looked about myself, just to make sure that I had covered all of my tracks. It was then that I noticed the mounds of chippings and tiny pieces of plaster, which had fallen from the ceiling and now covered the floor of my cell.

# Chapter Ten

If these tiny pieces of plaster happened to be seen, it wouldn't take too long to work out where they had come from and what I had been up to.

The keys jangled in the lock and with my heart pounding in my chest, I looked down at the chair.

*I love you Nik!* I thought to myself as I turned the chair upside down, and I doubted he knew he had unwittingly provided me with the tools that I needed to make my escape. Scooping the plaster chippings together with my hands, I piled them all together. I gathered them into my fist, and then poured them into the hollow leg of the upturned chair. A few tiny pieces dribbled through my fingers and back onto the floor, but these were so tiny, I doubted they would have been noticed. I poured the last of the chippings into the chair leg, snatched up the silver cap and rammed it back into place.

Just as my cell door swung open, I righted the chair, scooped up *'The Wind in the Willows'* and pretended I'd been reading all along.

Phillips came striding into my cell, and I continued to read my book as if I hadn't noticed him. Slowly, he circled me, and although I was pretending he wasn't there, I knew he was looking at me.

"Who gave you the chair and the book?'" he barked.

"A wolf," I said without looking up.

Without warning, he snatched the book out of my hands and tossed it across the room.

"Which wolf?" he roared so loudly, I nearly fell off my chair.

Guessing that Nik shouldn't have given me these items and not wanting to get him into trouble, I replied, "They didn't tell me their name."

"What did they look like?"

I met his gaze and said dryly, "Mmm…let me think about that…I guess they looked like a *wolf!*"

"Don't get smart with me, Hudson, or it will be the last thing that you ever do!" he grunted as he moved closer towards me.

"Well how am I supposed to know? As far as I'm concerned,

wolves all look alike," I tried to explain.

"Well you're not keeping them," Phillips growled.

*No! He can't take them away! What about my escape? I need them!*

"Please don't take them," I said. "I hate sitting on the floor all the time – it's so uncomfortable."

"Tough luck," Phillips snapped and pushed me off the chair with one shove of his claw-like hands.

I hit the floor hard and although my leg flared with pain, I noticed it was nowhere near as bad as it had been. But nevertheless, I gripped hold of it and screamed.

"Can't you see I'm in pain?" I cried.

Phillips just stood over me and puckered his large fleshy lips.

"If I had somewhere comfortable to sit my leg might heal quicker," I groaned.

Hearing this, he stared into my eyes and I saw a flash of something in them. It was as if I had said something that touched a nerve within him.

"The floor is hard and cold. How is my leg ever gonna heal if I'm lying on the ground all the time?" I told him.

I could sense that Phillips was thinking about this for a minute and then he said reluctantly, "Okay, you can keep it for the next few days, in the hope that it may aid your recovery. But if it doesn't, I'm taking the chair back. Besides, if your leg hasn't healed by then, you won't be needing it again."

On hearing this, I rolled over onto my side and rubbed my leg, "Thank you," I said. "I'm sure it will help."

Phillips just snorted in response and went back to the open door.

As he reached it, I called out to him and said, "What did you really come to my cell for?"

On hearing this, he stopped in the doorway and grinned at me.

"I came to tell you that you stink and it's time for a wash!" He then disappeared into the corridor and as he went, I heard him say to someone or *something*, "She's all yours!"

I looked at the open doorway as two Vampyrus appeared. It was only when I was hit in the chest with a powerful jet of water that I noticed the hosepipes in their hands.

The Vampyrus laughed between themselves as they hosed

me down. The force of the water was so strong that it pushed me across the cell floor and into the wall. The water was freezing cold and tasted salty, like sea water.

Once they had their fun and games, they turned off the water and left me alone, wet and cold on my cell floor. I rubbed my hands up and down the length of my arms to dry myself. My hospital gown was soaked through and clung uncomfortably to me. Moving to the centre of the cell where the sun shone through the hole, I lay on my back and warmed myself in the pool of light. I looked up at the hole and smiled to myself.

*So far so good! I'll be out of here by the end of the week!*

I knew that I would have to spend the next few nights chipping away, so I would have to sleep during the day to keep up my strength and give my leg a chance to heal. Phillips could open the zoo gates and give me an hour's head start, but if my leg was still infected, then any escape would be pointless as I wouldn't get very far.

The sunlight felt warm and soothing against my skin and as I drifted off to sleep I imagined that I was in a nice soft bed curled up under...

*...the blanket. It felt safe under the blanket.*

*I could hear the sound of sobbing.*

*"Bring me blood!" someone cried from down the corridor outside my room.*

*There was the sound of keys rattling in a lock.*

*"Have you brought me some blood?" the voice gasped.*

*Even from my hiding place beneath my blanket, I could hear the desperation in the voice – it sounded as if they were going out of their mind with cravings. I pulled my blanket tighter over my head.*

*Then there came a scuffling sound in the corridor outside. I peeked over the top of my covers and could see shadows darting back and forth under the gap beneath my door.*

*"She's gone," I heard a voice say and I knew it was one of those doctors talking, their voices sounding muffled as it seeped from beneath their surgical mask.*

*Climbing from under my blankets, I swung my legs over the*

35

*side of my bed and stood. Immediately, I grabbed hold of the mattress as my head swooned with a dream-like weightlessness. Composing myself, I inched my way towards the little window in my door.*

*I peered over the lip of the frame and watched as two of those doctors wheeled a stretcher from a room down the corridor and headed towards me. As they came nearer, I could see Kayla lying on her back, her head propped up against some pillows. Her lips were swollen and purple. But as they pushed her closer, I could see to my horror that her lips weren't swollen and purple, they were covered in blood.*

*They paused outside my door and I ducked down.*

*"Kayla, what have they done to you?" I whispered.*

*Then they were moving again and I stood up and looked back through the window just in time to see Kayla suddenly reach up with one bony hand. It looked hot and clammy and her fingers were twisted like claws. She waved her hand in the air as if acknowledging me. But that was impossible, right? How did she know that I was there? It was as if she had heard me whisper her name. And then the stretcher was gone and so was Kayla, as the doctors carried her away down the corridor and out of sight.*

*I crossed the room back towards my bed. Pulling the blankets back over my head, I closed my eyes again. I wanted to go to sleep and wished that I would never...*

"...wake-up!" the voice said in my ear.

I peered through my half-closed eyes and stared into the face of Nik. The wolf was standing over me. The cell was in semi darkness, as the daylight outside began to fade.

"What do you want?" I groaned, my stomach aching and my skin feeling hot as my body started to crave the red stuff again.

"To say thank you," he said softly.

"What for?"

"For not telling."

I pulled myself up onto my elbows and winced. My bladder was full and I desperately needed to take a pee.

"What you talking about?" I mumbled.

"For not telling Phillips it was me who brought you the chair and book."

"Oh, that," I said, as I got to my feet. I gingerly placed my right foot onto the floor and waited for the explosion of pain, but it didn't come. It still hurt and throbbed, but not as bad as before. My back continued to throb where I had been operated on, but it was bearable.

"Phillips was asking all sorts of awkward questions. He wanted to know which one of us it was," Nik said.

"What happened?" I asked, as I placed the flat of my hand against my bladder.

"He said that if he ever found out who had been kind to the half-breed, he would rip their throat out," Nik told me. "I'm going to have to be careful until Phillips has got everything sorted out."

"Got what sorted out?" I asked him.

"I don't know." he told me.

"How did I know you were gonna say that?" I said dryly, looking over my shoulder at the hole in the ground. The urge to pee was gnawing away inside of me now and I didn't know how much longer I could last.

"Are you okay?" Nik asked, looking at me with his yellow eyes.

"Yeah, I just need to pee." I told him.

"Well go then," he said. "What's the problem?"

"You are," I winced, as I tried to hold back.

"How come?"

"I'm not going in front of you," I assured him.

"Why not?"

"What do you mean, *why not*? It's private – that's why!"

"How strange," he woofed, and it sounded as he were laughing at me.

"Strange to wolves perhaps, but not to me. I don't like to be looked at while I'm going, if you know what I mean."

Nik turned away from me with a swish of his tail. "Happy now?" he asked.

"Not perfect, but better," I said hobbling over to the hole in the ground. "Promise you won't look?"

"I promise," he replied wearily.

Hitching up my gown, I peered over my shoulder just to make sure I wasn't being watched. Once I had finished, I turned round and made my way back to the middle of the cell.

"You can look now," I told him and although he hadn't watched me as promised, I still felt stripped away as if I had lost most of my dignity and I knew in my heart that I was living like an animal.

Turning around, Nik said, "I don't know what all the fuss was about."

"You wouldn't understand," I moaned, sitting on the chair.

"You'd be surprised how much I understand the situation you're in," Nik said, laying on the floor and resting his snout against his paws.

"What do you mean?" I asked him, his giant flanks easing in and out as he lay at my feet.

"I told you I'd been captured, right?" he said, glancing up at me. "It's like I've been caught in a photograph – trapped in that pose forever – unless..."

"Unless what?"

"Unless I make amends...for my past," he barked. "Until I do that I'm trapped in the guise of a wolf just like you're trapped inside these four walls."

"So if you make amends for whatever it is that you've done, the curse is lifted," I said. "But where does that leave me? What do I have to do to get out of here?"

Nik lay still on the floor and I watched how his long grey fur shimmered in the cool breeze from above us. Then looking down at his paws, he said, "You can't get out of here, Kiera; like me, you're trapped."

Glancing quickly up at the ceiling, I whispered, "What makes you so sure that I can't get out of here?"

"You might think about escaping," he said, still not looking at me, "but even if you did, you would only come back."

"You're kidding me, right?" I scoffed. "If I ever did get out of here, I couldn't think of one reason that would entice me back to this filthy, godforsaken place."

"I can," he said.

"And what's that?" I demanded.

"Human flesh," he barked softly. "You're an addict, Kiera."

Hearing those words made my stomach somersault, but this time not with hunger of desperate cravings, but revulsion. In my heart, I knew that the raw meat that had been passed to me through the hatch had been human flesh, but in my head I had convinced myself that it had been raw steak or anything but human. But to hear it spoken aloud by Nik had pulled the curtain aside that I had so conveniently hung over what was really feeding my addiction.

Not wanting to reveal my own self-loathing and revulsion at what I'd been eating, I swallowed hard and said, "I could find more if I really wanted to."

"Believe me, you really would want to find some more," Nik woofed and looked up at me. "But human meat is in short supply in these parts."

I shot forward in my chair and said, "How long has it been since you've seen a human?"

"Months," he said, flicking away a swarm of flies with his tail.

"What, they're all *dead?*" I asked, not believing what I was hearing.

"In this area, yes," he replied. "I don't venture out of the zoo much – but there is a town nearby to the east, its called Wasp Water. But all the humans there are dead."

Hearing him say this upset me and made me fearful for what I would find if I ever managed to escape from my cell. But unwittingly, he was giving me information just like the jailer's daughter had helped Mister Toad in *The Wind in the Willows*, and again I glanced down at the book where Phillips had tossed it. To know that the town of Wasp Water was to the east of the zoo told me that I was still in Cumbria in the north of England. Wasp Water had been one of the towns that Murphy had skirted us around on our way to the monastery, so I knew that I wasn't far from the lake and the Fountain of Souls.

It wasn't much, but it was something. It gave me some bearings – a direction to head in when I broke out of here. But if all the people were dead there, what would be the point? There would be shelter, cars, technology – anything that I might be able to use to get as far away from Cumbria as possible or at least tell the rest of the world what was really going on behind and beneath the Cumbria Mountains.

"So if all the people are dead in Wasp Water, where has the…the *meat* been coming from?" I asked him.

39

"The Vampyrus rounded up several hundred of them and they're being kept here at the zoo in cages," he said.

Hearing this reminded me of something my mother had said to me in my cell beneath the mountains. Hadn't she said something about keeping humans like animals in factory farms?

"But you can't keep people locked up in a zoo!" I hissed.

Looking at me with his yellow stare, Nik said, "It's the only zoo in the world where the humans are the exhibits and the animals come to visit."

"This isn't some kinda joke, you know!" I yelled at him. "We're talking about human beings!"

"Of which you're not one," he said, standing on all fours.

And every time someone or *thing* reminded me of that, my heart sunk a little bit deeper inside my chest and I couldn't help but reach round and gently poke those bony black fingers that protruded from my back. They were my constant reminder that Nik was right. I was fast losing my human side, and becoming just like them – an *animal*. But that didn't mean I had to behave like one of them. No longer was I going to eat that meat they pushed through the hatch at me. I wouldn't have another mouthful even if it meant killing me.

With a swish of his tail, Nik headed towards the cell door.

"What's going to happen to me?" I called after him. "What's going to happen to Kayla and Isidor?"

"If Phillips has his way, you and your friends will all soon be dead." Then Nik was gone, disappearing beyond the door and leaving me alone again.

# Chapter Eleven

"*Dead!*" I yelled at the closed door. Lashing out in frustration, I kicked the chair across my cell. Immediately my leg roared in pain and I dropped to the floor and held my shin.

My desire to escape was even stronger than ever and I looked up at the hole above me. I couldn't believe that the world just outside its walls was now being run by a bunch of talking animals who intended to kill me and my friends. I needed to find out for myself if it were all true. Finding myself locked up with the Vampyrus and Lycanthrope was enough to drive anyone insane – but to think that my friends might soon die on the strength of my scabby leg – that was more than I would or *could* comprehend.

The pain in my leg began to ease, so I shuffled across the floor to the chair. On the way, I noticed that a fresh bowl of food and water had been placed by the hatch and I guessed the paw had put it there while I had been sleeping earlier. I stopped long enough to devour half of the water, leaving some to aid me with my escape later. Looking down at the bowl of meat…flesh sitting in its bloody puddle, I reached out for it. But the images of people locked up in cages, being taken away and butchered to feed my cravings was enough to make me push the bowl aside. Even though I turned away, in the back of my mind, I knew that it was there, red and ripe and succulent.

"Stop it!" I hissed out loud as my stomach began to knot, my throat turning dry and my skin beginning to prickle with heat.

"I won't eat it!" I seethed.

Knowing that I had to stop thinking about the meat, I pulled the chair across the floor and stationed it under the hole. I tipped it up and removed one of the caps. I was mindful not to use the same cap from the previous night, as that leg was now full of the debris I had hidden in there.

Carefully, I climbed onto the chair and hoisted myself up. I removed the paper that I had put in place and began to scrape away at the edges of the hole.

Throughout the night I worked, stopping every so often to rest my aching arms and sip some of the water I had saved. I figured that I possibly had only one more night after this before Phillips came for me. I really needed to be in a position to make my escape before first light of the following day.

*But what about Isidor and Kayla?* I wondered. I had to take them with me. There was no way I was leaving them in the zoo. And what about Luke? Where was he? Then, remembering how he'd looked on the floor of my cell beneath the mountains, I feared that he might not be alive anymore. Not wanting to think about that, I pushed those pictures of his battered and cut body from my mind and focused on my escape.

*Once out of the cell where would I go?* I wondered.

I had no idea of my exact whereabouts in the zoo, but I reckoned that if I could at least find my way to the main entrance, I'd stand a good chance of escaping. I doubted that the animals would have locked the main gates. If what Nik had told me was true about there being no more humans other than me, Isidor, and Kayla, then the animals would have no reason to keep the gates shut – they could come and go as they pleased in their new world.

"But you're not one of them!" I heard Nik say in my head.

But I was human – in part at least- the better part. I'd always believed myself to be human and I wasn't going to stop believing that now. I feared that if I did, I would never get that half of me back. There was no way I was going to live like an animal, behave like an animal and eat like one. I was going to get out of this cell, out of this zoo and take my friends with me. *I'm Kiera Hudson.* I kept telling myself that over and over again in my head. I had to keep hold of that – I had to keep hold of me.

*But once I had escaped from my cell, what then? How would I find Kayla and Isidor?* I didn't have the answer to that. But nevertheless, I kept chipping away at the concrete around the wire mesh above me. I had to keep going, I had to keep thinking, planning as it took my mind off that bowl of red stuff that my stomach was now aching for, my throat was thirsty for.

*Keep planning Kiera – keep thinking ahead,* I told myself.

I'd already decided that once I was out of the zoo, I would head straight for the town of Wasp Water. I would be in familiar territory then – *human* territory. There would be a million and one places for Kayla, Isidor, and me to hide.

*What about food?* a little voice spoke up from within side me, and I glanced down at the red stuff. *Just one little bite wouldn't...*

There would be shops. The shelves would be stacked with cans of food – *normal* food. The cans would probably still be in date as they lasted for years. I would be able to find clothes and shoes in disused department stores. We would be alright.

*Then what?*

With sweat running off my brow into my eyes, the cravings for the red stuff in the bowl gnawed away at my insides. My stomach was beginning to cramp in sharp violent spasms, and several times I had to stop chipping away at the concrete to lean forward and double up until the pain passed. My throat felt as if it was on fire, but I couldn't even quench it with the water as I would need that later. Mopping my feverish brow with the sleeve of my hospital gown, I reached up and continued to scrape away the ceiling around the wire mesh.

By daybreak, I had completely removed the plaster around one entire edge of the mesh. I poked and pulled at it with my fingers and yanked it free. The wire gave under the strain and bent downwards revealing a gap big enough for me to put my arms through.

The urge to carry on throughout the day was overpowering, as the smell of freedom now seemed intoxicating. It was so strong that it even masked the stench from that hole in the corner of the cell, which I had been using as my toilet. But I had to be focused. If I were to be caught now, I would certainly never be given the chance to escape again.

So I climbed down from the chair, piled up the lose chippings and poured them into the hollow chair leg and replaced the cap. The hole in the ceiling was now twice as large as the one I had made the previous night and would definitely be noticed by any one of the animals that came into my cell.

Reluctantly, I ripped some pages from my book – or perhaps it was my escape manual? I worried that if Phillips, Sparky, or Nik happened to pick up *'The Wind in the Willows'* they would notice that the pages had been torn out.

Once I had ripped the pages into strips, I placed them in what was left of the water and filled in the gaps above me. When I had papered over the last of the cracks, I climbed off the chair and looked up. The paper was a different shade to the ceiling and it did look more obvious than the papier-mâché I'd created the night before. I now had to cover a larger area with it. Screwing up my eyes, I squinted up at my handy work, and like that it didn't look too bad. It looked like a big damp patch. That was the best I could do in these circumstances and I just prayed that none of my captors noticed it.

Confident that I'd hidden every trace of the work I'd carried out overnight, I curled up in the corner of my cell and closed my eyes. My stomach ached, and I felt as if I was going to be sick. My skin felt hot and clammy. I knew that I could make the pain go away and I looked over at the bowl that sat by the hatch. Turning away, I tried not to think about that red sticky meat and my head raced with thoughts of escape. Over and over again, I tried to plan for every conceivable outcome – but at no point did I ever consider failure – because for me, that wasn't an option.

The thought of being free of this stinking cell, to be wearing clean clothes, and to sink into a nice warm bath was overwhelming. I imagined walking free along a beach, with waves crashing up onto the shore and I could smell…

# Chapter Twelve

*...disinfectant. I knew it was disinfectant that they were spraying up and down the corridor outside because it wafted through the gaps beneath the door. It smelt bitter and it made my nostrils sore and my eyes sting.*

*Doctor Hunt sat beside my bed and read from a book. Mister McGregor was chasing a rabbit named Peter through the vegetable patch. Peter Rabbit was trying to escape!*

*With bleary eyes I studied Doctor Hunt's face, well the top half, as he continued to hide the lower part of his face behind that blue surgical mask.*

*His eyes looked older somehow as if since his last visit to my room much time had passed. Nets of wrinkles were engraved around the corners of his eyes and I was sure that they hadn't been there before. The Doctor's usually jet-black hair was now spattered with flecks of grey and his hands looked bony and worn as they curled around the edges of the book that he held in his lap.*

*"Have you gotten older?" I mumbled feeling half asleep.*

*Doctor Hunt closed the book and looked at me.*

*"No," he replied softly. But even his voice had sounded different, and I realised that it was worry – fear – in his voice that I could hear and see in the wrinkles around his eyes.*

*"How long have I been here?" I asked.*

*"Two months," he whispered and glanced over his shoulder at the door to my room, as if making sure that it was closed.*

*"What's wrong?" I asked, sensing his fear.*

*Hunt looked at me and his eyes smiled, but his look was insincere and hid his true feelings.*

*"I've performed a miracle, Kiera," he whispered, snatching another quick look back over his shoulder.*

*"What sort of a miracle?" I asked him, my foggy mind trying to make sense of what he was telling me.*

*"You're my miracle," he said. "They brought me here to finish off the work that Doctor Ravenwood and I started on a cure for the half-breeds – to help them survive and live past the age of sixteen. You, Kayla, and Isidor are the only known half-breeds that have lived past that age."*

45

"So what's the miracle?" I asked him, fighting to keep my eyes open.

"I cracked the code!" he whispered with excitement. "I've found the cure!"

"But that isn't a miracle- that's a curse," I told him, my speech starting to slur. "The Vampyrus will now be able to breed their army of half-breeds. I saw one, it looked like Kayla..."

"But I haven't given the Vampyrus the correct code. It works to a point, but it will never produce the perfect half-breed – not like you, Kayla, or Isidor. They will grow weak, become ill, and die."

"How come?"

"You were bitten on the leg by one of those murderous Lycanthrope," Hunt said. "The wound has become infected and spread throughout your system. Your leg will eventually heal – your immune system will fight off the infection. But I tweaked the DNA code that Phillips has, so in the half-breeds that they manufacture, the virus will slowly take over their system and kill them."

"But isn't Phillips going to figure out at some point that you've deceived him?" I asked.

"Not for a while," he said, "and by the time they do, it will be too late – I'll be dead."

"Dead?" I breathed.

"I know what the Vampyrus have planned for me once they think my work is complete," he said matter-of-factly.

"So why didn't you just drag out your work?" I asked. "You could have made your research last for years."

"The work was too important for me and Ravenwood not to finish," he said. "Remember, it's a cure for those future half-breed children that are born, and there will be more, Kiera."

"But let them kill you?" I yawned, fighting the meds that I'd been given. "You could escape."

"Ravenwood tried that with half of the completed code. Although the Vampyrus believe that they have the complete code, we separated the original," he explained. "I don't know how far Ravenwood got, I've not seen or had word from him since, but I'm certain he managed to hide his half of the code somewhere safe."

"How can you be so sure?" I asked him.

*"Because if Phillips had captured Ravenwood with anything that looked remotely like a DNA code he would have known that we were trying to deceive him," Hunt said.*

*"So where is the other half?" I said, staring at him through my half-closed eyes.*

*"I've given it to someone," he replied, glancing back over his shoulder again.*

*"Who?" I asked, feeling more confused than the drugs were making me.*

*"I knew I had to give it to someone," he said. "Someone I could trust – someone I knew who would have the sight to find a way to escape these Vampyrus."*

*"Who?" I asked again, wanting to hear their name before I lost consciousness again.*

*"I've given it to you, Kiera," he said. "You have it."*

*"What...where?" I slurred.*

*"I've written it amongst the pages of this," he said, holding up the book,* 'The Wind in the Willows.'

*Seeing the book in his hands...*

...I woke up and crawled over to the hole in the floor and was sick. I tried not to breathe in the stench that wafted throughout my cell from the hole. But it wasn't the smell that made me throw up, it was the agonising cramps in my stomach and the cool, feverish sweat that covered my skin that made me feel ill. It was my cravings for the red stuff and I didn't know if I could hold out.

*I had to!*

I felt dirty and I smelled, too. The hosing down the Vampyrus had given me had only freshened me up – it hadn't been a proper wash, not like relaxing in a hot bath with mountains of frothy bath suds while listening to my iPod.

Vomit swung from my chin and I knocked it away with the back of my hand. Standing, I crossed my cell to the chair. I was no longer hobbling and my leg was beginning to feel stronger. My hair was matted and I tried to drag my fingers through it, but it was impossible. The *'Wind in the Willows'* lay open on the dusty floor, and I looked down at the torn pages. In my dream – *memory* – Doctor Hunt had told me that he had written his half of the code in the book. But if he had, how much of it had I ripped out, mashed-

47

up into a soggy-pulp and filled the holes in the ceiling with? Reaching down, I picked-up the book and thumbed through the pages. Sweat ran from my brow where I was burning up with fever, dripping like rain drops onto the pages. Squinting, I looked down at the book but couldn't see anything that looked like handwritten code amongst what was left of the pages. To be honest, I didn't even know what I was looking for. What did DNA code look like anyhow? My cravings were what mattered and they felt all-consuming. But something inside of me, the part of me – Kiera – that was still holding on told me that the code was the most important thing. If discovered by Phillips and this *invisible man*, it would be used to breed more of those half-breeds and their special gifts would be used to destroy…

Dropping the book, I staggered over to the hole in the floor again and gagged as more sickness gushed from the pit of my stomach, up my throat, and into the hole. It burnt my mouth like acid, and it came out in thick, black, ropey streams.

*Just have some of that red stuff*, a voice whispered in my ear. *Go on, just a bite, you'll feel so much better.*

At first I thought it was that other part of me, the Kiera that wanted to give up and make the pain go away. But then I realised it was the voice of my mum talking inside my head, and I pushed the sound of her voice away.

Covering my ears with my hands, I rocked backwards and screamed, "No! I won't eat that shit!"

*"Go on,"* my mum's voice whispered inside my head. *"The red stuff will take the pain away."*

"But it's not just *red stuff* you want me to eat!" I screamed until my throat felt raw. "It's human flesh and I won't have anymore!"

Then her voice was gone – like a fine mist lifting away as the sun comes up.

Looking up at the square hole, I took comfort in the knowledge that in the early hours of tomorrow morning, I would be disappearing through it. I'd be getting away from this filthy, stinking cell, away from this zoo. This time tomorrow, Phillips would come to my cell and find me gone.

Through the hole I could see that it wasn't yet night, but the moon would only be a couple of hours away. I got a jittery feeling knowing that this would be my last night in the zoo.

What about Kayla and Isidor? I wouldn't leave without them. I needed a plan – but I couldn't think. It was like the pain in my stomach was stopping me from focusing, from *seeing* what I needed to do. Rolling over onto my side, I noticed that a fresh bowl of food – *red stuff* – and water had been placed in my cell and I wondered what type of creature that big white paw belonged to.

*A polar bear?*

Did they have polar bears in the zoo? I wondered. Why not? They seemed to have every other type of animal. I crouched down on my haunches and realising that this would be the last time that the paw would shove me my food through the hatch, I lent close to it and shouted:

"Thank you, white paw, for all of my food!"

I listened for any sort of a reply but there was nothing. A growl would have done.

*What was I doing? What was I thinking of?*

Why was I even concerning myself with what type of creature had been shoving that red stuff through the hatch? Why was I thanking them? They hadn't been doing me a favour – helping me out in some way. They were no more than helping feed my addiction. They were a part of all of this. And I knew, somewhere behind the pain that I was in, I was going mad – losing sight of escaping from my cell and fighting the cravings that I'd had since eating that flesh for my mother. But I hadn't eaten it for her – I'd eaten it for Luke. Where was he now? By eating it, had I saved him?

I looked at the bowl of meat sitting in a pool of black blood. Trembling all over, I reached out and touched it with the tips of my filthy fingers. The meat felt warm and moist and I just wanted to snatch it up and ram it into my mouth. To tear it into pieces with my teeth, taste the blood on my tongue and let it sooth my burning throat. With tears running down my cheeks, I stretched out my fingers and pushed the bowl away. Turning towards the water, I cupped it in my shaking hands and raised it to my cracked lips. I poked my tongue from my mouth and licked at the water and it felt cool and wonderful. Sitting on the floor of the cell, I sipped at the water, and let it wash over my tongue and down the back of my throat.

*"Save some!"* The Kiera that still wanted to escape said in my ear. *"You might need it to soak the pages of the book in."*

"But I need those pages," I whispered aloud. "It has a secret code written on them."

*"Save it – you've got a long night ahead of you and you need to be strong,"* the other Kiera said.

I took the bowl from my lips, and placed it back on the floor. I couldn't help but notice how the water looked so nice as it sloshed against the side of the bowl.

Trying not to think about the water and the other stuff – the red stuff, I thought of Nik and I wondered how nice it would have been to see him before I made my escape. I secretly hoped that he would come before nightfall. Although I had found him frustrating at times, he had been a friend to me.

Then as if my prayers had been answered, there was the sound of keys rattling in the lock and the door was slowly swung open. Glancing up, I hoped to see my friend. Instead, with what little strength I had left, I edged myself away from the door as Phillips and Sparky came towards me.

# Chapter Thirteen

I scrambled onto my chair as Phillips strode in with Sparky beside him. Both were in human form. Phillips wore a black shirt that was open at the throat, and I could see the scars that ran down the length of his face and neck. They still looked raw in places, pink and mauve and I remembered how I had watched from high up in a tree in St. Mary's graveyard as Potter had attacked him. That night seemed like years ago now. They circled me a couple of times, I noticed Sparky sniff the air as if his Lycanthrope instincts simmered beneath his Human form.

Phillips stopped in front of me and asked Sparky, "How's her leg healing?"

Sparky came forward, crouched down, and rubbed his nose into the scabs that had now completely formed over the wound. He then ran his tongue up the length of it. He smacked his lips together and then turned to face Phillips.

"I think her leg has more or less healed," he said.

"Are you sure?" Phillips asked, with a tinge of excitement in his voice.

"She'll be good enough," Sparky smiled at Phillips.

"I am right here, you know," I said.

Without warning, Phillips pushed me from my chair and sent me sprawling across the floor.

"What was that for!" I yelled.

Phillips came slowly forward and towered over me.

"Who gave you the book?" he asked, his black eyes boring into mine.

"I told you, I didn't catch their name," I protested.

"Liar!" Phillips roared. Sparky almost seemed to giggle behind him.

Phillips reached out and picked up 'The Wind in the Willows' and flicked through it. I nervously glanced up at the ceiling. Sparky caught my stare and I immediately looked back at Phillips. His long, bony fingers were methodically turning the pages, and then they stopped. He slowly raised his head and looked at me.

"There are pages missing," he grunted. "Why have you

ripped pages from the book?"

My mind raced and the pain in my stomach grew worse and it felt as if my innards were being ripped from me. I had to think of something and quick. Then looking up at him, I winced and said, "Well what do you expect when you don't provide any toilet paper? What am I meant to do?"

Phillips eyed me suspiciously, and then said, "You're a savage!"

"Why don't you get laughing-boy over there to go check out the hole?" I said with as much confidence in my voice that I could muster. "He's obviously got an *amazing* sense of smell!"

Phillips glanced at Sparky who seemed to have lost his sense of humour all of a sudden.

"Aw, Phillips you can't be serious?" Sparky barked.

Then looking back at me, Phillips said, "I'm taking the book."

"No you can't..." I started to protest, but then I realised that I didn't actually need it to assist my escape anymore, as I would be gone tonight and they would discover the hole tomorrow anyway. But if my dreams – *memories* – were true, the book had some deeper meaning – it had a code hidden within its pages.

Seeing my distress, Sparky began to chuckle again, and if I hadn't of needed all of my remaining strength for what lay ahead of me that night, I would have punched him straight in his fucking face.

"Tell me who brought the chair or I'll take that as well," Phillips said.

A surge of panic now swept through me, as I knew that without the chair my escape would be over.

"I don't know their name," I tried to convince him.

"This is your last chance! Tell me their name or the chair goes!" Phillips warned.

I looked at him and I knew that he meant every word. But I remembered Nik had told me that if he'd been discovered bringing me the book and chair, Phillips would have ripped his throat out.

*"They never told me their name!"* I shouted.

Phillips looked at me then turned and snatched up the chair.

"No!" I yelled. "You said I could use it to help heal my leg. Don't you need my leg to be better?" I pleaded.

Phillips turned at the cell door and grunted.

"Your leg is good enough for what I have planned for you!"

Sparky then turned, produced a large broom from the corridor outside and threw it at me.

"And clean this cell – it's disgusting!"

"You clean it, you piece of shit!" I shouted.

Phillips slammed the cell door shut, taking my chair and my chance of freedom with him.

*"No! Bring them back!"* I screamed. But it was no good, from within my cell I could hear Phillips stomping away down the corridor, Sparky chuckling insanely beside him.

I got to my feet and limped over to the cell door. I banged on it with my fists and roared over and over again.

"Let me outta here! I'm not an *animal* – it's you who should be locked up in here, *not me!*"

I slid down the door and settled on the floor, rolling into a ball. I looked up at the ceiling and wiped away the hot tears that ran down my dirty cheeks. The last shards of daylight shone through the square hole and I knew that my escape was over. The thought of spending the rest of my life locked in a zoo terrified me and I knew that the thought of escape was the only thing that had kept me going over the last few days. Now that had been taken away from me, I didn't know how I would get through tomorrow – let alone a life time of captivity. And what about the book with the code? He had taken it.

*What was it that Phillips had in store for me?* I wondered.

Tomorrow morning he would come for me and the thought of that moment filled me with dread.

I rolled onto my back and looked up at the square hole and the wire mesh. Over the last few days, as I had toppled on the chair, frantically scratching away the plaster, freedom had seemed so close – but it was something I now believed I would never have.

Closing my eyes, I pictured lakes, forests and mountains. I imagined running towards them, feeling the sun on my face, the rain on my skin, the wind tugging at my hair and the...*broom!* My mind screamed at me suddenly.

*I can use the broom that Phillips gave me to get out of here!*

Clambering to my feet, I snatched it up from the floor. I looked up at the square hole and could see only blackness outside. There was no moon tonight and I was grateful for that, because tonight I was going to escape and the darkness would hide me.

Taking hold of the broom firmly in my hands, I raised it above my head and began to jab away at the pages from the books that I had pressed into the holes. The paper began to fall away in large chunks and land on the floor of my cell. I continued to prod away at the papier-mâché until I had broken it all free.

Once I could see the edges of the wire mesh, I worked the handle of the broom under it and pulled it loose. The edge of the mesh hung down like a drooping lip and I turned the broom over and worked the head of it between the edge of the wire and the hole. I yanked on the broom and bent the wire mesh back on itself, so there was a gap. Standing back, I looked up at it, but could see that it still wasn't quite big enough for me to squeeze through.

If only I had that chair with its little silver caps for just one more night, then I would have been able to have scraped away enough of the plaster to release one more side of that wire mesh. But I hadn't one more night – I only had tonight and I would just have to improvise and make the best of the broom.

Then, I heard a growl come from behind the hatch. I froze in the darkness, my heart racing against my chest.

*The paw never bought food at this time of day – it had always been early morning!*

Maybe it had heard the sound of the broom banging away at the ceiling – perhaps that was what had roused its attention. I listened intently and I could hear whatever it was moving about outside the hatch. Pulling the broom away from the hole, I quickly swept the pieces of paper into the corner of the room and lay down on top of them.

I lay in the dark and waited. The paw beyond the hatch – if that's what it was – continued to move about, woofing and barking into the night.

*What was it doing?*

Maybe I had been discovered and it was signalling for Phillips to come quickly to my cell. Then I could hear movement in the corridor outside, there was an animal out there and it was coming towards my cell. I lay as still as I could, hoping that if it was Phillips and he did look in to check on me, he might think that I was asleep and leave me alone.

*But what about the hole?*

I opened my right eye and peered up at it. The wire mesh hung down, bent and twisted out of shape.

*Anyone would notice it – even a dumb Vampyrus!*

Then the sound of scraping against rust filled my cell as the black iron door was swung open.

# Chapter Fourteen

Nik came sauntering silently into my cell; the only sound he made was the soft whisper of his paws upon the ground.

"What do you want?" I asked impatiently. I didn't mean to be rude, but I was burning up with fever, my stomach was cramping and I didn't want my escape delayed.

"That's nice," he woofed. "I risk everything to come and see you every night and that's the thanks I get!"

"Why do you bother then?" I asked, as I continued to lay motionless on top of the pieces of paper.

"Because I'm curious,'" he purred again.

"About what?"

"You!"

I looked up at the hole and could see that he was standing directly beneath it. If Nik stayed there, I doubted he would notice it.

"Look Nik, I don't mean to be rude – but I think you should go," I told him. "I'm already in enough trouble with Phillips and if he finds you in here – we'll both get it!"

"Where's your sense of fun?" he asked.

"Sense of fun?" I asked disbelievingly. "I lost my sense of fun months ago," and I thought of how much life had changed since arriving at The Ragged Cove.

Nik came closer, stepping from under the hole above him. I looked up and then quickly back at Nik. He came closer still and then to my surprise, he nuzzled his head against my cheek. His fur was smooth like silk and as soft as pillows.

"I know what you are going through, Kiera. I know what it feels like to be trapped behind bars all day, unable to run free," he whispered into my ear. "Your prison is made of stone walls, mine is the coat of fur."

"What are you really like?" I asked him, trying to keep his attention so he didn't look up at the great gaping hole above.

"What do you mean?" he asked.

"You're a Lycanthrope, right?" I asked. "So what do you look like when you're not masquerading as a wolf? How old are you?"

"I'm sixteen-years-old," he said, fixing me with his piercing yellow eyes. "I stand about six-foot-seven in height. I have blonde hair and am quite scrawny."

It was hard for me to picture Nik as he described himself when not shaped as a wolf. It was hard for me to believe that he could look human at all as I'd only ever seen him as a wolf. But to think that there was a person beneath the thick coat of grey fur, made me feel sad for him. Like he said, he was trapped too.

"What was it that you did which was so terrible that you've been trapped?" I asked him, and this time I wasn't asking because I wanted to distract him from the hole in the ceiling – I really did want to know.

"I can't tell you that," he said.

"Why not?"

"What I did is too terrible to speak of," Nik barked at me, then with a swish of his giant tail, he slumped to the ground. "But I have cravings just like you do, Kiera. I understand your suffering – you want that flesh in the bowl over there as much as I want to rip your throat out."

"Rip my throat out?" I breathed, and if it wasn't for the fact that I was hiding the mashed-up pages of that book beneath me, I would have leapt to the other side of the cell.

"But it's more than just wanting to rip your throat out," he explained, never taking his bright yellow eyes off mine. And just like I'd stared into Jack Seth's eyes, I could see glimpses of Nik's true intentions. In those snapshots, I could see him hurting me – but it was more than just hurting me. He was torturing me, slowly and deliberately. He had me caught in his trance, and although my pain and suffering was unbearable, I couldn't help but tell him how much I needed him, wanted him. And even though in those glimpses I was bleeding and close to death, my whole being yearned for him.

Then those nightmarish images were gone, and Nik had broken my gaze.

"See, Kiera, I'm nothing more than a killer," he growled. "And like you, fight the urge to run to that flesh over there and devour it, I fight the desire to do all of those things to you that you've just seen in your mind's eye."

"What would happen to you if you did?" I asked him, my heart racing in my chest.

"Just like if you ate that flesh over there, you'd be lost to yourself forever. With each mouthful you would become like those other Vampyrus – Phillips and your mother – feeding off humans and creating vampires for the rest of eternity," he explained. "And if I were to murder you now, pleasure myself – the pleasure would only be short-lived as my father's curse would only embed itself deeper into my soul."

"Can the curse be lifted?" I asked him.

"Like your curse, Kiera, it can only be lifted if you beat your cravings for flesh," he said, "and mine will be lifted when I've beaten my cravings to murder and kill."

"So that's what all this is about?" I asked him. "You bringing me the chair, the book – being kind to me. It's your way of redeeming yourself somehow?"

"It's more than that," he said, still unable to look at me. "You don't know how much I want you, Kiera. Of all my victims, none have enticed me as much as you. To be in your presence drives me half crazy – I've never taken a half-breed before. The others have all been human. But with you, there is something different and it makes my heart race and fills me with nerves, anger, hatred; but most of all, desire. To be with you is overwhelming and every fibre of my being is screaming at me to take you – ravish you. So if I can fight the cravings that I have for you, then I can beat this – I can stop being a killer."

Then, looking down at the large, black scab that covered my shin, I said, "But it was you who bit me, right?"

Looking at me he said, "Yes, it was me – but it's not what you think."

"So you just bit a lump out of my leg for fun?" I hissed.

"Doctor Hunt got me to do it," Nik barked at me.

"Doctor Hunt?" I said, not believing what I was hearing.

"It has something to do with a code and that book I brought you," Nik said.

"I don't have the book anymore," I stressed. "Phillips has taken it."

"That doesn't matter," Nik woofed at me.

"But the code is in it!"

"No, its' not," Nik said, looking straight into my eyes.

Breaking his stare in case I succumbed to him, I said, "But I remembered Doctor Hunt telling me that he'd hidden the code within the pages of that book."

"And he did," Nik said. "But he was convinced that there was a spy amongst you and your friends – a traitor. You had a friend called Murphy, right?"

"Yes," I said, nodding my head.

"Doctor Hunt told me that this Murphy and he were friends. Murphy stayed with Hunt at his manor for a while. Hunt told him of his fears, but Murphy wouldn't believe that one of his friends could be caught up in all of this. Doctor Hunt said that he was close to finding out who it was, when suddenly he was captured and brought here to this zoo, never finding out who the spy was. But he is convinced that there is one amongst you. The book does hold a part of the code – but he made a second copy and hid it somewhere safe."

"Where is it?" I asked him. "I need to find it."

"I don't know," Nik said.

"Did Hunt tell you who he thought this traitor might be?" I asked him. "And why would he trust you?"

"No he didn't know who it was," he said. "And he trusted me because he knew that I was trying to make amends for my previous sins. Doctor Hunt understood how much I wanted to be free of my curse."

Staring down at my leg, I said, "So what is it that Phillips has planned for me tomorrow?"

"They started to breed the half-breeds in some desolate factory farm a few miles from here. But just as Hunt had planned, they didn't live very long – the infection from the bite I gave you attacks their immune system and they die, so they abandoned the factory," Nik said. "Although Phillips and his crew don't know that the infection was deliberately placed there by Hunt, they're smart enough to know that it's the infection in your leg that has destroyed the DNA that they had. So now they know your leg is better they plan to start breeding tomorrow."

"Breeding?" I said, my heart thumping in time with the jabbing pains in my stomach.

"Phillips is happy that he has the correct code now, so tomorrow they start the breeding process with you and your friends Kayla and Isidor."

"But what if my leg hadn't healed?" I asked him.

"They were going to kill you," he said. "They suspected that once you had died, the infection inside of you would have died too and they would have just taken the sample then."

"So why didn't they just kill me weeks ago and just take what they wanted?" I asked Nik.

"Whoever this traitor is – this invisible person without a face - wants you alive for some reason," he said, then looked away.

"So this invisible man is my protector? My saviour?" I scoffed

"Let's just say – whoever it is, doesn't solely have your best interests at heart – but for the time being, you are safe; for the time being, they need you," Nik barked over his shoulder.

"Need me for what?" I pushed.

Nik slinked back across the cell and stood under the hole. He turned to face me. "I don't know," he said, then left my cell.

# Chapter Fifteen

*Should I have told Nik about my planned escape?* I wondered. After all, he said that he was trying to redeem himself. But then again, he was a serial killer who wanted to torture and murder me! Could he really be trusted, when at any moment my ally might become my executioner? No. Even through the pain that clouded my mind, I knew that I had made the right decision in not telling him about my escape. He had spoken about trust, how Hunt had suspected that one of my friends was a traitor, and even though I knew that Murphy suspected the same – I couldn't bring myself to believe that. I mean, who out of them would do such a thing? And why?

With daybreak not far off, Phillips and Sparky would soon come for me to start their perverse breeding program. Knowing I only had a matter of hours to get free of my cell, find Luke, Kayla and Isidor and then find my way out of the zoo, I lifted the broom above me and forced the head between the gap I'd made between the ceiling and the mesh.

Placing all of my weight on the handle of the broom, I pulled. The wire gave a little but not enough. With one hand above the other, I pulled my way up the length of the handle, but my hands were clammy with fever and I slipped down the broom and landed in a heap on the floor. It was covered with dirt and dust, so I rubbed the palms of my hands across the ground until they were covered in muck. Taking hold of the broom again, I started to haul myself up towards the hole.

This time around, my hands gripped the handle firmly and I managed to heave myself up. Once I was level with the hole, I placed the fingers of my right hand through the mesh, and held onto the edge of the hole with my left. I then began to rip and pull on the wire with all my strength. At first, the wire showed no sign of moving, so I continued to pull at it. I yanked so hard that the wire cut into my fingers and they began to bleed. I looked at the blood, then turned away. I couldn't allow myself to think about that now, no matter how much my body screamed at me to slide back down the broom handle and eat some of the red stuff in the bowl. Bit by bit, tiny pieces of plaster began to fall away from the edge of the hole and the wire mesh began to loosen some more.

The growling on the other side of the hatch started up again and I knew deep within me that it was responding to the sounds of my breakout. It would only be a matter of minutes before Phillips came bursting through my cell door with Sparky cackling hysterically behind him.

Then a voice from my nightmares whispered in my ears as I remembered Doctor Hunt sitting beside my bed in the facility.

*"Someone I could trust," he said. "Someone I knew who would have the sight to find a way to escape these Vampyrus."*

I closed my eyes and understood the trust and belief that Hunt had placed in me. I couldn't let him down – I couldn't let myself down. So in sheer desperation, I began to rip the wire free. Taking hold of it with both hands, I swung from it like a monkey. I pulled at it with all my weight, as my feet swayed above the floor of my cell. My legs swung back and forth in the air, and I kicked out to give myself some momentum. I could feel a warm sensation running down my arms, and in the darkness I could just make out thick streams of blood oozing from between my fingers.

Then suddenly, just when I was about to give up hope – the wire mesh gave way and I fell to the floor. I landed on my back, squeezing the air from lungs. There was a noise from the corridor outside and the owner of the paw on the other side of the hatch released an agonising howl into the night. I got to my feet, doubled up in pain and fought to suck mouthfuls of air back into my lungs.

The broom lay on the floor beside me and I snatched it up. I pushed it through the hole and hooked it in one of the corners. Yanking on it to make sure it was secure, I began to hoist my way back up the broom handle. I didn't get very far before my hands began to slip again, as the blood continued to pour from my torn fingers. Dropping back to the floor, I hastily wiped my hands against my hospital gown.

Keys jangled in the lock of my cell door. I could hear laughing coming from outside and I could picture Sparky grinning from ear to ear in the dark. Turning my back on the cell door, closing my mind to that insane laughter, I took hold of the broom handle and started to climb. One hand over the other I went, as I shinned my way towards the hole above me with those words of Doctor Hunt whispering in my ears like a weak radio signal.

*"– someone I knew who would have the sight to find a way to escape these Vampyrus!"*

At the top of the broom handle, I reached out with my right hand and took hold of the edge of the hole. I then let go of the broom with my left hand and pulled myself up. My back scraped against what was left of the wire mesh, and I could feel those black finger-like bones recoil. I bit into my lower lip to stop myself from screaming out in pain.

Sweat ran into my eyes as I forced the upper half of my body through the hole. Immediately I felt my face caressed by a crisp cold breeze. It felt wonderful – like an angel stroking my face. I hoisted my way up onto my elbows and crawled onto the roof. To be out of that cell felt wonderful. At last I felt free and that feeling was incredible.

I looked back down into the darkness and saw Phillips charge into my cell, followed closely by Sparky. Phillips seemed to be momentarily confused, and then glanced upwards. Seeing me standing looking down at him, he screamed with rage. He brandished his fangs and even in the dark, they glowed yellow in his mouth. I watched as he raced across the cell, clattering into Sparky and sending him flying from my view. Phillips grabbed for the broom handle, but I quickly pulled it up through the hole and out of his reach.

"You won't escape me, Kiera!" he roared from below.

'You've gotta catch me first!" I spat and turning away from the edge of the hole, I ran across the roof of the cell.

# Chapter Sixteen

Teetering on the edge of the roof like a tightrope walker, I used the broom handle to balance myself. I looked down below, and in the gloom I could see something huge and white pacing back and forth.

*So I was right, that huge white paw did belong to a polar bear!* I thought. Just then, the creature looked up at me and howled and I could see that it was actually a wolf that was as big as a polar bear!

Staring up at me, it made a wailing sound in the back of its throat as if alerting everyone else in the zoo that I was making my escape.

"Where do you think you are going?" It called angrily up at me. "You can't escape!"

Looking all about me, I couldn't see any way off the roof. I began to panic as I raced along the outer edge of the wall. Running back in the direction I had come from, I saw that there was another building with a flat roof adjacent to the rooftop I was on. I ran towards the edge of the building and estimated the gap between the two to be about ten foot. Taking several paces backwards, I drew in a deep breath and ran as fast as I could towards the gap. A splinter of pain knifed its way up my right leg from the scabby-gash that had now mostly healed. If the pain had been a colour it would have been dark and purple, as it electrified all the nerve endings on its way up to my brain. Then suddenly, my legs seemed to take on a life of their own as they began to quicken. I looked down at them and they seemed almost a blur.

As I reached the edge of the building at an incredible speed, I threw myself into the air and soared across the gap. Landing with a thud on the other side, I rolled onto my back. The other Lycanthrope and Vampyrus in the zoo must have sensed something was up, as they began to roar, shriek, and howl.

I raced across the roof I had just landed on and didn't stop until I reached the other side. Looking down into the darkness, I could see water. It looked black and velvety, and would make a soft landing.

As I stood on the ledge and prepared to jump, a voice from

inside my head screamed, *"What's in the water?"*

Then from behind me, came the deep sound of roaring. I looked over my shoulder to see Phillips scrambling onto the roof. But he no longer looked like my old sergeant who had trained me back at training school; he had taken on his true Vampyrus form again. Turning away from him, I looked down at the black water, closed my eyes and jumped, the broom still firmly gripped in my hand.

I plunged in with an almighty splash. It was cold and I felt something large brush up against me. Instinctively, I kicked my legs out beneath the water to push whatever it was away. Holding my breath, I swam to the surface, and using my broom as a float, I paddled to the edge of the pool. As I climbed out, I looked back over my shoulder again to see Phillips leaping from the roof, his giant black wings rippling on either side of him.

"Come back!" he screeched as he swooped towards me.

From all around the zoo, I could hear the sounds of howling, barking, and gnashing of fangs and it was almost deafening. Then, closer to me, I heard the sound of screeching. It was coming from behind me. I whirled around, brandishing my broom in the air. It was then that I realised what it was that had swam alongside me in the pool. A vampire was climbing out of the water and it was racing towards me.

Sprinting around the edge of the water in a blur of shadows, I headed towards a door that was set amongst the rocks and boulders that had been built to recreate some kind of sea life area in the zoo. The sound of Phillips' beating wings was right behind me now and I dared not look back to see that mountain of muscle and black hair swooping out of the night at me.

The door was only feet away as I felt Phillips swipe at me with one of his mighty arms. His fingers ran down the length of my back, as he tried to take hold of my hospital gown. But I was just beyond his reach and I shot through the door and slammed it closed behind me.

The door rocked in its frame as Phillips crashed into it on the other side. I leant against the door as he tried to force it open. My bare feet began to slide across the tiled floor, as he smashed against the door. I turned slightly and barged the door closed with my shoulder. There was a bolt and I frantically fumbled with it in an attempt to lock the door. But Phillips was too strong and he rammed the door open an inch or two. I peered through the gap as he pressed his giant-sized head against it. I looked straight into one of his black eyes and he glared back at me.

"You can't get away," he growled and his breath was hot and stank of that same meat I'd eaten.

*"I won't be your prisoner!"* I yelled, as I jabbed the end of the broom between the gap in the door and rammed him between the eyes.

Phillips wailed in pain and fell backwards. Seizing my chance, I forced the door closed and locked it. No sooner had I slid the bolt into its housing then Phillips was crashing and banging on the other side again. The door began to bow and splinter under the weight of his pounding claws.

Fearing that the door would soon come smashing down, I ran frantically around the area that I now found myself in, desperately looking for another way out.

I found myself in a large room filled with metal cages. Some of them were stacked neatly on top of each other and some had been thrown across the floor. I raced amongst them and slipped over on several decomposing lumps of flesh that lay stinking on the ground. Ahead of me there was another door. I sprinted towards it and without thinking; I pushed the door open and went tearing out into the grounds of the zoo.

The night had started to fade and the first rays of daylight could be seen slicing through the clouds above. *That was good wasn't it?* I screamed inside my head. *At least the vampires wouldn't be able to track me in daylight.*

I found myself in a wide, open area, which had animal enclosures built all around it. Nervously, I looked around. To the right of me, I could see empty animal cages and to the left some kind of enclosure that was littered with hay and half-eaten pieces of meat. The huge metal bars, which had once kept the animals locked inside, had now been twisted apart or ripped down.

*What had happened to all the animals?* I wondered.

Then the sound of the door finally giving way under Phillips' weight startled me back into action and I ran down the concrete path that ran between the animal cages. I rounded a bend in the path and froze. Standing before me only feet away was a wolf. Its giant snout was buried in the stomach of a human corpse that lay spread across the path ahead of me. Slowly, very slowly I started to back away, not wanting to disturb it and draw attention to my presence. I'd only gone a few feet, when the wolf raised its huge head and glared at me. Its yellow eyes burnt with anger, and its razor-sharp teeth glinted in the early morning light.

"Stop right there!" it boomed in a thunderous voice.

I continued to edge away as the wolf licked the blood from its snout and began to kick at the ground with its front claws.

*He's gonna charge at me!* I screamed inside as I continued to shuffle backwards. Although doubting it would offer me any protection against this beast, I raised my broom into the air.

Then, as I had suspected, the wolf lowered its head and brandishing its teeth, it came racing towards me. Wheeling round, I ran back in the direction I had come. I raced back past the empty cages, and as I reached the door that I had only moments before burst through, Phillips came bounding out. He immediately swiped at me with his meaty arms and I dropped to the floor and rolled under them. I clambered to my feet and continued to run as fast and as hard as I could. My right leg began to burn as I propelled myself forward – faster and faster and *faster!*

There was a fork in the path and I glanced up to see a sign that read, *'Zoo Exit'*. I raced towards it. Souvenir shops, hotdog and ice cream stands looking derelict and unused whooshed past me in a haze.

I stole a quick glance back over my shoulder and could see both Phillips and the wolf were only feet away. I pressed onwards, my arms pumping up and down like pistons, my legs thrusting me onwards, creating a blaze of dust, which trailed behind me like smoke.

At last, ahead of me, I could see the turnstiles that the visitors had once used when visiting the zoo. Beyond these were a huge set of iron gates that towered up into the sky. I could see freedom waiting for me on the other side of those gates – I could smell it and my mouth almost watered at the thought.

Then there was something on my back, its paws were dragging me down by my shoulders. I frantically tried to look backwards expecting to see Phillips but he had slowed down along with the wolf some way back.

The sound of hysterical laughter filled my ears and I knew who it was that had pounced on me. I fell to the ground under the weight of Sparky, as he barked and snarled. I rolled onto my back and he lay across my chest, his huge pink tongue dribbling onto my face.

*"Get the fuck off me!"* I screamed. *"Let me go!"*

Sparky just looked at me wildly with his crazy yellow eyes and cackled with laughter and in them, just like I had with Jack Seth and Nik, I could see into his murderous soul. But unlike the others, when I looked into Sparky's eyes, I didn't *see* images of him torturing and murdering me – it was Mrs. Lovelace that I watched him butcher. My head jerked backwards as my mind splintered with graphic pictures of him leading her into Hallowed Manor, believing he was taking her to safety. I could *see* Sparky pushing open the giant drawing room doors. Then he was tearing at her throat, dragging his claws down the length of her wrinkled neck, her blood spraying his face.

Then he was moving away, sniffing the air like an animal - a wolf. I watched him as if I had been there the whole time, as he climbed the stairs that led from the great hall and made his way up towards the forbidden wing. But someone was waiting for him up at top of the stairs, shrouded in darkness. They stood on the landing, their head cast down, long black wings trailing from their back. Darkness cloaked them, and I tried to *see* through it. But the darkness masking their identity wasn't cast by the shadows at the top of the stairs, it was as if the blackness radiated from them - a darkness so dark that it blinded me from seeing who they were.

At the top of the stairs, Sparky dropped to his knees and clasped his hands together as if in prayer. He rocked back and forth on his knees as in worship. Who could demand such reverence, I wondered? But in my heart I knew who it was, it was that *invisible man* that Murphy, Luke, and Potter had talked about. But what was he doing at the manor? Had he been there all along, secreted into the shadows and watching all of us? Murphy had wondered how this man had always been one step ahead of us, been able to move his followers, like Mrs. Payne, into position – perhaps he had been there all the time?

Sparky glanced up at the figure that stood before him, his hands clasped together. But I knew, like me, Sparky couldn't see through the darkness that radiated from the figure. It was impenetrable - like a cloak surrounding him. Then the figure struck Sparky with his foot, sending him sprawling onto his arse. Turning away, the figure climbed the stairs to the secret hospital where the half-breed children lay dying, only kept alive by Doctor Ravenwood's and Lord Hunt's medicines.

As I lay captivated by Sparky's bright yellow stare, I could *see* the figure and Sparky enter the ward hidden in the attic of the Hallowed Manor. The children in their beds recoiled even before the figure or Sparky had come close. It was as if they could sense their hatred for them. I watched as Doctor Ravenwood came from his office at the end of the ward, and he begged Sparky and the other not to hurt his patients and it was then I knew how *blind* I had been - I hadn't *seen* it!

How had Sparky, on returning to the manor with Mrs. Lovelace, while my friends and I had fought the vampires in the clearing by the summerhouse, managed to single-handedly kill her and all the half-breeds? He also managed to overpower Doc Ravenwood and take two of the remaining children hostage. He had an accomplice – this *invisible man* had been waiting for him at the manor – they had acted together.

And the vision was over. No longer could I see Sparky and the winged stranger go from bed to bed, killing each of the half-breeds in turn. The pictures disappeared as quickly as they had come, like a T.V. being switched on then off.

With Sparky still astride me and grinning into my face, I reached out for the broom, which I had dropped. Curling my fingers around it, I bought the broom handle up into the air intending to bring it crashing down on top of Sparky's skull. But it was violently snatched from my hand.

I looked up to see who had taken it from me. Phillips was standing over me grunting and panting. He pounded the broom against his chest then threw it to one side. Sparky looked up at Phillips and drooled, "Let me eat the girl now – I can feel her heart beating in her chest – it will be ripe and bloody!"

Then Sparky yelped as Phillips knocked him flying off me with the back of one of his giant claws.

"Get away from her! She's not to be harmed – not yet anyway!" Phillips roared.

Sparky got to his feet and shook his head from side to side. He looked at Phillips and whimpered pathetically. He caught me looking at him and then giggled.

Phillips pulled me to my feet.

"Let me go!" I yelled, kicking and punching at him. "You can't treat me like this!"

But Phillips was too strong and his hold was like a vice. Then, out of the corner of my eye, I saw Nik. He stood in the shadow of a ticket booth, tucked away from view.

"You told on me! You saw the hole and told on me!" I roared at him. "You ain't ever going to be redeemed now. You'll rot in hell!"

Phillips, Sparky, and the wolf turned to see who it was I was screaming at, when two winged creatures flashed past me in a wave of shadows and clattered into Phillips and Sparky.

# Chapter Seventeen

Taken by complete surprise, Phillips crumbled to the floor, his giant black wings sending up a shower of dust and dirt from the ground. Sparky howled and the second werewolf darted away, all of them taken by surprise.

"Take these!" someone barked from beside me. Looking to my right, I could see that Nik had now appeared from the shadows of the ticket booth and was nudging what looked like a pile of rags across the ground towards me with his snout. I peered at the rags and could see that in fact it was my long black coat that I'd been wearing the day of my capture beneath the mountains. Snatching it up, I pulled it on and immediately checked the pockets. I was relieved when my fingertips brushed over my iPod, the CD I'd taken from the monastery and Murphy's crucifix given to me by Potter. To have some of my possessions back was incredibly liberating as if I'd already escaped from my prison – but of course I hadn't.

Pulling my coat tight about me, I looked at Nik, and with some distrust in my voice I said, "What's going on?"

But before he'd the chance to say anything he was springing through the air towards Sparky, who was lunging at one of the winged creatures that flashed all around him in a blaze of black shadows. Sparky was quick, and he snagged one of the creatures with his claws. The creature almost seemed to stutter in mid-air and slow, and as it did so, its identity became clear.

"Kayla!" I gasped, seeing her try and pull herself free from Sparky's grasp. Her wings beat furiously and her auburn hair rippled out behind her in the morning breeze. But I could see that her once brilliant flame coloured hair now looked dull and lifeless. Then she was gone, released back into the sky as Nik lunged at Sparky and took a bite of him with his huge gaping jaws.

There was a wailing behind me, then the familiar sound of stakes whizzing past me. Spinning round, I was overwhelmed to see Isidor, raining down a wave of stakes at Phillips. Phillips wrapped one of his wings around him as a shield, then raced towards Isidor who hovered in the air. But just as Kayla's hair had lost its brilliance, Isidor looked pale, gaunt, and weak. He was naked to the waist, apart from the rucksack thrown over his back, and his wings that trailed from beneath his arms.

"Isidor!" I shrieked in delight at seeing him. Whether he heard me or not, I didn't know, as he remained focused on Phillips who raced towards him. Within feet of Isidor, Phillips launched himself into the air, stakes zipping past him as Isidor released them from his crossbow. But Isidor's aim appeared to be off, either that or Phillips had lightning reflexes as the stakes flew harmlessly past him. Knowing that Isidor was in trouble in his weakened state, I rushed forwards towards the point from which Phillips was taking off from the ground. Even though he was more than a hundred feet away, I was upon him in an instant. It was like I had disappeared and reappeared on the other side of the walkway in a blink of an eye.

Before I'd the chance to fully understand what had just happened, I was yanking at Phillips' ankles and pulling him back out of the sky. He hit the ground with a sickening thud, and it sounded like I could hear every bone in his body rattle. Releasing him, he rolled quickly over, and seeing it was me who had thrown him to the ground, his face revealed a fleeting glimpse of surprise and shock.

Without taking his eyes from me, Phillips scrambled to his feet and I was sure I could still see that look of shock in his eyes. But he recovered quickly, spinning through the air like a rocket. Then, as if from nowhere, Kayla was plummeting from above, driving her feet into him and knocking him off course. Snapping my head to the left, I watched as Phillips flew out of control into the derelict, old ticket booth, his impact causing it to erupt into a shower of splinters.

Seizing his chance, Isidor swooped from the sky, and wrapping an arm about my waist, he raced me away over the walls of the zoo.

"We can't leave without Luke!" I yelled over the deafening sound of the wind that rushed over his wings. "We have to go back for him!"

"Not now!" Isidor shouted back. "We've only just managed to escape!"

Looking back, I could see Kayla tearing through the sky behind us, her wings rippling like two glittering sails. Then from above, l watched as Nik bravely continued to fight off Sparky as we made our escape.

Clinging to Isidor, we floated silently in a mass of low-flying cloud. Kayla was beside us, her wings almost folded close, but open enough to keep her airborne. She seemed to have come a long way since I spied on her in the grounds of Hallowed Manor when she had practiced using her wings. The bony black claws at the end of each wing opened and closed as if snatching at the air. She looked like some kind of prehistoric butterfly, if any such creature had ever existed.  On the other side of the cloud, I could see the shadows of the Vampyrus, as they soared back and forth in search of us. But we floated away with the clouds, unseen by our pursuers. Just like Kayla, Isidor was motionless, his wings slightly apart, just enough to keep him in the sky. It was then I remembered Luke telling Isidor about how the hunters amongst the Vampyrus used echolocation to track their prey - homing in on the vibrations that their giant wings made.

Holding my breath, we floated like that until we were cold and wet through from the cloud moisture. How long we hid like that, I couldn't tell; it was like time had stopped inside those giant clouds. We waited for the sounds of the Vampyrus to fade away. When the only sound was the wind tugging at the strands of my filthy, unkempt hair, Isidor and Kayla cautiously descended through the clouds and back towards the ground below.

The road we landed on was narrow and it twisted its way into the distance, finally disappearing between two hills. The world seemed eerily silent, only broken by the odd bark or growl that came from amongst the trees that grew tall and wild on either side of the road. This wasn't how I'd remembered the world to be – something had changed – but I didn't know what.

# Chapter Eighteen

I'd watched in awe as Kayla had fluttered out of the sky. She had landed softly, and I hobbled towards her and took her in my arms. At first we didn't say anything, we just stood in the cold wind and hugged each other. Like me, she wore a grubby-looking hospital gown, and her face, legs, and arms were covered in grime.

"I'm sorry, Kayla," I said.

"What for?" she whispered back.

"For not rescuing you," I told her.

"I knew you would come for me," she said, "even though it put your life in danger and you ended up being captured yourself."

"It wasn't just me - the others came in search of you, too," I told her. There was so much I wanted to - *needed to* - tell her. Her mother and father's death, the murder of Murphy. But now wasn't the time.

"I'm sorry I didn't believe you about Phillips," she said.

"You have nothing to be sorry for," I told her.

She pulled herself away from me, and over her shoulder I could see Isidor standing in the middle of the deserted road. Like all of us, his feet were bare, and he wore a baggy pair of striped pyjama bottoms. His body was deathly-white, and where I had once remembered a well-defined chest and stomach, I could see his chest plate and ribs almost seeming to poke through. The stubby-looking beard which grew from his chin was now long and black and the bottom of it nearly touched his chest. The black flaming tattoos covering his upper arms and neck looked as if they had been etched on the skin of a deflated balloon.

I looked at him and he met my stare.

Half-smiling at me, he said, "You look like shit, Kiera."

"It's good to see you, too," I smiled, and it was then I realised I couldn't remember the last time I had smiled.

Like I had embraced Kayla, I limped towards him, and threw my arms around his bony shoulders.

"It's good to see ya," he said and squeezed me so tight I thought my ribs were going to snap inside of me. Then in my ear he whispered, "She doesn't know I'm her brother – she doesn't know me at all."

"Okay," I whispered and squeezed him back. "I'll leave that for you to tell her."

"Thanks," he said back, then pulled gently away.

Turning to face Kayla, I said, "Hey Kayla, this is Isidor."

Coming towards us, her eyes wide and staring she said, "I've seen you a couple of times before - I think you tried to escape once, didn't you?" she said to Isidor.

"I tried a few times," he said, throwing his crossbow across his naked back, "not that it got me very far."

"So how did you both get out?" I asked them.

"That wolf set us free," Kayla said.

"Yeah, he came to my cell, just before dawn and said that if I wanted to escape than I should follow him. At first I thought it was some kinda sick joke," Isidor explained. "Then I saw Kayla was with him, and he had my crossbow and rucksack. So before he changed his mind, we went with him and he told us to wait in the shadows by the entrance to the zoo."

"I asked him what we were waiting for," Kayla cut in, "and he told us that we would soon know. It wasn't long before I saw you racing up that path towards us with Phillips and Sparky chasing you down. It was then that I realised that it was a breakout."

"Why do you think that werewolf helped us?" Isidor asked, rubbing the tops of his arms in an attempt to keep warm.

I thought of Nik and how he had been cursed by his father. I could only imagine the horrendous crimes he had committed, but he had been true to his word and he seemed to be in search of redemption in one way or another.

"He had to do it," I told them.

"Why?" Kayla asked. "Phillips will kill him for helping us."

"Maybe that's what he wanted," I whispered, almost to myself.

"But, why?" Kayla pushed.

Then meeting her gaze I said, "Just like us, Kayla, I think that all he wanted was to be free. And maybe he has his freedom now."

Cocking an eyebrow at me, Kayla said, "Whatever you say, Kiera. I won't pretend to understand what you're going on about and I'm too cold to be bothered to find out. Let's say that we find ourselves some meat."

Hearing Kayla say this, I gripped her arm and said, "What do you mean? What sort of meat are you talking about?" From the corner of my eye, I could see Isidor staring at the both of us.

"Whatever it was they were giving us back at that zoo," Kayla started, "I don't know what sort of meat it was, but it was delicious and I can't get enough of the stuff."

I glanced at Isidor and something struck me. He looked like a corpse that had been warmed-up – all bones and loose skin, and I looked pretty much the same. But although Kayla looked battered and bruised in other ways, she didn't look undernourished. Kayla looked as if she had eaten well during her time in captivity at the zoo. And although my whole being craved for the red stuff like an agonising itch that wouldn't go away however much I scratched it, Kayla was yet to understand that she was addicted to human flesh.

Knowing that this wasn't the time to explain to her what the Vampyrus and Lycanthrope had been feeding her, I dreaded the moment when I would have to tell her everything that had happened while she had been held prisoner. With my heart sinking in my chest at the thought of that conversation, I put my arm around her shoulder and said, "C'mon, we should find somewhere to hide until we can figure out how we get Luke out of that place."

Supporting me as I limped down the country road, Kayla said, "Kiera, why are you limping? Have you got something wrong with your leg?"

"It's a long story," I said back, "I'll tell you about it later."

"Okay, sure," she smiled, happy enough with my reply. Then, she added, "Hey did you meet my father at the zoo?"

"Uh-huh," I said, not knowing what to say.

"I think he musta escaped like us," she smiled at me.

"What makes you think that?" I asked her, knowing that by now he was probably dead.

"Because he stopped coming to see me," she said, and looking into her eyes, I wondered if she actually believed that.

I glanced back over my shoulder in search of Isidor, another person to join in the conversation, so I wouldn't have to answer all of Kayla's questions. But he walked several feet behind us, his head stooped low and I guessed he could hear all of Kayla's questions and he was wondering how he was going to tell her that he was her brother.

# Chapter Nineteen

The track leading away from the zoo carved its way through dense areas of woodland. I was grateful for the trees that climbed high above on either side of us, as they offered a natural camouflage against any of the Vampyrus that might still be searching for us high above. But all the while I kept heading east, towards the town that Nik had called Wasp Water.

When the trees thinned out along the roadside, I ushered the others towards the bushy hedgerows to avoid being seen, just like Murphy would have told us to. Thinking about him, I put my hand into my coat pocket and brushed his tiny silver crucifix with the tips of my fingers. We made our journey in silence, all us looking paler and weaker by the minute and I knew that like me, Kayla and Isidor were fighting their cravings for the red stuff. My stomach continued to cramp, and even though the morning air was bitterly cold, hot beads of sweat streamed from my forehead. Kayla's fiery red hair lay matted to her brow and cheeks in damp clumps and Isidor staggered along the uneven road, cradling his feverish body with his arms.

I don't know for how long or how far we had walked, but the meandering track that we had been walking on widened and we found ourselves on a road, which had signposts and markings on it. I prayed that we were nearing the town and hopefully some help.

A small cluster of houses appeared ahead but I could see no signs of life anywhere. The world seemed eerily silent, only broken by the sound of crows squawking from high up in the trees. As we drew nearer to the houses, I could see that some of them looked as if they had been smashed down, like buildings that had been bombed during the Second World War. Now all that was left was mountains of rubble, with the foundations protruding from the ground like twisted limbs. Even through the pain of my cravings, itching skin, and agonising thirst, that voice inside of me, the Kiera that was pushing me on, told me that something was terribly wrong. But my thoughts of searching for help – for Potter – nagged away at the corners of my mind and I knew that we must keep on going. We needed to find food, water and some clothes.

*A bath would be good too!* I thought to myself.

So we passed the deserted homes to the left and right and I walked towards the town. As we grew nearer we could see more deserted houses. The world seemed so quiet, only the sound of our bare feet could be heard smacking off the tarmac. Looking down, I was shocked to see that the road surface had split and cracked in places, leaving wild and untamed weeds and plants to sprout from them. Nearing the town, I noticed a sea of lights twinkling on and off up ahead. As we drew nearer, it became clear to me what these lights were. It was the glare of the pale winter sun glinting off the cars that lay strewn across the deserted road.

We walked slowly towards the cars. The wind blew amongst them and I could hear the creak of a car door as it swung open and closed. I took my hand and covered my mouth and nose as a rancid stench wafted towards me. A gasping sound came from behind me and I spun around to see Isidor doubled over getting sick. His sense of smell was far greater than mine and Kayla's, so the stench must have been overwhelming for him. Going to him, I rubbed his back, and his flesh felt burning hot.

Brushing my hand away, Isidor straightened himself and whispered, "It's okay, Kiera, I'll be fine." Covering his nose and mouth with his hands, he walked on.

Passing amongst the rows of cars, I dared to glance into some of them and then looked quickly away. There were people in them – *dead* people. Their faces were bloated and purple in colour. Black crusty lumps of blood had dried in streams around their noses and mouths. It was obvious they had been running from something – trying to escape the town with the people that they loved. I saw the broken windshields, the scratches running across the hoods of the cars, the hanging bumpers, the upturned faces of the dead, the desperate fingers forever frozen as if clutching the air. I could see the black tire tracks on the road and then my head was thrown back as if invisible hands had grabbed at my hair. And, closing my eyes against the glare of a cold winter sun, I could see what had happened to these people as if being played out like a movie on the inside of my eyelids.

They had come…

*…at dawn, just as the first shades of pink had spilt over the mountaintops. But there was something wrong! Why, on such a*

*beautiful morning, were there black clouds in the sky? The clouds were moving fast, racing over the horizon as if a storm were coming. Black and threatening they came, and as they grew nearer they changed shape. It was as if the clouds where breaking up – falling apart – and the shadows they created on the fields below were just as black and moved faster if that were possible. But they weren't clouds or shadows. It was Vampyrus that raced through the sky and Lycanthrope that sped over the mountains and fields towards the town. Swooping low, their giant black wings splayed on either side of them, the masses of Vampyrus flew over the town, their white fangs glistening like knives. The werewolves howled and barked as they bounded through rivers, leapt over gates and crashed through people's front doors.*

*Children sat up in their beds, rubbing the sleep from their eyes, as they stared in fear at the giant wolves that stood licking their giant snouts.*

*"Mummy...!" the boy cried, but before he'd had the chance to raise the alarm, he had been snatched away, carried like a rag doll in the giant jaws of a werewolf as it raced back across the fields and between the mountains with its prey.*

*The town of Wasp Water didn't wake to the sound of alarm clocks, letters being delivered, toast popping out of toasters, or the rustling of newspapers at kitchen tables. They woke to the sound of screaming, running, barking, howling, tearing and the ripping of flesh.*

*Half asleep, they ran from their homes, scrambling into their cars as the Vampyrus dropped through the air like stones above them. Windscreens imploding in showers of crystal glass as the Vampyrus ripped the occupants from the vehicles and fed on them. Blood jetted from throats, ears, and noses as the Vampyrus fed in a frenzy of excitement and hatred for these humans.*

*Cars crashed into each other as their owners fought like demolition derby drivers to get out of town. Some managed to get onto the main road, but the wolves were quick – super fast, and they raced along beside the cars, smashing their giant skulls into them. The cars crumbled as if made from cardboard, veering off the road and into ditches where the occupants were dragged kicking and screaming, until their life's blood was drained from them. And those who managed to outrun the werewolves were set*

*upon from above, as Vampyrus ripped open the roofs of the cars as*
*if opening a can of sardines. The families inside were snatched*
*away into the sky where they were torn to pieces by the Vampyrus.*

*More Vampyrus and Lycanthrope came like a plague of rats,*
*their squawking and howling deafening, making me tremble and*
*shake like a tree in a storm. I lurched to and fro as…*

…Isidor shook me.

"Kiera! Snap out of it!" he shouted, shaking me from side to
side. "Kiera – you've got to stop Kayla!"

Snapping my eyes open, I felt my knees buckle, and Isidor
steadied me. His eyes were grey and dark smudges circled them.

"Kiera – look at Kayla!" he shouted at me.

Still dazed and disorientated from my vision, I turned slowly
and looked at Kayla. She was standing in the centre of the road and
staring into one of the cars. Her arms hung motionless by her sides
and the wind blew her hair from her shoulders. She appeared to be
transfixed by the hideous sights hiding inside the cars. Then
slowly, she reached out and opened one of the car doors, spilling
one of the dead occupants onto the road. It lay half in and out of
the car, its head lolling to one side at an awkward angle as if its
neck had been snapped. But looking more closely, I could see that
the corpse's neck hadn't been broken, it was bearly there at all,
ripped away by one of the Vampyrus or Lycanthrope.

As if waking to find myself in a nightmare far worse than the one
I'd just woken from, I watched Kayla drop to her knees, brush the
hair from her face and lower her mouth to the festering hole
beneath the corpses chin.

Then, as quickly as blinking, I was pushing her off the body,
sending her crashing onto the road.

"No Kayla" I yelled. "You mustn't!"

Kayla sprung to her feet, and with fangs sprouting from her
gums, she launched herself at me. Isidor leapt at the same time as
Kayla and dragged her out of the air.

Wrapping his arms about her, Isidor screamed, "Help me, Kiera!"
Kayla kicked and clawed at Isidor, spittle flying from her fangs as
she fought against Isidor who tried to restrain her. "I can't hold her
for much longer!"

Seeing the desperation in his eyes, I raced towards him and pinned

Kayla's arms to her sides.

*"Get the fuck off me!"* she screamed with uncontrollable rage. Then she snapped her head forward as if to take a bite out of my face. Jerking backwards, I felt the spit from her fangs spatter against my face, and it burned like acid.

"Kayla!" I screamed back at her. "Calm down!"

"I'm thirsty!" she screeched, and her eyes rolled back, revealing the whites.

"She's burning up!" Isidor shouted. "And I'm too weak to hold her."

With Kayla's arms held fast to her sides, I looked into her face, and it looked flushed, like she had had too much sun. "Kayla, listen to me!" I roared at her. "You can't have that red stuff – it isn't going to help you. We've got to fight this!"

"Thirsty!" she screamed back and this time her eyes rolled down and she stared at me like she had gone insane.

Lowering my voice, I shook her by the arms and said, "Kayla, listen to me. I want that stuff as much as you do and so does Isidor, but we can't have it anymore."

"Thirsty," she groaned again, but this time her voice sounded weaker, as if the anger was leaving her and I guessed that her raging fever was beginning to sap her strength.

Sensing that she was no longer a threat to us, Isidor loosened his grip on her, and stroking the side of her hot face with my hand, I said, "Trust me Kayla, that red stuff you've been eating isn't like normal meat – its human flesh."

"Flesh?" she mumbled her eyes half open.

Knowing that I had to get her away from the corpses and the stench of their rotting flesh, I didn't answer her. Instead, I looped my arm around her shoulders and helped her up the road and towards town. Isidor followed and I could hear his teeth chattering in his gums as if he were freezing cold.

As I weaved my way amongst the parked cars, I came across corpses splayed from their vehicles as if they had tried to make a last, desperate attempt at escape during the remaining moments of their lives. Some had their hands gripped about their throats as if they'd tried to stop the blood that had pumped from them. Others clutched their chest with bony hands and I saw a sickening image of Murphy's heart being ripped from him. Pushing the image of

Murphy away, as it was too painful, I looked down at the bodies as I stepped over them, and was sickened at the sight of the flies crawling in and out of their open mouths and maggots wriggling from their nostrils and out of their ears.

I looked away in revulsion, shoving Kayla into Isidor's arms. I ran to the curb and puked what little of the red stuff I had left in my stomach into the gutter. It swung from my lips in clotted streams and I brushed it away with the back of my hand. My stomach cramped and I heaved again, but this time nothing came out. When I felt able to go on, I took hold of Kayla again, keeping to the edge of the curb. I tried desperately not to look upon those dead people again. I wanted to get away from them as quickly as possible. Not because of the way they smelled or how they looked, it was because I knew that if some of them had been bitten by Vampyrus, there was every chance that before long, they would wake as vampires.

# Chapter Twenty

The town seemed closer now and I could clearly see the individual outlines of buildings in the distance. Another mile or so and we would be lost amongst them. I continued to support Kayla; her fever had eased a little and she shuffled onwards, her head down, chin resting against her chest. Isidor walked silently beside me, his hands pressed over his mouth and nose to block out the smell, and every step he took was sluggish. The cars grew in number as we reached the outskirts of the town, and they stood either empty or contained dead passengers.

I spotted a police van, and with my heart leaping in my chest, I raced towards it. The word 'POLICE' seemed to scream 'HELP', 'SAVED' and 'AUTHORITY', but did I really believe that if there were any police officers left alive in that van, wouldn't they have tried to help these people? But we had to pass it if we were to reach the centre of town. So without thinking, I started off towards it as if it were calling to me like a mirage in a desert. Before taking too many steps, Isidor grabbed my arm and stopped me from going any further.

"What are you thinking of, Kiera?" he asked, his eyes wide and fearful.

"I'm going to checkout that police van," I told him. "There might be some police officers in there and they might be able to help us."

"Have you lost your mind?" he snapped. "Remember those vampire-cops we ran into? The ones who tried to run us off the road? The cops who shot at us?"

Realising that Isidor was correct, I shook my head and said, "Isidor you're right. I don't know what I was thinking of."

"It's okay," he whispered looking over at the police van. "I guess we're all going to be a bit cranky." Isidor hunkered down between two abandoned cars. I helped Kayla down into the gap, and we crawled amongst the cars towards the police van. As we drew near, I could see that its back doors were open and several of the cops, who were wearing boiler-type suits, were hanging out. They appeared to be lifeless and still.

"Look after Kayla," I said to Isidor, as I crept forwards on my hands and knees, not daring to get up in case it was a trap.

Dropping onto my stomach, I inched my way further towards the van, not taking my eyes of those bodies hanging out of the back.

When I got as close as I could without being detected, I peered around the rear wheel of one of the cars. Several of the cops had managed to climb from the van, but had landed in a heap on the road. To my horror, some of them stared up at the sky with half of their faces and throats missing. The lower half of their heads appeared to have been eaten away, leaving a huge, fleshy hole. Then, from behind me I heard a noise. Looking back over my shoulder, I could see Isidor crouching down with Kayla propped beside him. I sensed that Isidor had also heard the sound as his eyes were darting from left to right. The sound came again and I froze. Daring not to move an inch, I listened intently to the noise. The sound was coming from one of the cars several rows away.

*Was it one of those corpses waking up as a vampire?*

But what if it were a survivor – some child who had managed to survive the Vampyrus and Lycanthrope attack? Shouldn't we help them? It could be someone from the town, come in search of their family and they might know where other survivors are – there could be more – several more – even hundreds more who might be able to help us.

With these thoughts spinning through my mind, I got up slowly and crept between the cars. The noise came again, a shuffling sound like feet on concrete. I headed towards it. Then the noise came again, but from the opposite direction. I wheeled around.

"Hello?" I called out. "Is there anyone there?"

Silence.

I glanced back at Isidor, and he shrugged.

Crouching again, I shuffled deeper between the line of cars.

Then the sound came again and it was close. I gingerly poked my head over the edge of one of the car bonnets and found myself looking into the eyes of a tiger.

Its upper lip crumpled as it snarled at me. The tiger's teeth were like ivory daggers and they were covered in blood and flesh. Long, silver whiskers twitched around its snout, and it's orange and black coat glimmered in the sunlight. Seeing the blood smeared around its powerful jaws, I knew it had been feeding on the bodies strewn across the road and had probably escaped from the zoo when the Vampyrus had moved in.

I threw myself backwards in terror and clattered into one of the many cars. Regaining my balance, I darted between them and away from the tiger. It growled behind me, which was followed by the sound of its paws pounding against the roofs of the cars as it raced over to catch me. I saw Isidor peek out from over the hood of a car.

"Get down!" he screamed at me, as he raised his crossbow. But, in his weakened and frail state, Isidor looked as if he were having trouble taking aim. The crossbow wavered up and down and from side to side in his hands.

I weaved between the cars housing dead people and I had no intention of becoming one of them. My feet snapped off the tarmac, and as I rounded the front of a large four-by-four, I slipped and lost my balance completely. I hit the ground hard, knocking the wind from me. The tiger appeared on the roof of the four-by-four and snarled. Without taking my eyes off it, I inched backwards. The tiger looked down at me, and with a flash of those bloody teeth, it leapt from the four-by-four and flew through the air towards me. Closing my eyes, I waited for the tiger to sink its teeth into me.

There was a thud and a high-pitched wailing sound and as I opened my eyes, I saw something large and grey fleet across my line of vision, knocking the tiger out of the air. I turned my head to follow it and could see that the tiger had been bought down by another creature. They rolled about amongst the abandoned vehicles in a flash of colour and claws. The sounds of the creatures' woofing and howling were terrifying and I slid underneath the four-by-four for safety. From my hiding place, I could see the two animals clawing and biting at each other, but it was such a violent blur of rage, that it was hard to see exactly what was taking place.

Manoeuvring myself, I watched as a huge set of jaws came clamping down on the tiger's throat as it howled in agony. The other creature shook it violently to and fro and the tiger kicked out with its back legs. But its efforts were useless. The other creature was bigger and stronger and within moments had completely ripped open the tiger's throat in a spray of crimson. The tiger twitched and jerked for a few more seconds then became still as the other animal nuzzled its face into the open wound and began to eat.

I lay under the four-by-four and covered my ears against the sounds of ripping and tearing as the creature devoured the tiger. Not daring to move, I stayed there until I thought it was safe to open my eyes. Looking sideways, I gagged at the sight of the dead tiger now lying on its side, its stomach torn open and a mass of entrails spilled onto the tarmac. Then I heard the sound of woofing and breathing beside me. I slowly turned my head to see the bloody face of Nik staring at me.

"Are you going to lie under there all day or are you going to start looking for a way out of here?" he barked, licking away the blood and sinew that dangled from his whiskers.
"What are you doing here?" I asked him as I pulled myself out from beneath the four-by-four.

"To help you," he woofed.

"But I thought..." I started.

"You thought what?" he said, fixing me with his bright yellow eyes.

"But I thought you were dead back there," I said.

"And I probably will be if I ever go back, but it's too late for me to worry about that now. I don't think it took too much for them to work out it was me who gave you the chair and that book." Nik looked at me then turned away.

"Where you going?" I called out.

"I have something I need to do," he said with a swish of his pointed tail.

"What about my friend, Luke Bishop?" I asked.

"What about him?"

"Why didn't you save him, too?"

"I didn't have time," he said, licking the last of the tiger from his whiskers. "Besides you made so much goddamn noise escaping, the whole zoo came running." Fixing me with his yellow stare, he added, "If I were you, Kiera Hudson, I'd forget any ideas you might have about going back for your friend, Luke." Then he was gone, bounding away between the cars and out of sight.

"I can't forget about Luke!" I called after him. "I *won't* forget

86

about him – he's my friend!"

# Chapter Twenty-One

"What happened?" Isidor asked, as he came shuffling towards me, his arm around Kayla. And just for a glimpsing moment, I could see that they did look like brother and sister.

"There was a tiger," I told him, pointing to the remains of the giant cat.

"Did you do that?" Isidor asked, eyeing me.

"It was Nik."

"Nik?" Isidor said.

"The werewolf that helped us escape from the zoo," I explained.

"Where is he now?"

"Gone," I told him. I could see he was struggling to support Kayla, so I went to him and tucked my arm around her waist and her head flopped against my shoulder.

"Gone where?" Isidor asked me.

"I don't know," I said, then added, "look we should really try to make it into the town. There might be people – somebody that can help us."

"Why has this happened?" Isidor said, as we made our way up the road.

Remembering my earlier vision, I said, "The town came under attack by the Vampyrus and Lycanthrope. They took the children and killed the adults."

"But, why?" Isidor asked me from behind his hands which he'd placed over his nose and mouth again.

"Like Murphy warned us, they want to take over and rule the Earth. This looks like the start of it," I told him.

"But how have they gotten away with it? Why aren't the humans fighting back?"

With my heart sinking in my chest, I looked at him and said, "Perhaps there aren't any humans left."

"I can't believe we're the only humans left alive on Earth," Isidor said.

"We're not strictly human, remember?"

We walked on in silence, Kayla lent against me, her feet seeming to drag behind.

Just when I thought Isidor was lost to his private thoughts, he said, "Maybe they had their time – humans I mean. Perhaps it's the end of humanity."

"I can't accept that," I breathed, as I struggled to support Kayla.

"Maybe you're gonna have to!" Isidor said, and shuffled ahead.

I followed close behind him and we walked the rest of the way in silence.

Although Kayla was small, the weight of supporting her as we stumbled our way into the town made my arm go numb and I knew that once I had finally put her down, I would have the worst case of pins-and-needles ever.

I didn't have to wait long, as the road finally led us into the town of Wasp Water. The streets were narrow and the buildings that rose up on either side of us looked ancient. The roads were cobbled and we were met with the sight of cars full of the dead. Most of the shops lining the streets had the shutters pulled down, the shopkeepers and staff never making it into work on the morning of the attack. An odd piece of litter fluttered along the kerb, and apart from the sound that it made, the only other noise I could hear were the crows screeching in the distance. The stench of rotting meat wafted on the cold wind that whipped around the eaves of the buildings. Then I heard another sound; it was faint – but it was definitely there. I began to walk slowly to the right, my head tilted to one side as I homed in on the noise.

"What's wrong?" Isidor asked me.

"Shhh," I replied.

Isidor hobbled over and stood beside me. I could see that his bare feet, like mine, were raw and cold-looking.

"What is it?" he whispered, as he waved his crossbow before him.

"I can hear something," I said, as I continued to move towards the sound with Kayla. Then I had it, and I started to move as fast as I could towards it.

"What can you hear?" he called after me.

"The sound of running water!" I whooped.

I made my way towards a tall stone building, and as I drew

close I could see that it had once been a church, but the steeple and the crucifix that had once adorned it now lay in a pile of rubble on the ground. The church door was wedged open, and I had to look away at the sight of decaying bodies that were piled high in the doorway. I feared that if I looked at it for too long, then I would *see* them clambering over one another, desperate for the sanctuary that the church would offer against the vampires. Dragging Kayla past the front of the church, I followed a narrow path leading to the town square. There were tables and benches for people to relax on as they basked in the sun of long warm, summer evenings. But it was what was in the centre of the town square that I was interested in –a fountain. Water tumbled from it in thick, frothy streams. I gently rested Kayla on one of the benches, then taking off my coat, I climbed into the fountain and plunged myself beneath the water. It was ice-cold and my whole body tingled as if it were being shaken awake. I threw handfuls of water over my head and scrubbed away the dirt that covered me. Throwing his Crossbow aside, Isidor jumped in beside me and also began to throw water over himself. Isidor splashed with his hands like an overly-excited kid and showered me with it. I began to laugh as I stood under the fountain letting it wash the filth and the smell of that zoo from me.

Isidor flopped and danced around in the water and it was like it had breathed new life into him – into both of us. I watched as he shook his wings from side to side, sending forth a spray of water that glistened in the winter sunlight like a rainbow. Just like Isidor, I leapt from the fountain and shook the water from me. I ran my fingers through my hair and untangled it. My hospital gown was soaked through and it clung to me like an extra layer of skin. Once I put my coat on, I placed my hands back beneath the frothing fountain, and once they were covered with the freezing water, I went over to Kayla who sat slumped on the bench. Gently, I covered her cracked lips with my wet fingers. Instinctively, Kayla popped her tongue from her mouth and licked at the tiny droplets of water.

Seeing what I was trying to do, Isidor cupped his hands, filled them with water from the fountain and came over to the bench. Holding them out, I lent Kayla forward and said, "Kayla, drink some water. It will make you feel better." I didn't know if it would or not, it hadn't taken the cramps away in my stomach, but it had cooled my skin and made me feel more alert and awake.

Kayla lent forward with her eyes closed and sipped some of the water that Isidor had cupped in his hands. Some of it dripped from the corners of her mouth, but she swallowed some. Leaning back on the bench, Kayla slowly opened her eyes.

"I'm sorry, Kiera, about what happened," she said. "I didn't really want to hurt you."

"It's okay," I whispered and smoothed the hair away from her brow. "Come over to the fountain and have a wash, you'll feel so much better."

Closing her eyes on me, she shook her head. "I just want to sleep," she murmured.

Knowing that if I didn't get her fever down quick, she would be in serious trouble, I looked at Isidor and said, "You stay here with Kayla, I won't be long."

"Where are you going?" Isidor asked, and I could see that he was already burning-up again, as sweat ran from his temples.

"I'm gonna go and see if I can find some medicine," I said, "If Kayla doesn't get some help soon…" I trailed off.

As if he knew what I meant to say, he slumped down on the bench next to Kayla and said, "Don't be gone long. We shouldn't separate like this."

Heading back across the square, I looked back at him and with the best smile that I could muster, I said, "See you in a while, crocodile." I knew that Isidor was right, we should stay together, but Kayla was suffering more than we were, and if I didn't get her some medicine quick, she would only slow our escape.

I hurried as fast as I could through the uninhabited town, and at times, the silence seemed deafening. My whole body ached, and any benefits I had felt after showering in the fountain had now passed. The skin on my arms and legs itched and prickled with heat, and the scar on my leg throbbed. After some time, I came upon a street full of shops. I looked up at one of the buildings, and hidden amongst the grime and dirt, I could just make out a sign that read 'High Street'. Like all of the other buildings in town, they looked as if they had been built hundreds of years ago. Each of them had been constructed out of stone and beams of wood, but some of them looked as if they had been modernised, as the old lattice windows had been removed and replaced with big, glass windows and modern-looking name signs. There was a small boutique, a shoe shop, several classy-looking restaurants, and one small electronics outlet. I made my way along the deserted street until I came upon a department store. It wasn't as grand as anything I might have seen in a shopping mall, but in the front windows stood dummies dressed in the latest fashions.

Knowing that all of us would need some new and warm clothes, I pushed on the large glass doors and they swung silently open. The store stank and the smell was similar to the stench I had come across on the road. Next to the door there was a display of scarves, so I pulled one free and wrapped it around my nose and mouth.

I took a deep breath and crept through the store.

"Shit, this is creepy!" I whispered, trying to stay calm. But with every little noise I heard, I would freeze on the spot, my heart pounding. "Get a grip, Kiera!" I said aloud, "It's just a store with dead people in it!" I shuddered, but hearing the sound of my own voice kind of made me feel more at ease, as if I were having a conversation with someone; that I wasn't alone.

Further into the store, I came across cashiers slumped unceremoniously across the counters. A security guard lay slouched in the doorway of an elevator, and I had to step over a beautician from the perfume counter who lay face-down on the floor. I walked over to the clothing section, just wanting to get out of the store as soon as possible. I plucked myself a pair of jeans from a rack and pulled myself a sweatshirt from a hanger. Taking myself a pair of knickers, a bra, and some socks, I pulled off the filthy hospital gown and got dressed into my new clothes and they felt soft and fresh against my skin.

I took a pair of trainers from a display and held them against the sole of my foot.
"I think they'll fit," I said to myself, prising them on over my feet. I hurriedly tied the laces then grabbed a coat from the display. I put it on, and before ditching my old one, I removed my iPod, Murphy's crucifix, and the computer disc from the pockets. Then, snatching a rucksack from a display, I threw in some clothes and shoes for Kayla and Isidor. I had to guess their sizes and what they might like, but I figured anything was better than Kayla's dirt-

ridden gown and Isidor's striped pyjama bottoms. Glad to be leaving the store, I made my way out.

I pulled the scarf from my face and dragged my hair into a ponytail. I tied the scarf around my hair, and apart from the ever-increasing stabbing pains in my gut, I felt human – *half-human* – again.

I was conscious of the fact that the sun was beginning to fade behind the mountains in the distance and if there were vampires lurking in the town, they would soon come awake and start searching for food. A wind had picked up and I looked up at the clouds, which were turning gunmetal grey as they hung over the mountaintops.

Across the street I saw a supermarket. Without wasting another moment, I darted over to it. The automatic doors hissed open and I stepped inside. Just like the department store, the supermarket was littered with the deceased.

The freezers and fridges were still working but the non-frozen meat was rotting in pools of its own blood. This immediately gave me some idea as to how long I'd been held captive in the zoo. I had been taken hostage in October and the food looked at least six to eight weeks out of date. So that made it early to mid-December. I knew I had only been in the zoo a few days – so had I been in the facility prior to that? But where was it?

I picked up some of the meat and the sight and smell of it reminded me of the red stuff that the white paw would shove through the hatch and into my cell. Just thinking of that made my stomach leap and my throat burn with thirst. Gooseflesh covered my skin as those cravings that had been lurking just beneath the surface revealed themselves again. Dropping the meat with disgust, the sight of all those decaying bodies in their cars came flooding back into my mind.

*Perhaps I'll become a vegetarian!* I thought to myself and turned away from the stinking lumps of meat.

I hurried as fast as I could about the supermarket until I came across the canned tins of fruit. I opened up my rucksack and threw several cans inside. Then I went to the isle that housed the biscuits and crisps – sweet stuff would be good – a short burst of energy. I added these to my shopping but kept enough room for some bottles of water. Then to the medicine isle where I took several packs of

Aspirin and hoped that these would help control Kayla's, Isidor's, and my own fever.

Once I had everything I thought we might need, I took a can of tinned fruit from my bag and pulled back the ring. Plunging my finger inside, I hooked out a bright orange slice of peach and popped it into my mouth. I then ate another and another until the syrup was running off my chin and onto the floor. When I was full, I gathered up my rucksack and swiping a can of Coke from the fridge on my way out, I swallowed two of the Aspirin and then left the supermarket. It was almost dark outside, and I could hear barking and howling in the distance. The sound of it made my heart race and I knew that I had to get back to the town square and find somewhere for Kayla, Isidor, and me to stay for the night. But where? Then, glancing across the street, I saw the perfect place. It would be secure and was bound to have somewhere inside that we could lock ourselves away and be safe. But before I brought Kayla and Isidor all the way back across town, I would check it out first – just to make sure that it was as safe as I hoped it would be.
So, throwing the rucksack over my shoulder, I crossed the street and stepped into the police station.

# Chapter Twenty-Two

I hoisted myself over the front counter as the door leading to the rest of the station was locked. I walked as quietly as I could through a maze of corridors, pushing doors open as I went. In several of them, I found dead police officers curled on the floor. All of them, like the dead in the cars, were locked rigid in grotesque poses, as they silently grabbed at their throats and faces. Some of the police officers were dressed like the vampire-cops, in black boiler suits and thick, heavy boots. These must have been the real T.S.U. officers, not the ones I'd seen rip the throat out of the police sergeant while I had been hiding in the park with Potter, Luke, and my other friends. Some of them had guns clutched in their dead hands and I could see bullet holes sprayed across some of the walls.

"What's happened here?" I asked aloud, my voice echoing back at me off the walls. Deep down I knew what had happened, but I could *see* that these officers had fought to save the police station. It had become a fortress against the Vampyrus and Lycanthrope who had tried to storm it from outside. But the Vampyrus and Lycanthrope had been let in, they hadn't forced their way in. There had been a traitor amongst these police officers. Hunkering down, I could see that the officers' flesh wasn't as decomposed as much as those cocooned in their cars. They showed all the signs of only being dead a few days. The police station door had been left open, it hadn't been smashed down, which meant somebody had opened it from the inside. These police officers had retreated back into this room, where they had fired upon the Vampyrus and Lycanthrope that came for them.

I had seen enough. I closed the door and made my way deeper into the deserted police station. The florescent lights overhead flickered and buzzed, and I guessed that the station was now running on its emergency energy source. How long it would last before I was plunged into total darkness, I didn't know. My stomach was beginning to feel like I'd swallowed broken glass, and I wished that I hadn't eaten those peach slices. Sweat dripped from my forehead and stung my eyes.

At the end of the corridor, I found a set of stairs. Slowly, I climbed them and at the top, I came across a small landing with a door set into the far wall. Written across it were the words:

**Control Room**
**Authorised Personnel Only**

I doubted if the warning still held any relevance, and technically I had never been dismissed from the Force, so I pushed the door open and stepped inside. The room was circular in shape and in the middle, there was a series of control panels and computer screens. Radio headsets and microphones lay littered across the desks, entangled around the arms of the dead staff that had once worked in there.

Again the room smelled ripe of decomposing flesh, but I tried to block it from my mind. I walked around the central control panel, mindful not to step on any of the bodies that lay sprawled at my feet.

I looked at one of the computer screens and a message flashed on and off in green letters. It read:

**…all mobile phone lines down. No formal lines of communication open. Internet has gone off line…**

The next screen read:

**...the clouds seem to be alive. They are coming out of the clouds...**

And the last screen flashed:

**…they're animals. It's the wolves…and they are talking…**

I felt something brush up against my leg and I looked down to see Nik standing beside me.

"What are you doing here?" I gasped with surprise.

"Watching your back," he woofed, and he glanced at the message about the talking wolves.

"Why?" I asked him, still startled by his sudden appearance.

Then, staring at me with his crazy yellow eyes, he barked,

"Like I said, Kiera, it's all about redemption."

Breaking his stare, I picked up one of the radio handsets, which was attached to the array of control panels.

"What are you doing?" Nik asked.

"Calling for help!"

"But -"

"Look, there are dead police officers in here," I cut in, "And they only died in the last few days, which might mean that they were able to tell the rest of the world that exists on the other side of these goddamn mountains, what's been going on here." Then, turning my back on him, I pressed the talk button on the handset and spoke into it.

"Help! Somebody help us! If anyone is receiving this please come back to me!" I released the talk button and waited – no prayed - for a response.

Nothing, only static.

"If anyone can hear this, please help us!" I said again into the handset and again there was only silence.

There was a dial attached to the control panel so I turned it from left to right, hoping that I would tune into another signal – one that had a voice at the other end of it.

I pressed the talk button again and this time I said, "My name is Kiera Hudson and I've been locked up in a zoo…I'm in a town called Wasp Water set amongst the Cumbria mountains. There are dead people here – hundreds of them…please…"

Then suddenly, I heard a snapping sound and I looked round to see Nik chewing through the wire that led from the handset and into the control panel.

*"What are you doing!"* I screeched in disbelief. "Don't you want me to be rescued?"

"And that's exactly why I've bitten through the wire," he barked.

"What are you talking about?" I cried.

"Because those who come to save you might not be your friends," he said.

I was speechless and just shook my head in disbelief as Nik continued. "Doctor Hunt told me that one of your friends is a traitor- that they are working for this *invisible man*…"

"Look you've already told me this and…"

"Your friend Murphy was reluctant to believe what Doctor Hunt said and it cost him his life," Nik stared at me, his eyes wide and fiery.

"Look, Hunt got it wrong. None of my friends are working for this...*invisible man*," I snapped at him. "I trust them – *all* of them!"

"And so did your friend, Murphy," Nik said.

To hear those words made me realise that Nik was right. He was right because in my heart I knew that Murphy had come to suspect that one of us was a traitor. I could remember the conversation that I'd heard between Murphy and Potter in the signal box next to the disused railway line. Potter had been mad at Murphy as he believed that he suspected him of being the traitor. But knowing this, I still glared back at Nik, and said, "You're wrong about my friends and so was Doctor Hunt – none of them are traitors. I trust all of them with my life."

Nik shook his giant head and said, "Why don't you do what you believe is best, Kiera?"

"Sounds like a plan to me," I snapped and then threw the radio set onto the floor.

I stormed past Nik and left the control room.

"Where are you going?" he called out.

"To find a safe place for me and my *friends* to sleep!" I hollered angrily back over my shoulder. It was then that my head began to feel light and weightless. I started to retrace my steps back down the stairs, but halfway down, my stomach knotted and a searing bolt of pain cut through me. Gripping the handrail, I staggered down another two steps or so. The handrail felt ice cold against the burning skin of my hand. The world turned black, then came back into focus again and I could hear the sound of running in the distance. I glanced behind me and back up at the stairs. Nik stood at the top and silently looked down at me. I held out my hand towards him, as the sound of approaching feet grew louder. Everything swayed before me, and my whole body seemed to lock and go rigid as the cravings for blood consumed me.

With my hands outstretched before me in a feeble attempt to fight off whoever or whatever it was running loose in the police station, I lurched down the last few stairs. In the corridor, a figure loomed up in front of me and grabbed me by the arms. Too weak to fight them off, I collapsed against them, and as the lights went out inside my mind, the last thing I heard was someone whisper in my ear, "Take it easy, tiger!"

# Chapter Twenty-Three

*I woke to find the door to my cell open. The wire mesh was hanging from the hole in the concrete ceiling just like I'd left it, before making my escape.*

*But what was I doing back in my cell? Had I been recaptured?*

*My head hurt, and it felt as if my skull was being crushed in a vice. There was a dull thud behind my eyes, my throat was burning raw, and my stomach felt as if my intestines were being strangled by an invisible pair of hands.*

*Praying that no one would hear me, I crept towards the open door and out into the corridor on the other side. It was then that I noticed I was wearing the clothes that I'd taken from the store.*

*The sound of barking rebounded off the walls all around me. It made my heart beat so fast with fear that it felt as if it were trying to punch its way out of my chest. I tiptoed around a bend in the corridor. I stopped immediately and jumped back in the direction which I had come and pressed myself flat against the wall.*

*There was a wolf down there! And it was Sparky. How did I know that? I just did. I waited several seconds just to make sure that I hadn't been hallucinating and peeked around the edge of the wall. Sparky was still there, but now he was pacing back and forth outside an open door further down the corridor.*

*"I don't know how the doctor could have escaped," he whined.*

*With my head pressed flat against the wall, I watched from my hiding place as a winged man appeared from the room and approached Sparky. "We need Ravenwood!" he said, his voice low and husky, but there was a hint of anger.*

*I tried to stare at him, but his face seemed to be cast in shadow. But that couldn't be right? There were no shadows in this brightly-lit corridor. So how was it that I couldn't see his face? His upper body was naked, and I could see that it was taught with muscle. His legs were covered in a black pair of combat trousers, and his feet hidden by thick boots.*

*"I have hunters looking for him, but -" Sparky started.*

*"I don't want to hear excuses!' the man snapped. Sparky flinched backwards, his claws clacking on the tiled floor.*

*"They're not excuses, my -"*

Before Sparky had a chance to finish, the man with the long, black wings and the face masked in shadow gripped him by the throat. *"Close this place down. The half-breeds are no good to me in this state. We'll move our work to The Hollows."*

*"But what about the half-breeds we've been breeding?"* Sparky asked, and it sounded somewhere between a bark and grunt, unable to speak properly with the man gripping him by the throat.

*"Turn off their life supports like we did with the half-breeds at the facility,"* the man said, releasing his grip on Sparky.

*What facility? I wondered. Was that the place where I'd been operated on?*

*"But what about the virus?"* Sparky asked.

*"Once we have Ravenwood again, we'll have the cure,"* the man said, and his voice was low, almost a whisper again.

*"What about Hudson and the others?"*

Hearing Sparky mention my name, I slid round the edge of the wall, not because I feared that I might be seen, it was the thumping of my heart that I hoped they wouldn't hear.

*"They couldn't have gotten far, not in their conditions,"* the man said, and the tips of his wings made a whispering sound as they brushed against the ground. *"Don't concern yourselves with them, I'll worry about Kiera and her friends."*

*"What about us?"* Sparky chipped in nervously.

*"What do you mean us?"*

*"If you're heading back to The Hollows, where does that leave me and the rest of the Lycanthrope?"*

*"I need you to stay here and prepare for the final attack,"* the man said, and he sounded as if he were growing tired of Sparky's questions.

*"But..."*

*"I've told you, I'm not interested in excuses. What happened in Wasp Water was just the start – a practice if you like, for when we attack the bigger towns, cities - London,"* the man said, in his low husky voice, as if speaking from behind a mask.

*"If only we had..."* Sparky started, *"Somebody like Kiera. Now she is loose, she'll go looking for Ravenwood. She's not stupid – she'll know that he holds the key to breaking the code –*

she'll find him and the code. That's what she does, that's what she's good at – I've seen her in action."

"And so have I," the man said. "Don't you think I know that she'll go looking for the doctor? Why do you think her escape was made so easy?"

"So you let her escape?" Sparky sniggered.

"Of course – I needed someone to find the good doctor and she won't go far – she'll never even get out of Wasp Water," the faceless man said.

"And then you want us to go after her and bring her and the doctor back..."

"There will be no need for that," the man said, with a certain air of confidence.

"How can you be so sure?" Sparky asked.

"Because Kiera and I are friends now," the man said. "She'll bring Ravenwood to me of her own free will."

"Why would she do that?" Sparky barked, and like him I was curious to know why I would do such a thing.

"Because, Kiera trusts me," the man whispered.

"So she knows you then?" Sparky asked. "But nobody knows you – no one has ever seen your face."

"Kiera has seen it," the man almost seemed to laugh. "Kiera sees *everything!*"

Hearing a noise behind me, I wheeled round and shrieked in terror as I found myself staring into the menacing face of a Vampyrus. Stumbling backwards, I moved away from it. The Vampyrus came forward brandishing two hooked claws. Its muscles rippling beneath its black and silver flecked fur.

"I've found her!" he roared triumphantly.

Before his deep, menacing voice had stopped reverberating off the corridor walls, Sparky and the man with the shadow across his face were coming towards me.

"She knows where the code is!' the Vampyrus hissed.

My lower jaw began to chatter uncontrollably as I continued to move backwards up the corridor. My stomach began to cramp again, and I suddenly felt hot – as if I were edging my way backwards into a furnace.

I wanted to speak –but my lips flapped together as if I were blowing a raspberry.

"What is it you are trying to say?" Sparky asked smugly.

"R – R – RUN!" I screamed as I turned on the spot and raced away up the corridor.

I ran as hard and as fast as I could and for a moment – just the briefest of moments - my legs seemed to take on a life of their own as they began to propel me forwards at an incredible speed. But out of my peripheral vision, I saw something big and dark leap from one of the rooms that I sped past and come crashing into me. Whatever it was hit me with such force that I slammed into the corridor wall. I gasped as my head made contact with the floor with a sickening thud. I opened my eyes and screamed as I stared into the face of that man. But I couldn't see his face, not really. It was as if he were wearing a wide brimmed hat which cast a dark shadow across his features. But the shadows moved, twisted and contorted out of shape, as if whatever hid beneath them was writhing back and forth in pain.

Then, everything seemed to swirl in and out around me – from light to dark and back again as I fought to remain conscious. I dragged myself along the floor by my fingertips, desperate not to be caught by him. And then I screamed, the pain exploding like a bomb going off in my leg. I glanced back in horror to see that a wolf had sunk his razor-sharp teeth into my leg and was now slowly dragging me back towards him. But it wasn't just any wolf – it was Nik who was taking me back to my captors.

"What about your redemption?" I screamed at him.

I shut my eyes against the sight of his drooling and grinning jaws.

"No Nik," I pleaded. "I thought you had my back!"

My leg felt as if it was on fire. I could hear the grunts and the growls of the others as they approached. I needed to look...I needed to find out what they were going to do to me. I opened my eyes to see the Vampyrus bring his meaty fist down towards me. Everything went black and...

# Chapter Twenty-Four

…there was a red light winking on and off in the darkness.

"Who's there?" I croaked, sitting up on a bed. My body shivered uncontrollably, and I had never felt so ill. My skin was burning up, stabbing pains knifed through my stomach, and my back ached as if it had been stamped on. Crying out in pain, I swung my legs over the side of the bed, and the floor felt cold against my burning feet. That red light winked on and off again from the corner, but as my bleary eyes grew accustomed to the darkness, I could see a square of pale light just ahead. I stumbled towards it, my legs buckling beneath me. With my hands stretched out, I felt like someone trying to find their way blindfolded. Then my fingers brushed against something hard and cold – it was metal. A door. That square of pale light was coming through a hatch set into it. I was in a cell.

*Had I been captured again? Was I back in my cell in the zoo?*

My brains felt scrambled, and my heart thumped so hard that it felt as if my eyes were going to explode in their sockets.

I banged weakly on the door with my fists, and a dull thud echoed back at me. The red winking light moved in the darkness – it was coming towards me, then dropped to the floor and disappeared.

"Where am I?" I whispered, and knocked the cold sweat out of my eyes.

"You're somewhere safe," a voice said, and a strong set of arms wrapped themselves around me and held me close. My head rested against their chest, and the faint smell of tobacco coming from their shirt made me realise that the red light I had seen had been the end of a cigarette being smoked in the dark.

"Potter?" I barely managed.

"I've got you, sweet-cheeks," he whispered, guiding me back towards the bed in the corner of the cell.

"Where am I?" I asked again as he gently laid me down.

"In the cells beneath the police station," he answered, his voice was soft, like a dream floating over me.

"Police station?" I mumbled.

"That's right." he said, his voice still a whisper. "We're safe here."

"I'm thirsty," I told him.

"I'll get you some water," he said.

"I don't want water," I groaned as the pains in my stomach twisted like a corkscrew. "I want some…"

"No, Kiera," Potter said, and I could feel one of his strong hands stroke my sweat-dampened hair from my brow.

With my eyes closed against the pain, I gripped his arms and pulled him close. "Please Potter," I begged. "Just a little – it will take the pain away."

"No," he said firmly and pushed me down onto the bed.

"Please…"

"No," he insisted.

"I hate you!" I spat.

"Don't most people?" he said, and as I flopped back onto the bed, I could picture his face with that wry smile tugging at the corner of his lips.

I opened my mouth to speak and said…

*"…What are the odds of me escaping a cell only to find myself freely sleeping in one on my first night of freedom?"*

*"I'm sorry," I heard Nik say.*

*I opened my eyes to see him standing in the doorway. His giant fur covered frame almost blocking out the pale light that came from the corridor outside.*

*"Sorry for what?" I asked him.*

*"For biting through that wire," he grunted.*

*"Let's just forget it and get some sleep," I said. "Tomorrow I'm going to go and get my friends I left by the fountain and then go and find Doctor Ravenwood. You and me can both go our separate ways."*

*Nik came into the cell and lay on the floor beside my bed.*

*"Why don't you just run, Kiera – save yourself?" he asked.*

*I reached down and from my rucksack I pulled out a can of the tinned fruit that I had taken from the supermarket. On the front of the tin was a picture of a ripe juicy apple that had been cut in half.*

*"See that apple, Nik?" I asked.*

*"What about it?"*

105

*"You see those seeds? If you took them and planted them in the ground each one would grow into another apple tree. In turn those trees would produce apples and each apple would be full of seeds which again if planted would make several more apple trees and so on it goes."*

*"I'm not sure what you mean,"* he said.

*"Well if you just kept on planting those seeds, in the end you would end up with a world covered in apple trees. That's just the same as the vampires. The more the Vampyrus feed on humans, the more vampires will just keep on multiplying until in the end...I won't need to run, because there will be no place left to run to. The world will be infested with vampires. I will have to stop running someday – so today seems as good a day as any."* Closing my eyes, I turned towards the wall, and added, *"Instead of having a world of apple trees there will be a world of...*

"...pain," somebody said.

"Hopefully her pain has gone," another voice said.

I opened my eyes to see a teenage boy and man standing in the doorway of my police cell staring in at me. I blinked and rubbed my eyes, not believing what I was seeing. The boy was Isidor and he didn't look like a boy at all really, it was just that he looked dwarfed by the height of Jack Seth who stood beside him.

The first thing I noticed was that Isidor looked a lot better. His short dark brown hair looked freshly washed, and although his face looked tired, his blue eyes glistened, and his little beard was neatly trimmed beneath his chin. He wore a black jacket and combat trousers to match. I looked at Seth, and he looked older than I remembered him. He wore a baseball cap, which was pulled low across his brow and his eyes glowed yellow from his sunken eye sockets. His face still looked emaciated and his skin was waxy and pale. He stood bent forward, so as not to scrape his head against the ceiling of the cell. Seth wore the black denim jeans and blue denim shirt I'd seen him wear before. The red bandanna was still knotted about his scrawny neck and his body still looked painfully thin.

"How do you feel, Kiera?" Isidor asked, rubbing his unshaven chin with the back of his hand.

"Better...I think," I whispered, realising that those pains in my stomach had gone along with that incredible thirst. "How are you feeling?" I asked, realising that the last time I'd seen him, he sat slumped on the seat by the fountain in the town square.

"Not a hundred percent, but a million times better than I did," Isidor smiled at me from the doorway.

"And Kayla?" I asked, trying to stand up, but my legs still felt as if they were made from jelly.

"She's still sleeping," Seth cut in.

"Sleeping where?" I asked, not entirely trusting him.

Sensing my distrust, Isidor came forward and said, "It's okay, Kiera. Kayla is asleep in the cell next door."

"How long have I been out of it?" I asked, my mouth feeling dry and my tongue like an old piece of carpet.

"Four days," Seth said.

"Four days!" I croaked.

"You've been going cold-turkey," Seth almost seemed to grin and his yellow eyes sparkled.

"Kayla and I have been going through the same," Isidor explained. "I woke up from my nightmare yesterday."

"Nightmare," I whispered almost to myself. "I've had plenty of them."

"You were delirious," Seth said. "You've been shaking, convulsing, and God only knows what else as you battled your addiction to human flesh."

"Is it over then?" I asked.

"There will be a constant battle going on in your body, heart, and soul for the rest of your life," Seth explained. "You'll never be free of it, but you'll learn to control it. Then staring at me from beneath the brim of his baseball cap, his eyes took on a sudden glow and he smiled, "God knows, Kiera, that I have to fight my urges every time I'm near you." And just for the briefest of moments I knew he wasn't joking, as I saw those images again in his eyes – the snapshots of him with his hands around my throat, his skeletal frame lowering itself over mine.

Breaking his stare, I looked at Isidor and said, "Where's Potter?"

"He's gone to get more supplies, before nightfall," Isidor said.

"Supplies?" I asked.

"We're leaving at dawn tomorrow," Isidor said.

"Leaving for where?" I asked him.

"The Hollows."

"The Hollows? But what about Luke?"

Grinning, Seth looked at me and said, "When Isidor says we're leaving for The Hollows, he means, *us* – Potter isn't returning to The Hollows, he's going back to the zoo to rescue Luke."

Struggling to stand up, I said, "I'm going with him."

"He's already got a partner," Seth grinned.

"Who?"

"Eloisa," Seth said, still smiling. "Remember her?"

How could I forget that stunningly beautiful woman – Lycanthrope? "Yes," I told him. "I remember her."

"She'll look after your friend, Potter," Seth said. "And I'll look after you."

I straightened up, shoved past Seth, and I left the cell. Over my shoulder I shouted, "Potter must be going out of his tiny mind if he thinks I'm going anywhere with you!"

# Chapter Twenty-Five

Isidor came after me down the passageway that led between the cells.

"Does Potter really think I'm going to go anywhere with that freak?" I asked as I eyed Isidor.

Isidor took my arm gently and stopped me from going any further. Looking back at the cell we had come from, as if to make sure that we weren't being overheard, he said "Kiera, we don't have time for this. Potter has a plan."

"A plan?" I grimaced. "Who put him in charge?" I couldn't hide the anger I felt for Potter for even suggesting that I go anywhere with Seth.

"Potter will be back soon," Isidor said. "You should talk to him because he won't tell me anything. It's as if he doesn't trust me."

"I thought after what happened in the caves between you two that you were okay with each other now?" I asked him.

"Obviously not," Isidor sighed.

"Okay, I'll talk to him, but I'm not happy," I said. "Where's Kayla?"

"This way," Isidor said and he led me away down the passage.

"Does she know you're her brother?" I asked him as we walked.

"No, not yet," Isidor said. "I haven't had a chance to speak to her about anything. Like me and you, she's been out of it for the last few days."

"We're going to have to tell her that Sparky killed her mum – *your* mum." Then realising my mistake, I took Isidor's arm and looking at him, I said, "I'm sorry Isidor, I know that Lady Hunt was your mother too – but you've had a bit longer to understand things, you know, deal with what's been happening."

"What about our father?" Isidor asked me. "Do you think he is still alive?"

"This is going to be hard for you, Isidor, but I don't believe he is," I said, and gently squeezed his arm. "He told me that he was going to end his life once he had completed the DNA coding that the Vampyrus would use to create the half-breeds. But your father was a good man, Isidor. He helped me escape in his own way. Did you not speak to him about any of this at the facility?"

"I didn't see my father at the facility – it wasn't he who treated – *operated* - on me, if that's what they were doing. It was another Doctor called Ravenwood. But to be honest I was so drugged up on meds most of the time that I could barely speak. Then this Doctor Ravenwood stopped coming and they moved me to that zoo." Isidor explained. "Your mate Sparky got me hooked on the red stuff and I went kinda crazy. I knew I had to get off the stuff – so I guess, like you, I stopped eating it, although doing so made me feel as if I was gonna die. But you know what? I would have rather died than spend the rest of my life eating humans."

"How do you feel now, your cravings, I mean?" I asked him.

"They're bearable, I guess," he replied. "A bit like an itch that won't go away, so I try not to think about it. But it's still the early days, I guess."

"And it's that itch that will keep you alive, kid," someone said from the other end of the corridor.

We both turned in the direction of the voice to see Potter leaning against the custody block wall. Eloisa towered behind him, her perfectly shaped legs seeming to go on forever in a pair of tight-fitting jeans. Her long, blond hair spilled over her shoulders and down the front of the black jacket she wore. Her skin was pale, but this only highlighted her blood-red lips and golden eyes. Potter took a pack of cigarettes from his shirt pocket and lit one, his right eye closing as the blue smoke trailed up towards the ceiling. He jetted two streams of smoke from his nose and came towards me, Eloisa close behind him. I couldn't help but notice how *close* she trailed him, and I didn't like it.

"Good to see you back in the world of the living, sweet-cheeks," He said, coming towards me.

When he was close enough, I rolled my arm back, then punched him straight in the face.

His head rocked back on his neck, and the cigarette which had dangled from the corner of his mouth span away. "What was that for!" he snapped. "I've been trying to save you!"

"How hard?" I asked him, then shot a quick glance at Eloisa.

"What's that supposed to mean?" he said, rubbing his jaw.
"I was stuck in that filthy zoo for God knows how long while

you've been gallivanting around here!" I snapped.

Then, gently touching Potter on the shoulder, Eloisa said in the sickliest sweet voice that I'd ever heard, "Sean, I'll go and find Jack, you two look as if you need to talk." Then she was gone, striding away on those damn legs of hers, and out of the corner of my eye, I saw Isidor slope away too.

"Sean!" I hissed. "No one ever calls you *Sean*!"

"It's my name," he snapped back.

"Now I can see why you took so long in coming to find me!" I shouted.

"Now listen here, tiger," Potter shouted back, "storming that zoo wasn't my idea of a rescue – it would've been more like suicide! That place was like a fortress!"

"Oh, yeah?" I seethed. "We'll I managed to break out all right!"

"So what are you complaining about?" he said.

"What am I complaining about?" I almost shrieked in disbelief. "I've been operated on, bitten by a werewolf, imprisoned, beaten, forced to eat human flesh and to top it all off, I had to use a hole in the floor as a goddamn toilet!"

"I've heard that squat toilets are all the rage in places like France..." he started.

"But I wasn't in France!" I yelled at him. "I was in a freaking zoo being treated like some kind of animal, while you were living it up with *her*!"

"Her?" Potter said, looking now somewhat bemused. "Eloisa, you mean? She's not so bad."

"Well you've definitely changed your tune," I spat. "Only a few weeks ago you were babbling on about how you could barely forgive a girl for having hairy armpits let alone a hairy tongue!" Then, trying to hide an arrogant smirk that I *so* much wanted to knock from his face, Potter said, "Okay, I get what's going on here."

"Get what?"

"You're jealous," he said and his eyes glistened.

"Jealous! Me, jealous of *her*?" I blustered. Then, pushing him out of the way, I added, "I was right – you are out of your tiny mind!"

111

# Chapter Twenty-Six

I stormed down the corridor set between the two rows of cells, and finding the one Kayla inhabited, I went inside. Kayla was sitting propped up on the bed, and Isidor sat beside her.

"What was all the shouting about?" Kayla asked me, as I slumped down on the end of her bed.

I guessed with her sensitive hearing she knew what Potter and I had been arguing about, but I still replied, "Ah, nothing. Just forget about it – I am. More importantly, how are you doing?"

"Okay, I guess," she said, untangling her matted hair with her fingers.

Although, she did look better then when I last saw her semiconscious in the town square, her face still looked wan, and her eyes dull.

"Are the nightmares over?" she asked me.

"The nightmares?" I asked. Although in my heart, I knew what she meant.

"The Vampyrus, that zoo, the experiments?" She said, her eyes wide and fearful.

"That part of the nightmare is," I tried to assure her. I knew I had to tell her about her mum, her dad, and Isidor had his secret, too.

"What about my mum?" she asked. "My dad? Has he been found?"

"You dad was at that facility where they operated on us," I started gently.

"The facility?" she said, leaning forward to look at me. "What was he doing there?"

"He was captured, just like we were," I said. "Phillips captured him to finish work on a cure that your father and Doctor Ravenwood were working on."

"A cure for what?" Kayla asked, looking at me and then Isidor, wanting answers.

"I'm a half–breed just like you, Kayla," Isidor said. "Not many of us survive past the age of sixteen. As far as we know, there are only the three of us – me, you, and Kiera."

"So you're just like me?" Kayla asked, looking at me.

"Yes," I nodded.

"You have wings then?" She asked.

"Yes," and the thought of those bony fingers made my flesh crawl.

"You're scared about that, aren't you?" Kayla said staring at me.

"How do you know that?" I asked, staring back.

"You heart quickened when you mentioned them. I could hear it." Then turning to look at Isidor, she added, "But why is your heart racing, Isidor? What are you scared of?"

"Tell her," a voice said from the open doorway, and I turned to see Potter standing there.

"Tell me what?" Kayla said, swinging her legs over the side of the bed, and placing her feet firmly on the floor.

"Now's not a good time," Isidor said, standing up to face Potter.

"Time is one thing we don't have," Potter said, fixing him with his cool stare. "Nor sentiment."

"Potter, please," I said, now standing myself.

"If you won't tell her, I will," Potter insisted.

"Tell me what?" Kayla said, her voice now brimming with confusion.

I looked at Isidor; he was staring at Potter.

"Why do you always have to be such a prick?" Isidor snapped, taking a step towards Potter.

"Listen, kid, we don't have time to wallow in self-pity here, we've all lost people that we've cared about -" Potter started.

"Don't call me kid," Isidor snapped. "I thought we'd sorted that out!"

"Jesus, you sound like a tune that's been stuck on repeat," Potter said back. Then looking down at Kayla, he added, "Look, I hate to be the one to break it to you, sweetheart, but some spotty-faced arsehole called Sparky killed your mum, your father has probably topped himself because he helped Phillips come up with the magic formula that is going to wipe the human race from the face of the planet, and the dude standing over here next to me with the Shaggy-Do beard is your brother."

Without warning, Isidor darted forward and reached for Potter. But Potter was too quick and slammed Isidor into the wall of the

113

cell. Holding him there with one strong hand, Potter lent in close and said, "Listen to me, Eisenhower, or whatever your name might be, the girl needs to know the truth and she needs to know it quick. We don't have time to worry about people's feelings here."

"Why do you have to be so cruel?" Isidor shouted.

"Cruel?" Potter snapped. "I tell you what's cruel. Keeping the truth from the girl over there. Yeah the truth ain't pretty and its gonna hurt her, but with any luck that will make her angry – so fucking angry that she'll want to rip the head off the first vampire she comes across, because that's the only way we're gonna get out of this. This isn't some sorta game, you know. The Vampyrus and Lycanthrope are getting ready to shit all over this country from a great height, and we ain't gonna stop them if we're walking around booing and wooing for the people that we've lost. You need to turn those feelings of self-pity into rage – *hate* – my friend, because those are going to be the only emotions that are of any use to me. You don't think those Vampyrus and Lycanthrope are going to pity you, do you? They hate you, *us,* and anyone who stands in their way. So if you ain't up to it, go now because I'm not taking any flower-picking, peace-loving, tree-hugging, whale-saving, do-gooder with me!"

"I can't hate like you," Isidor said.

"Then improvise!" Potter snapped.

"Who put you in charge anyway?" Isidor said back, his eyes glowing.

"Phillips did."

"Phillips?" I asked, confused.

Then, releasing his grip on Isidor, Potter looked at me and said, "The moment he ripped Murphy's heart out."

"Murphy's dead too?" Kayla began to wail out loud.

"Yeah and so we'll all be, if the lot of you don't get your act together," Potter said and left the cell.

I watched as Isidor went to Kayla and slipped his arm round her shoulder, then with my body trembling with anger, I rushed out into the corridor.

"Potter!" I shouted after him.

"What?" Potter yelled back over his shoulder as he continued to walk away from me.

Rushing after him, I said, "I just don't believe you. How can

114

you be like that to her?"

Potter continued to stride ahead of me, and I had to trot to keep up with him. Leaving the cells behind us, Potter pushed against a door and disappeared into a darkened room. I followed him, the door nearly hitting me in the arse as it swung shut behind me. Even though there were no lights on in the room, I could see through the darkness. We were in a small, deserted cafeteria, where the police officers who were once stationed here took their meal breaks. Chairs lay upturned and on their sides like fallen skittles and tables had been pushed against the walls and windows. Potter stood alone in the middle of the room, a cigarette already burning in the corner of his mouth.

"What's gotten into you?" I demanded as I marched towards him.

"What's gotten into me?" he scoffed. "If I remember rightly, you smacked me in the face the moment you laid eyes on me!"

"Where do you get off on making decisions for me without even asking?" I roared.

"What decisions?" he shouted back.

"Deciding that I'm to go off hand in hand into The Hollows with that killer, while you go off to rescue Luke with that walking pair of breasts on legs!" I hissed.

"Breasts on legs?" Potter said, nearly chocking on a throat full of cigarette smoke as he stifled his laughter. "You mean Eloisa?"

"I see that you're on first-name terms with the werewolf – because that's what she is, Potter. She's also a child killer and so is her *lover,* Jack Seth!"

"You are jealous and that's what this is all really about," Potter smiled. "You're not pissed at me because I made plans without you – you're pissed because I've been spending time with her."

"Oh, please," I groaned, "Why don't you take your head from out of your own arse and -"

"And what?" Potter said, grinding out his cigarette with the heel of his boot.

"And kiss me!" I snapped.

Potter almost seemed to lunge at me as he gripped my arms and yanked me close. Covering my mouth with his, we kissed each other and I just wanted to be smothered by him; to be part of him.

Raking my fingers through his hair, Potter ran his fingertips down my spine, and I shivered with gooseflesh. I felt consumed by him, and it both thrilled and scared me at the same time, a cocktail of emotions that in some ways I hated, but in others, I passionately enjoyed. I was fearful that I wanted someone so much that in many ways I hated but who had another side to him that I couldn't help but be drawn to, and that scared me. But to be in his arms, to feel his hands roaming the length of my body, to feel his lips pressed hard over mine, took away the memories of my captivity, the operations that I'd endured, the addiction that I had overcome, the realisation that my mother was lost to the Vampyrus, that Murphy had been murdered and Luke...

I pulled away, gently, but I pulled away all the same.

"What's wrong?" Potter whispered, trying to keep me close to him.

"We shouldn't be doing this right now, not while there is so much to do," I said. "We should be planning on how we're going to rescue Luke."

Letting go of me, Potter looked into my eyes and said, "It always comes back to him, doesn't it?"

"He's our friend, Potter," I said, looking away. "We can't just leave him to rot in that prison."

"Don't you think I know that?" he said. "That's why I'm going back for him." After a short pause, he added, "And what happens when I bring him back?"

"What do you mean?"

"Is it going to be you and Luke again?" he asked, and he didn't sound angry, just confused. "What about me? Us? What about what happened between us in the caves?"

"How could I forget?" I whispered, but still couldn't look at him. "You have no idea how much that time we spent together beneath the mountains meant to me."

"So it wasn't just because you thought that you we're going to die this time?"

"Huh?" I said, looking up at him and hating the hurt that I could see in his eyes.

"You said before that you only kissed me in the summerhouse because you thought you were going to die," he reminded me, and I felt a stab of pain at the thought that I had actually said that to him.

"I didn't mean that," I confessed. "I kissed you that time because I wanted to and that's the truth. I've only ever kissed you because I wanted to."

"But do you really want me, Kiera, or is it Luke?" he asked me.

Looking at him with tears standing in my eyes, I whispered, "Don't ask me that, Sean, that's not fair."

"Sean?" he whispered back. "Nobody ever calls me Sean, remember?"

By the time I'd looked up to give him the answer that I knew he had the right to know, the door to the cafeteria was swinging closed and he had gone.

# Chapter Twenty-Seven

I crept from the cafeteria, and looking in both directions up the corridor, I could see Potter had gone. Half of me wanted to go and find him, to talk to him, but the other half of me thought that it would probably be best if I left him alone for a while. Potter was in a cranky mood, but wasn't he always? Still, I made my way back to the cells. As soon as I'd turned onto the passageway, I heard Kayla sobbing in the distance. Her cries echoing off the walls, and my heart ached.

Reaching the cell, I went inside to find Isidor holding her in his arms. She had her head rested against his chest, and I hoped that she was okay with the idea of having a brother. In some way, I guessed that it was probably the best news that she had received; after all, he was the only family she had left.

I sat on the edge of the bed and took one of her hands in mine. Looking up at me with her tear-stained face, she said, "Isidor said that you met my dad at the facility."

Nodding, I said, "Yes, I did."

"Why did he stop coming to see me?" she asked.

"Perhaps he couldn't bring himself to see you being treated like that, tested and operated on," I tried to explain.

"But why did he do those tests?" Kayla asked, cuffing away a silver stream of snot that covered her upper lip. "Did he really help Phillips like Potter said?"

"Phillips and the other Vampyrus thought that your dad was helping them. But really, he was tricking them."

"Tricking them? How?"

"Doctor Ravenwood and your dad had a plan," I told her. "They wanted to find the cure so they could help future children that were born like us. But they knew that once they had it all figured out, Phillips and this faceless man would use it to breed a race of half-breeds just like us so they could use them to fight the humans when they invaded above ground. You see, Kayla, me, you, and Isidor are very special with amazing gifts, and if the Vampyrus who want to rule the Earth had a whole army at their disposal with our unique abilities then…well, I don't even want to think about what might happen."

"So how did my dad and Doctor Ravenwood trick them?" she asked me, her tears now drying on her cheeks.

"I was bitten on the leg by a wolf, his name is Nik," I said. "The wound became infected, so your father corrupted the cure that he had designed with the infection. The real DNA code they wrote down. Ravenwood escaped from the facility with one half of the code and your father wrote the other half down in a book that he gave to me."

"Where's the book now?" Kayla asked me.

"I don't have it," I said. "I tore pages out of it to help me escape from the zoo, and what was left, Phillips took from me."

"Then he could have half the code?" Isidor cut in.

"I'm not sure," I told them both. "I mean, I tore a lot of pages from that book. For all I know, I could have destroyed the pages with the code on."

"But Ravenwood will know the complete code, right?" Kayla asked me.

"I don't know that either," I confessed. "I haven't a clue as to what this code looks like. It could be a few lines or pages and pages of numbers. I'm guessing that it wouldn't be something you could easily remember or your dad and Ravenwood wouldn't have written it down. But your father was a good man," I said looking at them both. "He encouraged me to escape."

"How?" Kayla asked.

"He read me passages from children's books, where the characters were escaping. It was almost as if he was afraid that he was being watched and listened to – so he had to give me the idea of escaping in a very subtle way."

"So we need to find Ravenwood." Isidor said. "But where is he now?"

"He could be anywhere," I said.

"He will be hiding out in this town somewhere," a voice suddenly said, and I turned around to see Jack Seth and Eloisa looming in the cell doorway. I didn't know how long they had been standing there and how much of our conversation they had overheard.

"What makes you say that?" Isidor asked him.

"This town has been sealed off by Phillips and his *special* police force. You know, the ones in the black boiler suits, who sprout fangs and wings and stuff," Seth said.

"What do you mean they've sealed it off?" I asked him, and it hurt my neck to look up at him as he towered over us.

"The rest of the country believes that those attacks on the London Underground were committed by some rabid animals that were smuggled into the UK," Seth explained. "The newspapers have reported that someone who was bitten down on the Tube Train managed to slip through the cordon back in London and get as far as here before they went half mad with the infection and started attacking the good people of Wasp Water. So to contain the virus, they have sealed off the town and destroyed all the animals in the zoo to stop the infection spreading."

"They can't do that," I said. "You can't just shut down a whole town without anyone asking questions."

"Oh, no?" Eloisa said. "Remember that outbreak of Foot-and-Mouth disease back in two-thousand-and-one and seven? Towns were sealed off all over the place and nobody asked any questions."

"But that was different," I said. "That was a genuine disease that was being spread by cattle."

"Exactly my point," Eloisa smiled. "You believed it just like everybody else."

"What are you saying?" Isidor asked her.

"There was no outbreak of Foot-and-Mouth disease," she smiled. "It was a series of towns that had...how can I say it? A little problem with vampires."

"See, the government at the time couldn't let the rest of the country know that," Seth continued, "And it was rather fortunate at the time for the Vampyrus that one of their own was Minister for Agriculture and Farming and was invaluable at cleaning the mess up."

"So you're telling me that the government knows what's really going on here?" I asked.

"No, of course not," Eloisa said, as if I were some dumb first grader. God, I really disliked her. "The Prime Minister is far too concerned about saving Europe from collapsing beneath a pile of debt, he hasn't got time to concern himself with a tiny little town like this. He leaves that up to others – the Vampyrus who have infiltrated the government. People will believe whatever they are told – just like you did back in two-thousand-and-one and two-thousand-and-seven. The rest of society is happy to wander along with their little lives as long as what's happening in the sleepy town of Wasp Water doesn't impact on them."

"And boy, have they got a surprise coming their way," Seth half-smiled, and his crazy-looking eyes almost seemed to spin in their hollow sockets. "Anyway, me and my good lady are off to bed," he said. Then fixing his wild eyes on mine he said, "Perhaps you should get some rest too, Kiera, after all, we have to make a long journey together tomorrow.

Just the thought of spending any time on my own with him made my flesh crawl and I looked away.

# Chapter Twenty-Eight

I left Isidor and Kayla alone in the cell, as I guessed that they would have plenty to talk about and would need some time to get to know one another. I didn't feel tired – I'd spent enough time out of it over the last few days. So, picking my coat up from my cell floor I rummaged in my pocket and fished out my iPod. Sticking in the earphones, I switched it on and started to listen to *Grenade* by Bruno Mars. Dropping my coat onto my bed, I saw something bright and shiny fall onto the floor. Reaching down, I picked up the disc I had taken from the monastery. I turned it over in my hands and left the cell.

I made my way back past the cafeteria, pushing open doors on each side of the corridor. Some of the rooms still held sights that I'd rather not have been reminded of, so closing the doors I made my way further down the corridor. At the end, I found a door which had the words, *Report Writing Room*, written neatly across the front of it. I eased the door open. Relieved that there weren't any corpses strewn about the place, I crept inside and closed the door behind me. With the lights out, I made my way across the room towards a long table that housed a number of computers. Sitting down in front of the first computer I came to, I switched it on. The screen blinked white in the darkness, then came to life. Two boxes appeared on the screen, one for my user name, the second for my password. Knowing what I.T. departments were like in the Force, I hoped that they hadn't yet removed me from the database. I typed in my details and hit the return key. The screen went black, then lit-up with the Force logo and badge.

"Yes!" I whispered, taking the disc and placing it into the hard drive. I listened to the computer whir to life. Another box appeared on the screen which read '*View Files*'. Clicking onto the box, the screen revealed a series of files. There were hundreds, no thousands. I scanned my eyes over them, not knowing what exactly I was looking for, but hoping that one of them would grab my attention.

I dragged the cursor down the page, and about halfway down, I saw a file that had been named, '*Facility 1*'. Opening up the file the screen became awash with diagrams of what looked like big, glass pods. With Bruno Mars singing in my ears, I scrolled down the page, and was baffled by the series of technical diagrams of what looked like a hangar full of racks, on each one there was row upon row of these glass pods. I had no true idea of what they were, but they looked like a series of glass coffins. Then beneath the diagrams, there was a drawing, similar to something that an architect might draw of the monastery. Then, as I looked at the diagram more carefully, I could see that built into the foundations beneath the monastery was a chamber, which held a mass of these glass-like coffins I'd seen above. I clicked on the image and it increased in size. I continued to zoom in until I gasped at what I could now clearly see.

In each of the coffins lay what looked like a person. It was hard to tell because these were just computer images and not photographs, but each of the people inside the coffins, were featureless. As I sat and stared at the images, I remembered something that one of the monks had said when Potter had been pretending to freak-out for some of the red stuff.

*"Brother, take him to the crypt, there is plenty of human flesh for him there,"* the monk had said.

*Were the images on the screen in front of me what he had been referring to?* I wondered. *Row upon row of humans, waiting to be fed upon?*

At the bottom of the page, in bright red letters as if in warning, the following message had been written.

### FACILITY CLOSED

I shut down the file and beneath this there was another which had been named *'Facility 2'*. Just like I had with the first, I clicked on it and the file opened. Again, I was faced with a series of diagrams of the same pods come glass coffins. But this was slightly different and had thick umbilical type cords coming from them. I scrolled down the page until I came across another technical drawing of a building. It looked like a large hangar, the type that you might find on an airfield. Again, the diagram had been drawn in such a way that you could see through it and all the hundreds and hundreds of pods that lined the walls. But there was something else. Beneath the building, there seemed to be a tunnel of some kind. It didn't show or say where it led to.

I enlarged the image and zoomed in. There was an upper level to this facility and it had been divided into corridors with rooms leading from them. Some of the rooms had been named. There were examination rooms, laboratories, and an operating theatre. As I sat and stared at the picture, I wondered if this wasn't the facility where Isidor, Kayla, and I had been kept before moving to the zoo. Scrolling to the bottom of the page, I came across a similar message to the one that I had seen before, but this was more of a warning. In bold, red letters it said:

## FACILTY CLOSED
## BIOHAZARD – NO ADMITTANCE!

Just like I had before, I closed down the file, and was just scanning over the others, curious as to what else I might find on the disc, when a shadow loomed over me, casting the screen in darkness.

Switching off my iPod, I gasped and said, "You nearly scared the hell out of me!"

Without looking at me, Potter leant over the table and switched the computer off.

"I was looking at something," I said.

"Shhh!" he said, raising a finger to his lips. "There mustn't be any light. Not even from the screen."

"What are you talking about?" I whispered.

"Come with me," he said, and walked towards the windows.

I followed him, and turning to look back at me, he said, "Keep your head down or they might see you."

Crouching over, I made my way towards the window. Peering over the ledge, I looked out. The window gave a view of the street below, and just opposite I could see the supermarket that I had taken the tins of fruit from. The lights inside were now out. The shop looked in complete darkness, but as I looked into the gloom I could see figures walking about inside amongst the isles and displays.

"Who are they?" I whispered, not taking my eyes off the view below.

"What's left of the townsfolk," Potter said. "Yet, they're not people anymore, they're vampires."

I remembered all those dead people in the cars that cluttered the road leading out of town, the bodies in the store and supermarket. My fears had been right; they had woken as vampires, created by the Vampyrus.

"They've been coming out every night now, for as long as I've been hiding out here with Seth and Eloisa," Potter whispered.

"What are they doing?" I said, as I watched a group walk into view from further down the street.

"They're looking for food – *blood*," Potter hushed. "I guess they're thirsty."

I continued to watch the vampires from the window as they almost seemed to roam the street in packs. Their faces were deathly white, their hair and clothes dishevelled. All of them bore the injuries that had been inflicted upon them by the Vampyrus and Lycanthrope. Some shuffled down the street, their heads resting against their shoulders. Others had limbs missing, and I watched one as he tripped over his own entrails that hung from his guts and fell flat on his face in the middle of the street. Then, something bizarre happened and I leapt back from the window. Seeing the vampire fall onto the road, the other vampires raced over to it and began to feed. With their arms swinging up and down, they ripped and tore the flesh from the fallen vampire. It screamed in pain, and I covered my ears with my hands in an attempt to block out its ear-splitting cries. Peeking over the lip of the window frame, I watched with sickening horror as the vampires in the store raced out onto the street at the smell of blood. Some of them were so eager to feed, that they simply crashed through the widows, sending a shower of glass across the pavement.

"What are they doing?" I whispered at Potter, but unable to tear my eyes from the gruesome scene below.

"I told you they were thirsty," he whispered back.

"But they're eating one of their own!"

"All the good human flesh has run out," he said glancing at me. "All that is left is each other."

"So what you're saying is that their cravings will get so bad they will eventually eat each other?" I said.

"That's exactly what I'm saying," Potter grinned at me. "They can't leave the town as it's been sealed off by Vampyrus and Lycanthrope, so in the end they will turn on each other to feed their thirst. Every night, once making sure that you were okay, I'd sneak from your cell and come in here to watch them. At first there were hundreds of them, but as the nights have passed their number has grown smaller. Look!" he said, "There goes another one!"

I glanced back out of the window, to see a pack of the vampires leap through the air and attack another of their own. The vampire went down in a flurry of shadows as it frantically thrashed its arms and legs about. Within seconds it had fallen still, and the others gathered around it like a pack of wild hyenas that had made a kill.

Not wanting to see any more, I turned away, sliding my back against the wall to sit on the floor. "You know we're not the only people hiding out in this town, don't you?" I said to Potter.

Joining me on the floor, Potter said, "Who else then?"

"Ravenwood, for starters," I told him.

"How do you know that?"

"Hunt told me Ravenwood had escaped with half of the DNA code that they had developed," I answered. I sat and told Potter about everything that I could remember from my time at the facility. I explained to him that most of my memories of what had happened had come to me in nightmares or visions, as I had been constantly drugged. Potter listened with a grim look on his face as I recalled how I'd been treated by Phillips and Sparky at the zoo. He smiled knowingly as I told him how I'd figured out my escape from my cell, but his smile soon faded as I described my last nightmare to him – the one in which the faceless man had said that he had let me escape so that I would bring Ravenwood and the missing part of the code to him.

"What did this man look like?" Potter pushed, his eyes the colour of an overcast sky bloated with snow.

"I've told you, I couldn't see his face," I said. "It's always cast in shadow. It's like he knows that I can see through the dark, so he has this way of blocking me out from *seeing* him."

"But why would he do that?" Potter asked thoughtfully, then added, "Unless…"

"I'd already met him before – I would recognise him," I said. "In my dream he said I'd seen his face because I could *see* everything."

"So there was nothing that you recognised about this man?"

Potter asked sounding frustrated. "What about his voice? You heard him speak in your dreams, right?"

"Sure," I said, "but he always kept his voice low and shallow as if to disguise it in some way. But knowing that isn't good."

"What do you mean?" Potter asked, taking another cigarette and popping it between his lips.

"Don't you see?" I said. "Whoever this faceless – *invisible man* – is, for him to go to such lengths to disguise himself from me means that he isn't someone that I've met just once or twice – he is someone that I know extremely well. So well, that just the briefest glimpse of his face or the tiniest sound of his voice would reveal his identity to me."

Blowing smoke from the corner of his mouth, Potter turned to face me and looking me straight in the eyes, he said, "Got any ideas?"

"None," I said back. And fell silent.

"What's up?"

"Nothing."

"You must think I was born in the early hours of this morning if you think I'm going to believe that," he said, and moved closer. "Tell me what's wrong."

"Remember Murphy thought that there was a traitor amongst us?" I said, staring at him.

"Yeah?" Potter said thoughtfully.

"Well, Hunt thought the same thing. It was he who first gave Murphy the idea," I pushed.

"So that's where Murphy got the idea from," Potter said with bitterness in his voice. "That Doc is just an old quack. What does he know?"

"But what if he was right?" I said, still looking at him. "What if there is a traitor amongst us – reporting back to this invisible man exactly what we're planning, where we are heading next?"

Potter broke my gaze and sat silently for a moment. Then, with his head bent low, he whispered a name. "Isidor."

"Do you know how crazy that sounds?" I said. "I'm mean do you have any idea what you're saying?"

"Look, like I've said before, there's just something about him," Potter said, turning to face me again. "He just turned up out of the blue like that back at the manor."

"He saved us," I reminded him.

"I had everything under control," he said.

"He told me that he came looking for his sister – Kayla," I said not wanting to believe what Potter was saying. Then I stopped, and I felt as if I couldn't breathe.

"What?" Potter asked, eyeing me.

But all I could think about was my dream, the one where Sparky went back to the manor and killed Mrs. Lovelace, then met the man at the top of the stairs. The faceless man that helped Sparky murder the half-breed children. What if Potter was right? What if it had been Isidor at the manor and once he'd finished helping Sparky, he had come to the summerhouse? It couldn't have been Luke, Murphy, or Potter as they were with me, fighting off the vampires. So that did only leave Isidor.

"What are you thinking about?" Potter pushed, again sounding impatient.

"Nothing," I lied. I couldn't share my fears with Potter as I couldn't be sure that I was right about Isidor. Potter disliked the guy enough without me provoking him. No, I wouldn't say anything until I was sure. However much my heart ached to even think that Isidor might be the traitor, I knew that I would have to watch him, *see* exactly what he was up to.

"Okay, keep your thoughts to yourself," Potter sniffed. "I'm getting used to that these days, but I'm telling you that kid has got more fiddles going on than the London Philharmonic Orchestra."

"You don't know that for sure," I said.

"What I do know for sure," Potter growled, "is if he is the bastard that's been tipping this *invisible man* off, I'm going to personally nail his scrotum to the floor!"

"You have such a wonderful way with words, Potter," I sighed.

"Thank you," he snapped.

"That wasn't meant as a compliment," I told him. "Whatever happened to innocent until proven guilty? Didn't we learn that in police training school? Isn't that meant to mean something? Don't we need some evidence?"

"I have evidence," Potter said.

"And what's that?" I asked. "Go on, enlighten me."

"He's a pain in the arse!" He snapped. "Good enough for

you?"

"No!" I snapped back.

"I tell you something for nothing, Kiera," he said. "You're a beautiful-looking girl, but that Miss Marple thing you insist on doing don't go with the posh French knickers you like wearing!"

"Why do you have to be so impossible sometimes?" I asked, and got up to walk away. But before I'd even reached the door, Potter had grabbed my arm.

"What about the other one?" he said.

"The other what?"

"Person hiding out in this town. You said there were two," he reminded me.

"Nik," I said, almost forgetting all about him.

"Nik?"

"He's a Lycanthrope," I told him.

"I didn't think you were a fan of that particular species," Potter said, drawing deeply on his cigarette.

"This one's different," I started.

"What do you mean, he isn't a murdering son-of-a-bitch like the rest of them?" Potter grimaced.

"No, I think he's done his fair share of killings, but like I said, he seems different."

"Don't you believe it," Potter said, grinding his cigarette out on the office floor.

"Nik's looking for redemption," I tried to convince him. "He helped me, Isidor, and Kayla escape. I'm surprised you didn't see him, he was here the day you found me."

"Apart from Seth and Eloisa, there was no werewolf, sweet-cheeks," Potter said.

"That's strange," I wondered aloud.

"Why?"

"I don't know," I said back. "Anyway, I thought you and Seth and what's-her-face are the best of friends."

"Don't you believe it, sweet-cheeks," Potter said, his voice low.

"What's that supposed to mean? Aren't I meant to be going down into The Hollows with Seth while you swan off with his girlfriend?" I said, trying to mask my bitterness.

Pulling me close, he whispered in my ear, "Seth ain't ever

129

going to make it down into The Hollows – I'll see to that. And as for Eloisa, she won't ever be coming back from that zoo, once I've rescued Luke."

"What are you talking about?" I whispered confused.

"You don't think I've forgotten what that scum did to Murphy, do you?" he said. Then letting go of my arm, he left the room.

"Potter!" I called after him. "What are you going to do to them?"

Without even so much as looking back at me, Potter continued down the corridor to his cell and closed the door.

# Chapter Twenty-Nine

My sleep was restless and I spent most of the night rolling onto my side, onto my back, and then my side again. My stomach still lurched from time to time with hunger and my mouth and throat would turn dry. I knew it was my body still craving the red stuff – but it was easier. Would I have these cravings for the rest of my life? Potter told Isidor we would, and it would be those feelings that would keep us sharp – alive.

In an attempt to take my mind off the red stuff, I thought of Ravenwood. I had already figured out where he would more than likely be hiding out in Wasp Water. But what would happen when I found him? The man in my visions said that I would take Ravenwood to him, but how would I ever do that? I'd never lead Ravenwood and the code to my enemy. But who was that? I know Potter suspected Isidor, but I wasn't convinced – not yet.

Rolling onto my side again, I picked up my iPod and turned it on. Closing my eyes, I started to listen to *Shake It Out* by Florence and the Machine and the line, *'It's always darkest before the dawn'*, couldn't have seemed truer at that moment in time.

I must have eventually fallen asleep, because I woke to find Kayla sitting at the end of my bed. Either my iPod had fallen out or she had taken it, because she was now listening to it. Kayla was dressed in the clothes I'd taken for her from the department store, and I could tell that she had showered and fixed her hair, as it now shone its usual brilliant red as it cascaded over her shoulders. Although her skin still looked pale, her eyes had more of their emerald sparkle and it made me feel happy to see her looking better.

Seeing that I was awake, she removed the earphones and said, "Potter says that we're good to go when you're ready."

"What time is it?" I yawned, rubbing the sleep from my eyes.

"Nearly nine," she smiled.

Pulling myself up onto my elbows, I looked at her and said, What are you smiling at? What's so funny?"

"You," she chuckled. "You've got the worst case of bed-head ever!"

"I didn't sleep too well last night – so give me a break," I smiled back. "Where's everyone else – Isidor and the others?"

"They're in the canteen having some tea and coffee before we set off for The Hollows," she said. "Potter's keen to get going."

Swinging my legs over the side of the bed, I said, "I'm not going to The Hollows – not yet, anyhow."

"But Potter..." Kayla started.

"Potter can think what he wants," I said back, as I pulled on my jeans and top. "He doesn't tell me what to do. He's not my keeper."

"Where are you going, then?" she asked me.

"To find Ravenwood."

"Can I come with you?" Kayla asked.

"I wouldn't have it any other way," I said back.

"What about Isidor?"

Looking down at her sitting at the end of my bed, I said, "Sure, why not."

"Good," was all she said.

"You like him, don't you?" I asked.

"Sure," she smiled at me. "But just my luck though."

"What is?" I frowned.

"The first cute guy to come along since, like, forever and it turns out he's my brother," she groaned.

"Too bad," I grinned at her.

"Don't I know it!" she grinned back.

Heading towards the cell door, I looked back at her and said, "Give me five and I'll see you in the canteen – I'm just gonna take a shower. And tell Potter, I take my coffee strong and sweet!"

As I made my way down the cellblock to the showers, I could hear Kayla giggling behind me.

I stepped into one of the shower stalls, and removed my clothes. Turning on the water, I threw my head back and let it splash against my face and it felt wonderful. With my fingers, I started to untangle the worst case of bed-head ever. Then, very carefully, I felt for those little black bones that had been sticking out from between my shoulder blades. With my eyes screwed shut, I felt for them. To my relief, they had gone. I opened my eyes again and saw a shadow fleet past on the other side of the shower block. I reached up and turned off the water. Standing with my arms covering my chest, I listened. I could hear the sound of movement on the other side of the cubicle I was in. Keeping my breathing shallow so I could hear the slightest of sounds, I hurriedly pulled on my jeans and yanked my top over my head. My clothes clung to me and I felt uncomfortable in more ways than one.

Easing open the cubicle door, I peered out into the room, which was now empty. I opened the door leading to the passageway that ran between the cells and I could see by a set of damp footprints who had been spying on me. With my heart thumping in my chest, I raced down the passageway, following the footprints as I went. But as I reached the corridor that led to the canteen, the footprints had faded, the moisture evaporating into the air.

With my blood almost seeming to boil in my veins, I threw open the canteen door and rushed inside. I could see him sitting at one of the tables, sipping coffee from a mug. *How dare he?* I screamed inside and raced towards him. But no sooner had I taken my first step than I was upon him and knocking the mug away from his lips with my fist. Jack Seth looked startled as the mug flew from his hands, and hot coffee splashed against his face. His eyes blazed brilliant yellow as he pounced from his seat.

It all happened so fast, I think it had taken everyone in the room by surprise. All I could hear was the sound of chairs skidding backwards across the tiled floor.

"What was that for, you crazy bitch!" Seth snarled, his top lip rolling back to reveal his black rotten teeth.

"You filthy, freaking pervert!" I screamed, and clawed at his face. As my fingers flashed before my eyes, I could see that my fingernails were no longer clear–looking and neat, but now long and ivory-looking, like claws.

Seth saw me reaching for his eyes, and snatched my arm away, twisting it down by my side. His grip was fierce like a vice, but with one lightning snap of my wrist, I had pulled my arm away as easily as if I were being held by a baby. I saw the surprise in his eyes at how easily I had gotten away from him, and he took a step backwards.

Leaping into the air, I took hold of his scrawny neck and launched him through the air. He spun away from me like a child's

133

toy and smashed into the wall on the opposite side of the canteen. Plaster and brick dust exploded into the air, as the wall cracked beneath the force of him colliding with it. But Seth hadn't even hit the floor before he was coming at me, his eyes burning in their sunken sockets. He came towards me in a flash, and I stood my ground, back straight and arms and legs rigid. And in my mind's eye, I knew exactly what I was going to do when he reached me, I was going to…

Then as if being plucked from the air, Seth flew from the room as Potter clattered into him. They hit the side the wall with such speed and force that the whole building shook.

"What's going on here!" Eloisa suddenly roared as she pounced into the air, landing on top of a table, her nails making a clicking nose against its surface.

"Why don't you ask your lover over there!" I shouted back at her. "He was watching me take a shower!" And inside, I could see those images again of him hurting me, laying on top of me, and the thought of it made me want to puke.

"What the fuck are you going on about?" Seth growled as Potter fought to restrain him from coming at me again.

"Ever since I met you, you've been staring at me with those fucked-up eyes of yours!" I roared back. "Filling my head with disgusting images of how you want me – of how you want to slowly torture then murder me. We'll I'm not having it anymore, you sick bastard. It ends now! It ends at this moment!" Then, before I knew what had happened, I was standing before him, as Potter held him back. I looked up into his crazy eyes and whatever he saw in mine made him flinch. It was only there for the briefest of moments, but it *was* there.

Leaning in so close that I could feel his hot breath against me, I hissed, "You *ever* look at me like that again, you won't believe what happens next."

Seth stared into my eyes and I refused to break his stare. Then smiling down at me, he ran his grey coloured tongue over his cracked lips. "I look forward to it, Kiera Hudson. Now, whoever you thought you saw watching you, it wasn't me. I've been here the whole time. Your friends will testify to that."

"But I saw paw prints leading away from the shower block," I insisted.

Shaking his head from side to side, and not taking his eyes off mine, he said, "Not my paw prints."

"How can I be sure it wasn't you?" I snapped.

Then looking me up and down as if he were undressing me with his eyes, he licked his lips again with his dead-looking tongue and chuckled, "Kiera, if it had been me that had had the pleasure of seeing you washing yourself in that shower, you'd be dead now – I wouldn't have been able to stop myself."

"Okay that's enough, you sick pup," Potter snarled and pushed Seth away. "Why don't you do everyone a favour and go and die somewhere?"

Straightening the bandana around his throat, Seth smiled and said to Eloisa, "C'mon my dear, let's go and get some air, I need to cool down – perhaps a cold shower might sort me out."

"Yeah, why don't you go and do that," Potter yelled.

With my heart racing in my chest and my breathing coming out in short, sharp breaths, I watched Seth and Eloisa leave the canteen.

When they had gone, Isidor and Kayla came rushing across the room towards me.

"Where did you spring from?" Isidor breathed.

"Yeah, what just happened?" Kayla chipped in. "It was like one minute I was sitting there listening to your iPod and the next minute the werewolf dude was flying across the room."

"I don't know what happened," I whispered, looking down at my hands, which had now gone back to their normal shape and size.

"You threw Seth across the room like he was made of straw," Isidor said.

Looking at the three of them, I said, "I don't know what's happening to me."

Then lighting a cigarette, Potter said, "You're changing – that's what's happening." Turning to Isidor and Kayla, Potter said, "Okay, the show's over. Go and get your stuff, we're moving out in five minutes."

Without saying anything back, Kayla and Isidor looked at one another, then silently left.

"Help me, Potter," I said looking at him.

"You don't look like you need any help, tiger," he said, and blew smoke from his nostrils.

"Please, just for once, can't you stop the wisecracks?" I pleaded. "I'm scared."

Pitching out his cigarette, Potter came close and cupped my face in his strong hands. "There isn't anything to be scared of, Kiera. I've got your back."

"Someone was watching me," I told him.

"But it wasn't Seth this time," he said.

"Then who else could it have been?"

"Didn't you say there was another Lycanthrope hiding out in this town?" Potter reminded me.

"Nik?" I said. "Why would he be here? Why would he be watching me?"

"Maybe he wasn't *watching* you – perhaps he was guarding you?" Potter suggested.

"Guarding me?" I breathed. "Guarding me from whom?"

"Whoever it is amongst us that's the traitor," Potter half-smiled, but I could tell he was being serious for once.

"Isidor, you mean?" I asked.

"Now why would you go and say a thing like that?" Potter said, removing his hands from my face. Then leaning into me, he kissed me softly on the forehead. "Come on, tiger, we've got to get you below ground before sundown."

"I'm not going down to The Hollows," I told him. "Not yet, anyway."

"You've got to," he said, sounding alarmed. "You'll be safe there."

"Am I safe anywhere?" I asked him. And before he could answer, I said, "I'm going to look for Ravenwood."

"But you don't even know where to start looking," Potter said, sounding frustrated with me.

"I know a good place to start," I answered.

"Where?"

"Back at the facility," I smiled.

"The facility?" he asked, raising an eyebrow. "What makes you think that he would go back there?"

"Do you remember that disc I downloaded at the monastery?"

"The one we all nearly died for while it was downloading – yeah I remember it," he said dryly.

"Well, when you snuck up on me last night, I'd been looking at some files on it," I started to explain. "Anyway, that facility has been closed down due to some kind of biohazard. I'm guessing that the biohazard is the infection that Hunt and Ravenwood spread amongst the half-breeds they were developing. The infection probably spread amongst them, and the Vampyrus got scared enough to think that it would spread to them – that's why they moved us to the zoo."

"So why would Ravenwood go back if there is this potentially dangerous biohazard floating about?" Potter asked.

"Because he helped to create it and knows that it's not dangerous to the Vampyrus, just to the half-breeds that are injected with the DNA code. See, it's like this self-destruct button for the half-breeds. They grow so much – then wham – the infection kicks in and they die. We can't die from it because our immune system will fight it off, but Hunt and Ravenwood were savvy enough to alter the DNA coding in the half-breeds so as not to be able to fight off the infection. So where is the one place that the Vampyrus won't go back to?" I said.

"You've lost me," Potter said with a frown.

Slapping my forehead with the flat of my hand, I cried, "The *facility*! Ravenwood knows that they won't go back there for fear of becoming ill and dying – so he knows that's the one place that he is safe."

Staring at me, Potter said, "I'm coming with you."

"What about Luke?" I said. "He needs to be rescued from that zoo."

"Where is this facility?" Potter asked.

"I'm not sure, but from the diagrams on the disc, it looks as if it's been built to look like some kind of airplane hangar," I told him.

"The old Military of Defence place," he said thoughtfully.

"How far away is it?" I asked him.

"A few miles away, just north of here," he said. "Seth and I scoped it out a while back while we were searching for you. But the place looks derelict."

"That's where Ravenwood is hiding out," I said. "I'm sure of it."

"Well I guess we'd better get going then," he said heading

towards the door. "But you better be right about this, sweet-cheeks. We don't have time to waste and Luke has even less."

Catching up with him, I took hold of his hand and said, "Thanks."

"For what?"

"For coming with me. Seth gives me the creeps." Then briefly kissing him on the cheek, I made my way out of the canteen.

# Chapter Thirty

We gathered on the front steps of the police station. If the town had been full of people like it would have been only weeks before, we would have made a very odd sight to them on this cold December morning.

The six of us stood beneath the bruised and battered looking sky, great dark clouds almost seeming to hang above us. The air was so cold, that within moments it had turned my nose and ears numb. I pulled the collar of my coat up about my neck and blew into my hands to keep them warm. Isidor and Kayla stood on either side of me, both were dressed in thick jackets and dark combat trousers and boots. Kayla's hair blew about her shoulders and Isidor's eyebrow piercing twinkled back at me. Over his back, he had the rucksack I had taken from the store and a mass of sharpened stakes protruded from the top of it. I guessed he must have been busy collecting branches from nearby trees and sharpening them over the last couple of days.

Jack Seth and Eloisa stood on the bottom step, both of them dressed as before, as if the cold didn't bother them. Seth looked at me and winked, and I looked away. Eloisa's stare was as cold as the air that blew about us. Potter, dressed in a long, dark coat and jeans, explained to the team that the plan had altered slightly and that we were going to make a short detour via the old Military of Defence site. Then he and Eloisa will go in search of Luke, and the rest of us are to go below ground into The Hollows. Potter didn't explain to Seth and Eloisa why we were taking the detour and they didn't ask.

Following Potter, we made our way down the steps at the front of the police station and walked single-file up the street and out of town. The remains of the vampires that had been fed upon last night lay strewn across the street, and there was so little left of them, that if I hadn't of seen them being attacked, I wouldn't have known where the scattered pieces of bone and flesh had come from.

As we reached the end of the street, I looked back and was startled to see Nik slinking down the front steps of the police station and out onto the street.

I instantly called out to him but my words were lost in the wind that roared all around us.

"Did you say something?" Isidor shouted at me.

"No, it was nothing," I replied. I looked back once more only to see that Nik had gone.

As we made our way out of town, it started to snow, and ahead I could see the never-ending stream of abandoned cars snaking away into the distance. I wished that the snow came down faster so it would cover the windows of those cars we had to pass. I didn't want to see those disfigured and bloated faces anymore.

We passed a small children's park and the swings listed back and forth in the wind, the chains crying out on rusty hinges. Apart from the swings and the crows that squawked from nearby fields, the world was silent – too silent. We eventually left the deserted town behind us and Potter led us over many fields, which were fast turning white. Banks of hills lay ahead and it was difficult to make out their peaks as the snow that now covered them blended in with the colour of the sky.

In silence, we walked through fast-running streams and stomped through the thickening snow. Every so often, we would pass deserted farmhouses and barns, and from the outside, each one of them looked so snug and cosy. I had to do everything in my control to stop myself from suggesting to the others that perhaps we should take a break and warm ourselves inside. But I knew what might lay behind the walls, the victims of the Vampyrus and Lycanthrope and worse still, sleeping vampires who were waiting for the night to come alive again. It wasn't just the thought of those vampires that kept me moving, it was the gathering clouds above us. They were so dark now, almost black, and the storm raging behind them was only hours away.

So we pushed on in silence, each of us lost to our own thoughts and plans. On several occasions, I glanced sideways at Isidor and wondered what he was thinking about. Did he have a plan? If so, what kind of plan was it?

With the snow falling harder and the wind turning colder, I thrust my hands into my coat pockets, bent forward and pressed on. All of us were now covered in a layer of snow. Just as I was beginning to wonder how much further I could go on without finding somewhere warm to defrost, Isidor stopped dead in his tracks and raised one hand in the air.

"Hang on!" he shouted over the roar of the wind.

"What's up?" Potter asked as he turned and came back down the hill towards Isidor.

"I can smell something," Isidor said, sniffing at the air, like a dog.

"Good for you," Potter snapped. "Come on, we haven't got time for -"

"No, wait a minute!" Isidor insisted. "I can smell burning, like some kind of fire."

"What, like some kind of campfire?" I asked him, wondering if I'd been wrong about Ravenwood hiding out at the facility and when in fact he was camping out in the woods that rose above us on the brow of a hill.

"Perhaps," Isidor mumbled, shaking his head and sniffing at the air again. Then he was off, taking the lead.

"Wait up!" Potter shouted after him, but Isidor carried on like a bloodhound that had fixed on its prey's scent.

With our feet crunching through the snow, we followed Isidor up the hill, Kayla panting beside me and the Lycanthrope following us from behind. With my cheeks flushed red with the cold and plumes of wispy breath seeping from my mouth and nose, I looked down into a large, open valley. In its centre was the hangar that I had seen in the diagrams. A tarmac road led away from the hangar, but it was too narrow to be a runway like I had originally suspected. But all the same, it was there to support large vehicles that had once come and gone from the hangar.
The whole facility was surrounded by fencing that stretched up into the sky and all of it was covered in razor wire. At each corner of the fencing stood search towers, but these looked to be unmanned and disused just like the rest of the facility. Inside the perimeter, set some way to the side of the hangar, was a cluster of tiny houses and I guessed that these were purpose-built homes for the staff who had once worked here. The place was pretty remote and I couldn't imagine the commute to work each day to be easy one for some of them.

"There!" Isidor said, pointing down at the cluster of houses below. "See the smoke coming from that chimney?"

"Someone's at home," I said.

"Let's go and pay the good doctor a house call," Potter said starting off down the hill.

The road led directly to the gates of a large, sprawling military site which was flat and now covered in snow. Glancing back, I could see our footprints winding their way down the hill to where we now stood in front of the two large gates that towered above us. Attached to them was a warning in bright red letters which read:

## MILITARY OF DEFENCE PROPERTY
## TRESSPASSERS WILL BE MET
## WITH DEADLY FORCE!

*Or fangs and a set of giant claws*, I said to myself. Despite the warning, Potter pushed against the gates, which swung open. Like the rest of the world, the site was eerily quiet, and the gates wailed on unoiled hinges. We made our way across the open area that stretched out in front of the hangar. I glanced over at it, and from ground level, the hangar looked huge. I could see that its vast doors were slightly open revealing a black slit of darkness, and it almost seemed to look at me like an eye. I couldn't remember being in there, tested and operated on, and despite the freezing cold, I shivered at the thought of what we might find inside. Turning away, I followed Potter and the others towards the house with the smoke that tumbled from its chimney.

A white picket fence circled the little house, which was smothered on all sides with brambles and moss which covered it like green, bony hands. A twisted, gnarled-looking tree stood in the front garden, and it towered over the house like a giant, misshapen spine. It cast a shadow over the house and created a feeling of great sadness. I glanced up at the tree and thought that I saw something moving through its knotted branches – but whatever it had been was now gone in a flurry of powdery snow.

Something spoke inside of me - that inner voice of mine that had guided me during my torment in the zoo, was talking to me.

*There's something wrong, Kiera!*

"Are you okay?" I heard someone ask me.

I turned to find Isidor standing next to me.

142

Nodding, I said, "Yeah, I'm fine."

Seth and Eloisa joined us at the gate.

"Seen any more werewolves?" Seth asked, and his voice was so expressionless that I didn't know whether he was being serious or having a joke at my expense.

"Not yet," I said back, "But you can be sure that you'll be the first to know when I do."

Hearing this, Potter smiled to himself. Then, swinging the gate open, he made his way up the path towards the house.

"Be careful!" I called out as the rest of us made our way after him.

# Chapter Thirty-One

Potter pushed against the front door, but it was locked tight. Brushing him aside, I said, "Not so fast."

"What's wrong now?" Potter groaned.

"Kayla, can you hear anything?" I said, turning to look at her.

Kayla came forward through the falling snow, and swiping her hair behind her ear, she turned her head towards the front door.

"Nothing," she whispered.

"Now perhaps we can get this over and done with?" Potter moaned, reaching for the doorknob again. Then, looking at Isidor and me, he said, "Or perhaps Sherlock Holmes and Doctor Watson want to have a snoop around?"

Ignoring him, I said, "Someone has been here and it wasn't long ago. They flew here – so that makes whoever it was a Vampyrus. They were male and known to Doctor Ravenwood. He knew them well, so well that he trusted them."

"How do you know all that?" Eloisa asked, staring at me with her brilliant eyes.

"There are no tracks leading to and from the house, apart from ours, that is," I told her. "But there was a set of footprints in the snow just in front of the door. So whoever it was, flew here and landed just outside the door." Pointing down to the footprints, I added, "They are too big to have been made by a female, and they haven't yet been covered by fresh, falling snow so they were only here a short time ago. They've gone now, or Kayla would have heard them. Even if they weren't moving, she would've heard the blood running through their veins."

"But how can you be so sure that this Doctor Ravenwood was friends with this Vampyrus – that he trusted him?" Seth asked with a sneer.

"The door is still intact," I said. "Whoever came here, came here for a reason and they wouldn't have gone away if Ravenwood hadn't have let them in. They would have, more than likely, broken the door down. It's quite easy for me to surmise, then, that Ravenwood knew this person. Ravenwood is on the run – in hiding – he wouldn't have just opened the door to anyone. No, it was a friend, someone he trusted."

Slowly clapping his hands together, Potter said, "I like your style, Sherlock," then glancing at Isidor, he added, "And what about you, Watson?"

Fixing Potter with a stare, Isidor said, "I can smell blood." Hearing this, Potter brushed Isidor aside, stepped up to the front door and without any hesitation smashed his fist into one of the wooden panels. His hand cut through the door as if he were tearing through a sheet of soggy paper. He eased his arm through up to his elbow, twisted it slightly, and then the sound of the lock being released could be heard from the other side. Potter withdrew his arm, and gently pushed open the door with his fingertips.

Without apprehension, he marched inside the house. I started after him and as he was about to step into the hallway, I grabbed hold of his arm.

"Be careful," I said and looked into his dark eyes.

He looked down at my hand, and then looked back at me. "So you keep telling me," he smiled and shrugged my hand free. The others followed us inside and closed the door behind them.

We stood in the gloom of the hallway and the only sound breaking the silence was our breathing. To Kayla, that sound must have been deafening. I glanced about. There was a staircase to our right and I peered up into the darkness. Potter followed my gaze and looked up. He stared back at me and his eyes were as black as the landing above us.

"Wait down here," he told us.

Without giving anyone a chance to object, he began to stride up the stairs two at a time.

Isidor wandered away from me and pushed open a door which led into a lounge. Looking down, I saw a trail of blood leading from beneath the door, and I feared what might be waiting for us on the other side. But before I had a chance to say anything, Isidor went inside. He disappeared from view and I waited. No sound came from the room, so I carefully peered around the edge of the door and looked inside.

Isidor was looking at a body that lay lace face-down on the floor. Beneath the body was a worn-looking rug, with frayed and turned-up corners. A set of bay windows shed a slither of milky light into the room. It was furnished with comfortable chairs and a sofa. There were chocolate brown bookshelves stuffed with leather bound tomes and a large coffee table that had sheets of paper scattered across it. A fireplace was carved into the wall, and behind the grate were lumps of coal that glowed hot and red, sending a spiral of smoke tumbling up the chimney.

Isidor turned to face me as Kayla and the two Lycanthrope entered the room. Seeing the body on the floor, Kayla gasped, and clapped a hand over her mouth.

"Are you okay?" I asked her.

She nodded, not taking her eyes off the body sprawled before us.

"This couldn't be the work of a Lycanthrope," Seth said smugly, "His injuries don't look that bad."

"He's dead, isn't he?" Potter asked as he strolled into the room and lit a cigarette. "I'd say that was pretty bad."

"Maybe he collapsed?" Isidor said, eyeing the body.

Toeing the body with the tip of his boot, Potter rolled the figure over and said, "Yeah perhaps you're right, Watson. Maybe Ravenwood hit the corner of the coffee table as he went down, and ripped half of his face off and throat out!"

"He was killed by a Vampyrus," I whispered, dropping to my knees to examine the floor. I brushed the tips of my fingers over the rug that Ravenwood was stretched across, and ran them around the edges of his body. His face was torn open from the top left corner to the bottom of his ear and I could see his teeth grinning back at me. An opening ran from beneath his chin to his navel. The open cavity didn't smell as much as I feared, as his intestines had been taken or more than likely, eaten. Glancing up Isidor, I could see that he had covered his mouth and nose with his hands.

"Well?" Potter asked.

"He wasn't attacked here, not in this room anyway," I started, as I ran the palms of my hands down over Ravenwood's open eyes and closed them. "He crawled in here from another room in the house, the kitchen probably, but his killer thought that he had left Ravenwood for dead in the kitchen. Ravenwood crawled in here after the Vampyrus had left. His attacker was right-handed, about six-foot-one in height, but no more than six-two. The killer didn't come here to find the code, he came here to give me a warning – he wanted me to know that, again, he was one step ahead of us. He knew we would come here for Ravenwood. And I can *see* where

Ravenwood hid the last part of his code."

"How do you know all that stuff?" Kayla asked.

"She's making it up," Seth sneered.

Without looking at Seth, I said, "Ravenwood didn't die here because there is very little blood on the rug and no blood splatter marks on the walls or ceiling."

"The good-old blood splatter book," Potter said, the cigarette dangling from the corner of his mouth. "I'm pleased to say I missed that spellbinding class at training school."

"The size and severity of his injuries show that there would have been blood, and lots of it, but there is hardly any here. The blood leading from the door and up the hallway is undisturbed. If he had been killed in here, the killer would have surely left some footprint or trace as he exited the house."

"They could have flown out?" Isidor suggested.

"Wingspan," I said back, shaking my head. "The room is too small and the hallway too narrow. No, he was definitely killed in the kitchen. Ravenwood was struck on the left side of his face, and the tears in the flesh show that he was attacked from the front – therefore his killer was right-handed."

"Let me guess," Potter cut in, "you know the killer's height by the spread between each of the footprints?"

"You're learning, but there are no footprints, remember? Now pay attention," I said. "When people write a message on a wall, they write it at eye level, so this leaves a good indication as to the height of whoever left the message."

"What message?" Kayla asked.

"That message!" I said pointing to the wall, cast in shadow by the open door. At once, they all turned around and looked at the message that had been scrawled in blood across the wall.

In a breathless voice, Kayla read it aloud. "Kiera, I got to the Doc first – now bring me the code!"

"What does that mean?" Isidor asked, as we watched the bloody letters drip down the walls.

"It means what it says," I whispered. "He's telling me that he knows my every move and that he knows I'll take the code to him."

"But you won't, will you?" Kayla asked, looking at me, her eyes wide.

"Not intentionally," I said thoughtfully.

"But if this Vampyrus killed Ravenwood in the kitchen, why leave the message in here?" Eloisa asked me.

"By leaving it here, behind the door, he is telling me that he knows how my mind works. The killer knew that I would search the house, leave no stone unturned. That's my nature. So he hid the message behind the door. It's also his way of informing me that he got away – disappeared without revealing himself. It's his way of making contact with me, but not directly. He's trying to taunt me."

"Okay, enough of the psychology," Seth sneered, "You said you could see where Ravenwood had hidden the code. I can't see it."

"That's because you look – but don't *see*," I said. "If Ravenwood was able to crawl out of the kitchen, why didn't he go to the front door to get away and find some help? That would be the natural thing to do, right? But he didn't, he came in here and sprawled himself face-down on this rug. Remember how his arms were spread out, almost as if it was his dying wish to protect something – to conceal it with his body?" Then, kneeling down again, I pointed to the turned-up end of the rug. "See this? It's been rolled back, and often, as the corner has failed to roll flat again. And if you look really closely, you can see that the colour of the floor beneath the rug is exactly the same shade as the rest of the floor. If the rug had been here for many years, wouldn't the colour of the floor beneath the rug be lighter?"

Taking hold of the corner of the rug, I said, "Ravenwood put it here recently to hide something." Then, pulling it back, I revealed a hatch that had been cut into the floor.

# Chapter Thirty-Two

I peered over Potter's shoulder and could see a set of wooden stairs leading down into darkness.

"I wonder what's down there?" I whispered.

"Why are you whispering?" Potter whispered back.

"Dunno," I shrugged, and followed him down into the pitch black.

There was a wall to my right and I could see a banister attached to it. I gripped hold of the banister and moved down. The stairs cried out beneath us as the others followed down behind. At the bottom, I nearly collided with Potter's shoulder as he suddenly came to a halt in front of me. For a moment there was silence, stillness, nothing. Then I heard a click as Potter pulled on the light switch that hung from the ceiling just above him. My new surroundings appeared before me in the dim glow of the naked light bulb.

My throat made a shallow wheezing sound as I sucked in a mouthful of air in shock at what had just been revealed to me. Along each wall of the basement stood metal shelves from floor to ceiling. On each of these shelves sat guns, in neat rows, gleaming in the light of the bulb.

"Whoa!" I whispered, as I approached the racks of guns.

As I drew near to them, they didn't look like the guns I had seen in the old black and white westerns that my dad had forced me to watch as a kid. These guns were bigger, powerful, and more deadly – like the guns those vampire-cops had shot at us.

"What is this place?" Kayla asked, eyeing the guns.

"Some kind of armoury, I guess. This is part of a military base after all," I said.

"But this just looks like a regular house," Kayla frowned. "Why so many guns?"

"Maybe whoever lived here, thought that one day they might need them," Isidor said.

"Against what?" Kayla pushed.

"Us, probably," Potter half-smiled.

Isidor came forward and stuck out his hand to touch one.

"Don't touch," Potter snapped.

Isidor immediately withdrew his hand and stuck it in his

149

trouser pocket.

"They're not toys," Potter said looking at the racks of guns.

"Lighten up, Potter," Seth said picking up one of the weapons. "These things are heavy."

"They could also be lethal in the wrong hands," Potter said, swiping the gun from Seth and placing it back on the shelf.

"Look, Potter, if you're heading back to the zoo with Eloisa to rescue the boy, Luke, you're gonna need something to protect yourselves with," Seth spat.

"I'm a Vampyrus and she's a werewolf for Christ's sake – what more do we need to protect ourselves with? Besides, we didn't come here to arm ourselves – we came for the code."

"Does anyone even know what this code looks like?" Kayla asked.

"No is the simple answer..." I started.

"If no one knows what this code looks like, then this whole detour is just one big waste of time," Eloisa said. "I mean, we don't even know where to -" but before she'd had a chance to finish, the basement was filled with the sound of pounding.

I turned around to see Potter consumed by a cloud of dust as he forced one of his arms into the brick wall.

"What are you doing?" I asked, crossing the basement.

"There's a chamber beyond this wall," he said.

"How do you know that?"

Looking over his shoulder at me, he said, "You're not the only one around here that can figure things out. See those old bags of half-used cement and that pile of bricks?"

I glanced into the corner of the basement and smiled.

"This wall has been built recently," he said with some pride. "See, I'm one step ahead of you, sweet-cheeks!"

The dust began to settle and I could see that Potter's arm was bleeding. At the sight of his blood, my stomach lurched, and I felt my throat turn dust-dry. I swallowed hard and looked away. It was then that I noticed Isidor sniffing the air as he absorbed the fragrance of the red stuff that seeped from the cuts along Potter's forearm. He caught me looking at him and covered his nose with his hand. But it was Kayla who concerned me the most. Like me and Isidor, she had seen Potter's blood, and she now stood mesmerised as she watched it drip onto the floor. I watched as she parted her lips and wetted them with the tip of her tongue, and I doubted she even knew that she was doing it.

Potter's arm disappeared through the wall up to his shoulder and at last the blood was hidden. Almost at once, Kayla's eyes flickered and she glanced around the room as if waking from a dream.

"Are you okay?" I asked her.

"Sure," she smiled back.

But I knew she wasn't okay, just like Isidor wasn't okay. I knew how the sudden sight of Potter's blood had made me feel inside. The silky redness of it and the way it had glided down over his wrist, dripping in thick streams onto the dusty floor had made my stomach somersault as if I hadn't eaten for a week. The cravings were nowhere near as bad as before, but it was a reminder that I still craved the red stuff.

Potter turned his head to one side and I met his black gaze. He wasn't looking at me; he seemed to be concentrating on something that had grabbed his attention on the other side of the wall. I could hear the sound of his claws tearing and scratching and it sounded like long fingernails being dragged across ice. Then without warning, Potter jumped back from the wall, bringing most of it down before him. Bricks clattered to the ground all around us, sending up billows of dust. I covered my nose and mouth as some of it got into the back of my throat and stung my eyes. As the dust and debris settled, I saw Potter's uncovered arm again. He saw me looking at the streaks of red that ran from his wrist to his elbow, and covered them with the sleeve of his coat. He then kicked the rubble away that lay at his feet and peered into the hole that he had made in the wall.

"There's something in here," he said, shoulder barging the remainder of the bricks away and disappearing into the space that he had discovered.

I looked at Kayla and she raised her eyebrows and shrugged. Within moments, Potter stepped back into the basement holding three glass tubes of thick, pink-red liquid.

"You three look as if you could do with some of this," he said, handing out the tubes of Lot 13.

Kayla snatched it from his hands, and removing the stopper with her teeth, she spat it away, tilted her head back and poured the

Lot 13 into her mouth. It dribbled like glue from her lips, and she wiped it away with her fingers, which she then licked clean.

I wasn't sure if taking Lot 13 was the answer to our cravings. By taking it, weren't we in some small way feeding the habit? Wouldn't it be better to just get the stuff completely out of our system – to be rid of it forever? I looked across at Isidor and he was slowly removing the stopper. Like me, I could tell that he felt unsure about drinking it.

"I know what you're thinking," Potter said looking at me. "But Kiera, those cravings won't ever go away. You're going to have to live with them for the rest of your life – we all are."

"But what about when Lot 13 runs out?" I asked, looking down at the tube of pink slime. "What happens then?"

"You go beneath ground, to The Hollows, until the feelings subside," he said. "But seeing as we're not in The Hollows – down the hatch it goes!" Then, flicking the stopper away with his thumb, he raised the test tube to his mouth and poured its contents down his throat. He shook his head as if just swallowing a large glass of whiskey and wiped his lips with the back of his hand. "What you waiting for?"

Isidor looked at me and shrugged, then raising the test tube to his mouth he started to drink. I watched his Adams apple bob up and down in his throat as he swallowed Lot 13.

Handing the glass tube back to Potter, I shook my head and said, "No, I'm not going to be a slave to anyone or anything. I'll find another way of dealing with my cravings."

"Kiera, you don't understand -" Potter started.

"I said *no*! What's the matter with you – are you deaf?" Pushing him out of my way, I climbed through the hole in the wall and stepped into the chamber beyond it.

# Chapter Thirty-Three

There was a room hidden behind the wall. It looked like a poky laboratory of some kind and reminded me of the science labs at college. The room was lit from above by a series of florescent lights that flickered on and off like lightning. One moment the laboratory was brightly lit, the next it was thrown into darkness. Either way, I could clearly see what lay hidden behind the wall. There were two metal work benches running horizontally down the middle of the room. Each was covered in an array of test tubes, Bunsen burners, microscopes, glass beakers, and a whole assortment of other equipment. Along the walls, were shelves crammed full of books, microwaves, plastic boxes, and rows of tubes containing Lot 13.

The others followed me into the secret laboratory and Seth made a whistling sound as he looked around the room.

"Someone has been keeping themselves busy," he said.

"What is all this stuff anyway?" Eloisa asked, but no one answered her.

I watched Potter cross the laboratory, and start taking down handfuls of the test tubes that contained Lot 13. "Give me your rucksack," he said to Isidor without looking at him.
Isidor handed it over, and Potter filled the bag with as many of the tubes as he could. Handing it back to Isidor, it made a clinking sound as the bottles jiggled about inside. Kayla went to the work benches and started to thumb through notebooks and sheets of paper that had been scattered across them. Holding up a sheet of paper that was covered in undecipherable scribbling, Kayla said, "Hey, Kiera, could this be what you're looking for? Could it be the code?"

"How would she know?" Seth sneered. "She's already admitted that she hasn't a clue what this code looks like."

"It could be staring her straight in the face and she wouldn't see it," Eloisa added.
Without looking at either of them, I whispered, "I do see it!"
Looking over Kayla's shoulder there was a small alcove set into the wall. Beneath it there was a comfortable-looking armchair, a small electric heater, a coffee table, and an old fashioned

lampstand. This setting looked at complete odds to the rest of the laboratory. It was like somebody had a made comfortable little rest area, where they could take a break from their scientific experiments and relax with a good…book! And it was that which I could see resting on the arm of the flea-bitten armchair.

With my heart racing in my chest, I hurried around the work benches and made my way into the snug little alcove. I snatched up the book, and before I'd even turned it over in my hands I knew what it would be. I looked down at the cover and read the title on the front.

### *The Wind in the Willows*

Frantically, I thumbed through the pages, and it was identical to the one that I had in the zoo. But that was the problem, there didn't appear to be any numbers or odd-looking shapes and symbols on any of the pages of this book, either.

"What's wrong?" Kayla asked, coming to stand beside me.

"This is the story, the book your father read to me as I slipped in and out of consciousness," I told her, as I skipped through the pages hoping that something, some sign would jump out at me. "I thought the code was hidden within its pages –but just like the copy I had in the zoo, I can't see -"

Then I saw it, a message written on the inside of the dust jacket. Taking the book in my hands, I sat in the armchair and read the message.

*Hello Kiera,*
*If you are reading this, then my good friend, Doctor Hunt was right in his theory that you would escape your cage and find this book. I should have been here to greet you – that was our plan – but my time is short, I know that. It is only a matter of time – days or hours – before I am found.*
*So I'll try and explain everything here and I hope in some way this will help you on your journey that lies ahead. I knew after meeting you at the manor that you were special, but I could also tell that you had no idea how special you are. Did this surprise me? No. Neither did it surprise Doctor (Lord) Hunt as we both knew that there is still so much that you do not know – so much*

*that has not yet been explained to you.*

*Some of the Vampyrus history was explained to you in The Ragged Cove by our friend, Luke Bishop, but I don't believe at the time that even he understood your significance. To be honest, I don't think any of us did. I know that Luke cares for you deeply, and I believe that, in part, this was why he held back some of the truth from you. He told me that you might have been frightened and he didn't want to lose you.*

*Luke was right in what he told you – the Vampyrus have lived beneath ground for thousands of years – too many to remember. But we were not here first- nor were the humans for that matter – we evolved together. But as we grew and spread across the Earth, the Vampyrus and the humans fought over the planet for thousands of years, until eventually a truce was made. It is written in legend that the gods were so displeased with how our two races had almost destroyed the planet that they had given to us, they decided to separate the Vampyrus and humans. They banished the Vampyrus underground and the humans above ground.*

*You may think that the Vampyrus got a bad deal – but believe me, Kiera, when I tell you that The Hollows are majestic and stooped in mystery, a beautiful world just as glorious as above-ground – if not better!*

*The truce lasted many thousands of years and it was as if the humans and the Vampyrus forgot about each other – in fact they did. It was as if to each other, neither existed. But as time passed from one generation to another, a Vampyrus was born who was named Elias Munn. Some say that he wasn't born at all as he cannot be traced to any other members of the Vampyrus race. Legend says that, as a boy, he got lost in the many caverns and tunnels in The Hollows. For weeks he wandered, hungry and cold until by chance he happened upon a tunnel that led above ground. To his amazement, he discovered a whole new world above the one he had lived his short life. He kept this discovery a secret and over the following years he would sneak above ground and discovered that, free of The Hollows, he looked like the creatures that lived above him. Gone were his wings, his black bristling fur, claws and fangs. So enchanted by this new world he had discovered, he made a life for himself and eventually fell in love with a human female. They loved one another deeply, until one fateful day he made a mistake. He revealed his true identity to her. She was overcome with revulsion and fear at the sight of him, she ultimately rejected him. Driven mad with hurt and despair, Elias Munn plunged his fist into her chest and tore her heart out, screaming that if he couldn't have her heart then no other man could. Even though she lay dead at his feet, Elias ate her heart to make sure that no other would ever have her heart again.*

*From that moment on, the gods cursed him for taking a human life and breaking the truce. But it wasn't only Elias they punished; they cursed the entire Vampyrus race. Because he had eaten human flesh – we were all cursed with the thirst for it. It was the gods' final attempt of stopping us from venturing above ground. Within The Hollows the cravings fade. But those of us with good hearts can resist human flesh for a time above ground, before needing to return to The Hollows. Those with hate and fear in their hearts can go only hours, at the most, days, before they need to return to The Hollows. But the gods' plan failed as Elias, bitter and twisted with hate for the humans because of his lover's rejection, encouraged other like-minded Vampyrus to go above ground and feed, which brought about the creation of vampires.*

*So, over the centuries, there have been outbreaks of vampire attacks above ground. Fearing that humans would once again remember the Vampyrus and come in search of us, bringing war to The Hollows – the elders and lawmakers sent teams like Murphy, Luke, and Potter to hunt down this bloodthirsty Vampyrus and bring him back to The Hollows.*

*But Elias Munn is rumoured to have become immortal from the blood that he drank from his lover's heart. He has never aged since that day. No one now knows his true identity or name, as over the centuries he has adopted many different guises. It is he who now threatens the fragile peace that exists between the humans and Vampyrus. But it was prophesied that if the humans and the Vampyrus couldn't live together in peace, the gods would send a 'half and half' – part human and part Vampyrus – a half-breed to settle the conflict once and for all. The gods would let that half-breed decide which race should survive and which should perish. But the half-breed wouldn't come alone – there would be two others sent to help and guide this half-breed as their journey would be hard and long and fraught with many battles and dangers.*

*So, if you were hoping to find a code, a series of numbers or words hidden amongst the pages of this book, then you are mistaken. Kiera, you are the code! You are the half-breed who has been sent to decide which of our two races will survive while the other perishes. Myth and legend says that the gods believe that only you can be impartial as you are the best of both of our races. Kiera, the gods are leaving it up to you to decide which race lives and which one dies. The Vampyrus know this and that is why they had you locked up in that zoo. They wanted to strip you of your humanity – the human part of you. They wanted you to become an animal, to think like an animal, get you addicted to human flesh so you would see that race as nothing more than animals to feed on.*

*Doctor Hunt and I knew we had to get you away from there before they broke you completely. He wanted you to save his two children, the half-breeds that have been born, to help and guide you. He didn't want their humanity taken away – it was all that was left of their mother – the woman that he loved and who was murdered. But we were being watched. Everything we said or did was being monitored. So many times Doctor Hunt wanted to tell you what was happening – what they were trying to do to you. Hunt had heard about your gift – your ability to see things – to work situations out by seeing what everyone else failed to notice. So he was convinced that if he gave you enough clues, enough subtle hints, even in your almost catatonic state you would be able to piece them all together.*

*So he came up with a plan. Doctor Hunt would read you books in which the heroes escaped. Time and time again, he read you those chapters about Mr. Toad escaping from the prison and Peter Rabbit fleeing Mr. McGregor, hoping that you would take the bait and figure out your own escape. Hunt also needed you to make an emotional connection to the books, in the hope that if you ever saw one of those books again, it would remind you of the times he spent reading to you and the message that he was hoping you would see. He hoped that if you ever saw this book again, it would trigger something within you. That's why he got Nik to bring a copy to you in your cell. I wasn't convinced, but if you are reading this now, then you must have escaped and you must have picked up this book the moment you saw it, and my dear friend and colleague, Lord*

*Hunt was right about you.*

*Hunt figured out who you were and your purpose after studying your DNA in the facility. Your DNA almost blew our minds. We'd never seen anything like it. I don't have the time to explain what we discovered, but believe me, Kiera, when I tell you that you are going to be incredible!*

*But what now? The Vampyrus have samples of your DNA, but as you know, Doctor Hunt had it corrupted with the infection that came from the werewolf's bite. The Vampyrus will continue to try and create other half-breeds like you, Kayla, and Isidor, but as you well know, they will grow ill and die. It won't take long for the Vampyrus to realise that they have been deceived and what they have to work with is useless. So for now, go to The Hollows. You will be safe there. Let your friends, Luke and Potter guide you. Seek out a friend of mine called Felix Coanda. He is expecting you. Coanda will be able to help you. I'm sorry that I won't be alive to help you myself. But go quickly, Kiera, because he will come for you. Hunt believed that someone already close to you is a traitor – I was never convinced of that. Maybe he was right and I didn't want to see it.*

*But be careful, Kiera, of who you befriend and love on your journey, for it is said that if Elias Munn can get the half-breed to love him, as a father, or a brother, or a lover, then just like his first love – he would have taken your heart as his own and he will be given the power to choose which race lives and which race dies.*

*I have nothing more to say and I know that I will be dead very soon. Therefore, whatever decision you make won't affect me – but, Kiera, it will change you. Whichever race you decide to live, will be the species that you solely become. You will no longer be a half-breed – you will either be a human or a Vampyrus. As for Kayla and Isidor, your decision will permanently change them, too.*

*I do not have to tell you that the burden on you is a great one. The fate of two entire races lies in your hands. The decision to destroy an entire race is not an easy one – so choose wisely, Kiera Hudson.*

*Doctor Thaddeus Ravenwood*

Trembling with fear, anger, or maybe revulsion, I clawed the pages that Ravenwood had written on from the book. I screwed them into a ball with my hands.

"What's wrong?" Potter asked. "What did it say?"

Without looking at him, I held out my hand and said, "Give me your lighter."

"Why?" he said.

I looked at him and his face was a mask of confusion. "Just give me the lighter!" I spat.

Rummaging in his trouser pocket, he handed me the Zippo lighter and said, "Kiera, what did the message say?"

Ignoring him and with a trembling hand, I held the lighter to the corner of the pages and watched them start to burn. If I destroyed them, then perhaps those words had never been written and the burden would pass me by.

"But what about the code?" Kayla asked, watching me drop the ball of burning pages to the floor.

"There is no code!" I shouted at her, and at once regretted it.

"So what was the goddamn point in coming all the way out here?" Seth barked.

Looking at him straight in the eyes, I raised my finger and said, "Don't even start on me, Lycanthrope! I'm so not in the mood for you!"

"But Kiera," Isidor said, stamping out the remains of the blackened pages, "You said we needed the code."

"How many ways have I got to say this?" I yelled at him. "There is no code – I'm the freaking code!"

Unable to say another word, I raced from the laboratory, through the basement, and up into the house. Ravenwood lay face-up on the floor.

"Why me?" I shouted down at him.

I stepped over his corpse and ran from the house. The sky was almost black with clouds and the snow fell harder now in thick, white torrents. With my breath escaping my mouth in wispy streams, I headed through the snow. On the other side of the garden fence, I saw something big move behind the tree that I had seen earlier.

"Who's there?" I called out.

There was a howling sound, but I couldn't tell if this was the wind of a wolf close by.

The movement came again. I headed towards the tree and as I got closer with my heart pounding in my chest, I saw who was hiding there.

"Nik?" I whispered. "What are you doing here?"

Without saying a word, he met my stare with his brilliant yellow eyes, then he was gone, bounding away until I lost sight of him in the falling snow.

# Chapter Thirty-Four

"Who were you talking to?" someone asked over my shoulder.

I spun round to find Potter standing behind me. "No one, I guess," glancing back through the snow in the direction that Nik had bounded away.

"What's going on?" Potter asked, and placed one hand on my shoulder.

Brushing it away, I said, "I need some time alone."

"Why?" Potter pushed. "Has it got something to do with what was written in that book?"

"Please, Potter," I begged, staring into his eyes which were as dark as the clouds above us. "I just need some time."

"But that's something we don't have," he said. "I need to go after Luke and you need to get to the -"

"The Hollows," I finished for him. "You're not the only one who says I should be down there."

Shaking snow from his jet-black hair, Potter looked up into the battered looking sky and said, "It's going to be night soon, and with this storm, I don't think any of us will be going anywhere – it wouldn't be safe. Besides I have something I need to do before I set off to rescue Luke."

"And what's that?" I asked, and for the first time ever in Potter's company I felt the smallest pang of suspicion. But I strangled it deep inside of me.

Looking at me through the falling snow, Potter said, "You're not the only one around here who has secrets they don't want to share." He then turned and headed back towards the house where the others gathered in the doorway.

"Where are you going?" I called after him.

"Like I said, it's too dangerous to travel tonight," he called back. "We go at first light."

I caught up with him, my boots crunching in the snow. Taking Potter by the arm, I said, "Okay, but I don't want to stay in that house. Not with Ravenwood."

As if searching my eyes with his, he said, "We'll stay in the hangar." Then he was gone, making his away across the snow-covered front yard, towards the facility that loomed in the distance.

Looking at the others huddled in the doorway, I called to them and said, "This way!"

Wind screamed across the open plain that lay before the giant hangar, and all of us pulled our clothes tightly together to protect ourselves from the driving snow. Seth and Eloisa didn't appear to be bothered by the snow and they followed us at a distance, walking upright as the bitter wind blew hard at them.

We reached the facility doors, which loomed high above us. They were slightly apart down the centre and a strip of yellow and black tape flapped in the wind. Across the tape were the words, **"KEEP OUT. BIOHAZARD"**. Undeterred by the warning, Potter tore the tape free and slipped between the gap in the doors.

Before following him inside, Kayla gripped my arm and said, "Kiera, this is where we were kept, right? Where they did those tests on us?"

Clawing my fringe from my eyes, I looked at her and said, "I think so."

"Then should we really be going back in there?" Isidor spoke up. "Look it says to stay out – Biohazard."

"There is no hazard to us, Isidor, I promise," I tried to reassure him. "The Vampyrus think there is a virus that's going to kill them, but there isn't – not really. It's the infection that your father took from my leg and spiked the DNA formula with. It kills the half-breeds that the Vampyrus are trying to mass produce, but not us."

"Are you sure?" Kayla asked, not sounding convinced.

"I'm sure," I told her and slipped through the gap in the doors.

The facility was vast, seeming to stretch away into the distance for miles. Emergency lights flickered overhead. I could see that stairs led away immediately to my right up to a metal landing that lined the inner walls of the hangar and branched off into different rooms and corridors.

"Does any of this seem familiar to you?" Potter asked.

"Not at the moment," I whispered back. "How about you two?" I quizzed, looking at Kayla and Isidor. They both shook their heads as they glanced about.

Jack Seth and Eloisa stepped in from the cold, and both stood brushing the snow from their hair and clothes.

"Another detour?" Seth asked Potter.

"Just for tonight," he said. "The storm is too bad and it will be night soon."

"Are you sure they're the only reasons?" Seth pushed.

Looking away, Potter said, "What other possible reasons could there be? Now let's have a look to see if we can't find somewhere to bed down for the night."

I looked at Seth and Eloisa and they shared a knowing glance with each other.

Potter led us up the stairs and through a maze of corridors and passageways. Pipes ran along the walls and some of them hissed steam in short, smoky bursts. The corridors were lit from above by a series of neon lights and water dripped from the ceiling and ran down the walls. The facility looked as if it had quickly fallen into disrepair.

Stopping abruptly, Potter turned to face the wall. He pressed a series of buttons set into a panel on the wall next to a door. A red light flashed on and off, barring us entry to whatever lay on the other side of the door. Sucking in air, Potter sighed, rolled up his sleeve and smashed his fist into the panel. Sparks shot from behind it, then the door slid up and opened.

Turning to face us, Potter said, "Follow me," and then slipped through the gap he had opened.

The door slid closed behind us with a hiss. I looked around to discover that we were now standing in a room that was oblong in shape. Down the length of one of the walls were two windows, which both looked out into a large glass container filled with water.

Potter glanced at me, raised an eyebrow, and then led us to the first viewing window, where we all peered into the murky water on the other side of the glass. I immediately jumped backwards with fright and had to stifle a scream. Behind the window floated a white *thing*. Initially it looked human with two arms and two legs. But it was its face that was all wrong. It looked like a disfigured version of Isidor.

The head of this half-breed, although similar in appearance to Isidor, was bloated and misshapen, elongated and stretched. It had two black eyes that swivelled blindly in two sunken sockets. Its mouth was huge and open like a flapping gash. But this was nothing compared to the umbilical cord that snaked from an open wound on the crown of its head. The cord coiled upwards and was attached to an underwater panel that flashed with a series of lights.

"What is it?" Seth asked, and I caught a smile tug at the corners of his mouth as he glanced at Isidor.

Knowing that Seth was probably taking some perverse satisfaction from this, Isidor swallowed hard and walked closer to the window. "I'm surprised you don't recognise it," he whispered, as if fearing that he might wake the half-breed on the other side of the glass. "It's meant to be me."

"This must be one of the failed attempts at breeding a copy of Isidor from his DNA," I spoke aloud.

I looked through the glass at the half-breed and watched as its jaws flapped loosely open and closed beneath the water. I couldn't tell if this was a deliberate act on behalf of the creature or not. I hoped not. I hoped that it was dead and wasn't suffering in some way.

Potter remained silent, and turning his back, he moved away from the window and came to rest in front of another set of glass panels. Again, it looked into an underwater chamber and inside this one floated what appeared to be a human girl. I gazed at her and she looked as if she were asleep. This time though, I had no difficulty in recognising who it was floating behind the glass. It was me, aged about eight-years-old.

On seeing the girl behind the glass I began to tremble.

"What's wrong?" Potter asked, brushing my hand gently with the tips of his fingers.

Yanking his hand away, I pointed at the girl floating behind the glass and shouted, "That's me! That's me as a child!"

"What?" Kayla asked looking around at me.

Isidor was still staring blankly in at his deformed half-breed, his head tilted to one side. I knew that, just like me, seeing this other version of himself had disturbed him.

Seth seemed unmoved and said to me, "So this was you as a child? Cute!"

"Back off, Seth!" Potter ordered. "Can't you see Kiera's upset by this?"

"I was just admiring the Vampyrus' creativity," Seth smiled and winked at Eloisa.

"You call that thing in there *creative*?" I snapped at him.

164

"That's cruel. Whatever that might be in there is – was – living. It would have had feelings and emotions. How dare the Vampyrus do this to her – to *me!*"

"That's like the Kayla-thing Isidor killed in that room at the monastery," Potter said.

"Kayla what?" Kayla suddenly said. "What are you talking about, Potter?"

"Sorry, did someone forget to mention it, but there was a half-breed who looked just like you at this monastery we came across," Potter started to explain. "Well, she had less hair than you and she was…"

"Potter!" I shouted at him. "Don't you have any tact?"

"The girl needs to know the truth," Potter said back. "You know the kid is like sixteen – you can't protect her for the rest of her life."

"What are you both talking about?" Kayla said, forcing her way between us.

"See that girl in there," I said pointing to the eight-year-old me floating in the water. "That was just what I looked like as a girl. But what's important, Kayla, is that in there *isn't* me. That's something the Vampyrus have tried to breed from my DNA."

"So there are things out there that look like me?" Kayla asked, searching my eyes for the truth.
"Yes. But however much they try, they will never be able to make another me or you – we're unique – and those things are just worthless copies."

"It's alive!" Eloisa suddenly said, and for the first time since meeting her, I could sense fear in her voice – but then again, maybe it was revulsion I could detect? I followed her bright yellow stare as she pointed at the younger-me floating in the water. The girl had opened her eyes and was staring at me. Although she looked like me in almost every way, her eyes were not hazel like mine but cold and black. Her skin was corpse white and wrinkled from being submerged in the water for too long. Her jet-black hair fanned out in the water like a mermaid's fin. Kicking her legs, she swam towards the glass and looked at me. It was then that I noticed that it wasn't just her legs that she used to propel herself through the water, but a set of fins – no – wings that grew from her back. Raising her one hand, she tapped slowly on the glass and the sound of her knocking sent gooseflesh down my spine. As if captivated by her stare, I inched towards the glass. With the tip of our noses almost touching, I felt an incredible wave of sadness come over me. I pitied her – I pitied me – but wasn't that the same thing?

The girl opened her mouth as if to smile, but her lips turned upwards forming a cruel grin. I could see a row of razor-sharp teeth protruding through her gums. Then, without warning she began to smash her head into the glass as if trying to break it with her face.

"She's alive!" Kayla shrieked, jerking backwards and away from the glass.

Shaking his head, Potter said, "Not alive like us. She doesn't have feelings or senses."

"How can you be so sure?" Kayla asked, not able to take her eyes off the glass.

"You try smashing your face in like that, and see if you feel it! She just exists," Potter said, as he flipped a series of switches that were fixed to the wall by the window. "But not anymore."

No sooner had he turned off the switches, the water drained out of the tank, like a bath having its plug removed. Sensing that she was in danger, the girl behind the window began to swish about, clutch at the water with her claws. As the last of the water drained from the tank, the girl collapsed onto her side. Drawing her knees up to her chest, she gasped several times, closed her eyes and fell still.

Potter turned away from the window and I followed. I couldn't bear to look upon her – *me* – any longer. In my mind, I kept telling myself that she wasn't *me* – she was a monster created in a laboratory like '*Mary Shelly's Frankenstein*'. The girl had been a creature without a soul, just like the mutant back in the monastery. Potter had been right in turning off this girl's life support. She had no right to life. But who was I or any of us to make that decision? Who had given us the power to play God? And then I thought of the choice that I would soon have to make and I almost had to stuff my knuckles into my mouth to stop myself from screaming.

Kayla, Seth, and Eloisa followed us across the room. As we reached the door that led from the chamber, I looked back to see Isidor still standing by the glass and looking at the boy who floated behind it. Isidor stood only inches from the glass. He had his hand pressed flat against it as if trying to make contact with the creature on the other side. Then to my surprise, Potter headed back towards him. He slowly raised his hand, flipped off the switches on the wall next to the tank. Then, placing his arm around Isidor's shoulder, he guided him from the room, and as they went, I could see the silver streaks of tears on Isidor's face.

# Chapter Thirty-Five

We sat together in a large dining hall which I guessed had been used by the staff at the facility. Kayla and I finished the remainder of the tinned fruit I had taken from the supermarket. That seemed so long ago now. So much had changed, and my head and heart were trying to play catch-up. However much I tried not to think about Ravenwood's letter to me, it kept worming its way to the front of my mind. All I could think about was the decision he had left me to make.

*I do not have to tell you that the burden on you is great. The fate of two entire races lies in your hands. The decision to destroy an entire race is not an easy one – so choose wisely, Kiera Hudson.*

Over and over again those words kept going around and around in my mind, like a broken merry-go-round that couldn't be stopped. I thought that if I burnt that message, then those words would fade away like ash on a breeze, but if anything, it had only seared those words into my mind like a brand on a farm animal. Isidor sat alone at one end of the table. He wasn't eating. He sat and stared at the blank wall in front of him. Potter had taken one of the bottles of Lot 13 and was drinking from it. He rolled one down the length of the table towards Isidor, but Isidor just let it roll on by.

"You need to keep your strength up, kid," Potter said, but Isidor just kept staring at the wall. Part of me wanted to go to him and talk to him about what I had read in that message left by Ravenwood. I wanted to tell Kayla, too. But, I knew in my heart that it wasn't the right time. How could I talk to them rationally about our importance if I didn't really understand the consequences of it myself? No, I would wait – get everything set in my own mind before I burdened them with it. So, getting up from my seat, I took one of the opened cans of fruit and went to him.

Hooking my finger into the can, I plucked out a slimy, crescent-shaped peach slice and popped it into my mouth. "You know, although these things are bright enough to light up the dark, they taste good."

Isidor ignored me.

"Isidor…" I started.

"They had no right," he suddenly said, his voice soft but firm.

"Sorry?" I said back.

"Phillips and the others had no right to take my DNA, to operate on me, do tests on me, just so they could make that deformed-looking creature back there," he said.

"They've done it to the three of us," I said. "I know that doesn't make it any easier, but you don't have to go through this alone."

"What do they want from us?" he whispered, not taking his eyes off the wall, as if deep in thought.

"We're special, Isidor, but you already know that," I said. "This man – Elias Munn – I think that's his name or it used to be – believes that he can copy us, take our uniqueness and harness it in some way. But the thing is, Isidor, that isn't you back there and it never will be. I know it's hard, but just think of it as a bad piece of sculpture. It might bear some faint resemblance to you or even look just like you – but it can never be you."

"I guess," he said turning to look at me. "I hadn't thought of it like that."

"Isidor, if there is one thing that I've learnt on this journey, it's that whatever happens, all you can do is be true to yourself," I said, "You can't ever be more than that."

With a faint smile, he said, "Thanks, Kiera."

"What for?" I asked him.

"For being you," he said. "Now where are those peach slices?"

I pushed the can towards him. "How are your cravings?" I asked him.

"Okay," he said, pushing some peach into his mouth. "That Lot 13 Potter gave me back at the house has taken the edge off it. What about you?"

"I'm coping," I lied, eyeing the tube of Lot 13 Potter had sent rolling down the table. "I don't know if Potter was right."

"About what?" Isidor asked me.

"That we'll have to take Lot 13 for the rest of our lives," I said.

"Well, he was right about one thing," Isidor said.

"And what was that?" I asked him, curious.

"It does help if you're angry," he said looking at me. "It does

169

help if you hate the ones who have hurt you."

"How do you figure that out?" I asked, glancing back at Potter who sat some seats away with a cigarette dangling from his mouth.

"Because I'm not going to stop until I've taken Phillips' heart out!" Isidor said.

I looked at him and it was as if he had lost that boyish look of his. He appeared older somehow, and in his once blue eyes, I could see pain. But it was more than that; it was like he had said – it was hate.

Feeling tired and wanting to be alone so I could think about everything I had learnt from Ravenwood's letter, I left the others sitting in the dining hall and went to look for somewhere to sleep for the night. My whole body ached with tiredness, and my head thumped with a dull thud.

I wandered along the empty walkways and corridors, and as I did, I had snapshot memories of the facility with its plain white walls and sterile floors. I came across a row of rooms and each one of the doors had a circular window set into them, just like the one from my dreams. I remembered again looking through the window as Isidor had stared in at me, his face haunted and scared looking. *"Kiera!"* Isidor had screamed. *"Help me!"* he had begged and banged weakly against the window. *"We have to get out of here, Kiera!"* and it was almost as if his screams were still echoing off the walls and down the corridors in the desolate facility.

Stopping in front of one of the doors, not knowing why I picked that particular one, I pushed it open and went inside. There was a bed set against the far wall and the blankets had been pulled back. There was an upturned chair and it made me think of Doctor Hunt sitting next to me as he read from those books. Righting the chair, I noticed something under the bed. I crouched and picked it up. I looked down at the book in my hands and didn't know whether to laugh or cry. The book was *'Peter Rabbit'*. I thumbed through the pages and looked at the watercolour pictures of Mr. McGregor brandishing his rake as he chased Peter Rabbit across the allotment.

"Go on Peter, run!" I whispered aloud. "Don't let him catch you!"

Closing the book, I placed it on the bed that I had once

occupied. Knowing that I would be too uncomfortable ever sleeping in this room again, I closed the door behind me and looked for somewhere else to rest. I climbed down the stairs to another level and found myself in another passageway. Just like the others I'd searched, there were doors leading off of it. Pushing against one of them, it opened to reveal a narrow room with a small bed. There was no bedding, but there was a pillow. Stepping into the room, I closed the door behind me. Along the opposite wall sat two small lockers. One of the doors was ajar and I pulled it open. It was empty but attached to the inside of the door was a faded photograph of a young woman holding a smiling baby.

"Who's that?" I asked aloud.

"What does it say on the front of the locker?" someone asked. I looked up to see Potter standing in the doorway.

"What are you doing here?" I asked him, startled by his sudden appearance. I felt a little angry that he was here when I just wanted to be alone, but another part of me was glad, too. I swung the locker door closed and read the name that had been stencilled across its front. It read: *Coanda*

I recognised the name as being the person who Ravenwood said I should seek out in The Hollows. I said to Potter, "Who is Coanda?"

"The person who used to own that locker, I guess," he said. "Why, is there a problem?"

Still not ready to discuss what I'd read in that message from Ravenwood, I shrugged and said, "No, there isn't a problem."

Closing the door behind him, Potter came towards me. "I think there is a problem," he said.

"What makes you think that?" I asked, looking away.

Taking my chin in his hand, he gently turned my face back towards him. "Please, Kiera, talk to me."

"Why, so you can turn it into some kind of joke?" I snapped at him.

"That's not fair," he said, taking his hand away from my face. "You've changed."

"I've changed?" I scoffed. "What about you?"

"What about me?" he said, lighting a cigarette.

"You're always so freaking cranky," I said.

"Is that it? And I thought you were being a stroppy-cow

171

because you were struggling with how you felt about me," he smiled.

Dropping onto the bed, I said, "See, that's exactly what I mean! You never take anything seriously unless it involves smashing a door down, tearing up some vampires, or kicking some werewolf's arse."

"I take a lot of things seriously, Kiera," he said, and his smile had faded. "Just because I don't go around all day long weeping and wailing, it doesn't mean I don't care."

"Look at the way you were with Kayla back at the police station," I reminded him. "There was no need for that."

"Listen, sweet-cheeks, just in case you haven't noticed, we're in serious fucking trouble here," he snapped, blowing smoke through his nose. "You're not doing that girl any favours by being soft with her. This ride we're on is going to get a whole lot worse before it gets better! If she doesn't toughen up, she's gonna get herself killed, or worse."

"What could be worse than that?" I said.

"Getting *you* killed," he shouted back at me.

"I can look after myself," I yelled back.

"Not while you're watching her back," he said, his voice lowering but still remaining firm. "And then there's Isidor."

"So you do know his name then?" I bitched.

"I know his *name* but I'm not prepared to see it etched on a gravestone. Because believe me, Kiera, that's exactly what's going to happen if someone doesn't have the bollocks to take his head out of his arse. Jesus, that boy wanders around in a trance most days. So he's good with his crossbow, but that ain't gone help him against what's coming. That boy needs to man-up, because I'm not going to sit back and watch him get himself killed, or anyone else for that matter."

"So you do have feelings?" I snipped at him.

"Feelings!" Potter almost roared at me. "You have no idea about how I really feel!"

"So tell me!" I shouted at him.

"I love you!" he bellowed at me and his eyes turned black. "Happy now? I love you, okay? I love you so fucking much that it hurts! It's driving me insane! I loved you from the moment I saw you doing your Miss Marple impression in those woods back at

The Ragged Cove. But I could tell you were sweet on Luke and hey, why not? He's the good-looking one, right? I mean, I'm just the hired muscle. I'm the one who gets everyone else out of the shit. But I couldn't help my feelings, I'd never felt like that before. So yeah, okay I stole a kiss from you in the gatehouse – big fucking deal! But you know what? That was the biggest mistake of my life, because that one kiss from you drove me out of my tiny freaking mind! So, I'm sorry if I give the boy a hard time and ain't too gentle with the girl, but I'm not going to sit back and watch you risk your life just so you can blow their noses and wipe their arses!"

I looked at Potter and he seemed almost out of breath after his rant. Once he had finished, he put out his cigarette and lit another one. Standing, I looked at him and said, "Potter, I had no idea..."

"Ah, forget it," he said, waving me away with his hand. "I shouldn't have said anything. Besides, I'll be moving out at first light in search of Luke. Once I've rescued him, I'll bring him to you in The Hollows and you won't have to see me again."

"What does that mean?" I asked, my heart skipping a beat at the thought of him leaving.

"I don't want to get in the way of you and Luke," he said. "I know how you feel about him."

"Luke's my friend..." I started.

"And Murphy was mine, but you didn't catch us swimming nude together in a lake!" he snapped.

"You know about that?" I gasped.

"Yeah, but don't go getting your posh French knickers in a twist. I wasn't spying on you, I was looking for stuff to make a fire with in the overhang," he said.

"Why didn't you tell me before?" I asked, still reeling from his outburst.

"What, so you would think I was some kind of pervert who went spying on -" he started.

"No, not that!" I cut over him. "Why didn't you say how you felt about me?"

"Did I really need to say anything, Kiera?" he said, taking a puff on his cigarette. "For someone who's meant to see stuff – you *see* diddly-shit. How many times have I saved Isidor's bacon because you asked me to? You know I might like a good scrap but

Kamikaze missions aren't my idea of fun. How many times have I got you out of the shit? Christ, I stood on the bonnet of a speeding car while homicidal vampire-cops sprayed me with their machine guns! How much more have I got to do before you'll *see* how much I love you? I thought getting your car out of the snow back in The Ragged Cove would have done the trick – but you're obviously a hard nut to crack!"

"I'm sorry," I said, going to him. "I never meant to…"

"I don't want your apologies, Kiera," he said, his voice softening.

"What do you want?" I asked him, looking into his eyes.

"I want to know what it is you listen to on that goddamn iPod the whole time," he smirked.

Taking the iPod from my pocket, I handed it to him and said, "Why don't you take a look?"

I watched Potter scroll down the list of songs with his thumb. "I don't suppose you have *'I'm your man'* by Wham, do you?" he smiled.

"No," I smiled back.

"Oh, okay, what about this?" he said, removing the earphones so we could both listen to the song that he had chosen. Placing the iPod on top of the locker, he took me in his arms as *'Just the way you are'* by Bruno Mars started to play.

The music filled the tiny room, and Potter brought his lips close to mine. Slowly, we started to sway against each other as if sharing a dance. Although his lips hovered just above mine, he didn't kiss me. I listened to the words of the song that he had chosen, and closing my eyes, I kissed him. We turned around and around to the music and it felt as if I were at a prom instead of in a hangar.

The song swept me away to another place, and I let Potter take me there as he held me in his arms. Those feelings of nervous excitement and fear washed over me again, like they always did when we were together. My stomach fluttered, and this time it wasn't the cravings making it summersault. My skin prickled and my heart raced. Entwining his strong hands in my hair, he kissed my face and then in my ear he whispered, "What I really want, Kiera, what I've only ever wanted, is you."

Easing me down onto the bed, the song continued to play, and at that moment in time I felt a feeling of such intense happiness, that I didn't want to let him go, because I believed that if I did, that happiness would go with him. Tugging at each other's clothes, I ran my hands over his chest and stomach, up his back, and through his hair. The last time that we made love, we had been manacled in the caves below the mountains. This time was different – I felt free to explore him and for him to explore me. With the gentle voice of Bruno Mars singing in the background, we made love; and unlike in the caves, our love-making wasn't rushed and desperate. This time it was gentle, caring, and seemed to last forever.

We lay facing each other on the narrow bed, and held each other. The music had stopped long ago and all I could hear was the sound of our breathing as it fell in time with each other.

"So, what's your secret?" he asked me, his voice just a whisper in the dark.

"What do you mean?" I asked, although I knew exactly what he meant.

"What was written in that book?" he brushed my hair with his fingertips.

"Have you ever heard of the name Elias Munn?" I asked.

He was silent for a moment as if contemplating his answer. "That story is just a myth," he said. "Is that who Ravenwood believes is behind all of this?"

"Yes," I told him.

"But that's like saying Father Christmas is real," he whispered. "The story of Elias Munn is a fable – a ghost story the Vampyrus tell their kids to spook them – it's nothing more than that."

"Do you know the story about the half-breeds?" I whispered.

"No, I've missed that one," he said.

So, as we lay in the dark next to each other, I told him what was written in the message left by Ravenwood. At the end, Potter lay quietly for several moments, then said, "Kiera, I don't know how much of this is all true, but it just sounds like a fairy tale to me. I've heard loads of different stuff about the humans and the conflicts that they had eons ago, but I've never heard one about a half-breed that has to make a choice between the Vampyrus and the humans. I mean, how does that work, exactly? What if you chose now? What if you just snapped your fingers and said, "I want all Vampyrus to die", is it gonna happen? I don't think so."

"Maybe it's not that easy," I said. "Perhaps there is some kind of test – something I have to do first."

"Like what?" he replied. "Run the hundred meters? Come first in a fancy dress competition? Win the X-Factor? The whole thing sounds ridiculous if you ask me."

"Putting it like that, it does sound a bit odd," I said, running my fingertips across his chest.

"Kiera, Statler and Waldorf were just a couple of crazy old men..."

"Who?" I asked.

"Hunt and Ravenwood – you know Statler and Waldorf?" he said.

"Who are they?"

"The two old men from The Muppet Show," he said, sounding bemused that I had no idea who they were. "They are just like Hunt and Ravenwood – to crazy old men."

"Hunt wasn't crazy," I said.

"No?" Potter whispered. "Then why did he give his son away as a baby? Why did he send his daughter to those schools where she was bullied? Why did he experiment on them, for crying out loud? I'm telling you, Kiera, the guy wasn't too tightly wrapped."

"He was trying to find a cure," I said.

"It sounds to me that his work was more important to him than anything else," Potter said.

"But he helped me escape," I insisted.

"Oh yeah, I was forgetting – a kids book about some toad with cross-dressing tendencies is just the thing you need when trying to escape. I must have missed that episode of Prison Break!"

I rolled on to my back and looked into the darkness. Although I was glad I'd confided in Potter and he had put things into perspective like only he could, I still felt unsure and didn't think that Hunt or Ravenwood would have lied to me. Whatever the truth, once I was in The Hollows, I would seek out this Felix Coanda. After all, the very room I now lay in had a locker with that name on it. Turning my head against the pillow to face Potter, I said, "So, what about you? What's your secret?"

"I'm not sure that I have one," he said.

"Yeah, you do," I said, and pinched his arm.

"You'll find out what it is tomorrow," he said. "I can't tell you what it is now."

"Why not?" I asked him.

"Because you would only try and stop me from doing what it is that I have to do," he said.

"You're scaring me now," I whispered and rested my head against his firm chest.

"There's nothing to be scared of," he hushed, folding his arms around me. "I'm just doing an old friend a favour."

"Has it something to do with Seth and Eloisa?" I whispered. "You said that Seth wouldn't be coming with me into The Hollows and Eloisa wouldn't be coming back with you and Luke from the zoo."

"Wait until tomorrow," he said. "Everything will seem clearer then."

"Have it your way," I said, yawning, now too tired to press him on the point any further. I closed my eyes, and the steady sound of his heartbeat soon had me drifting off to sleep. As I was about to slip into unconsciousness, Potter whispered, "I love you, Kiera – do you love me?"

"I'm not allowed to fall in love," I mumbled. "Ravenwood...

# Chapter Thirty-Six

*...grabbed hold of my right leg and I wailed out in pain. It was dark and I was outside. I could see the facility I had fled from on the other side of the field. I could hear the sound of running and the gnashing of pointed teeth in the undergrowth all around me.*

*The wolves, they're coming after me!*

*I looked down at my leg and could see a long, open wound running the length of my shin. The blood which poured from it glistened black in the dark. There was something silver and metal-looking in the cut.*

*I must have tripped and ripped my leg open on some barbwire fencing and some of it had got entangled in the wound.*

*To look at the gaping hole sent splinters of pain through my body. My stomach began to lurch and the urge to throw-up was almost impossible to resist.*

*The sound of woofing came, and out of the darkness came hundreds of brilliant yellow eyes. I dug my fingers into the long grass and tried to drag myself away from them, but in every direction I turned, a hundred pairs of those evil eyes came out of the darkness at me.*

*My leg continued to burn with pain and my head began to feel woozy. The world began to seesaw around me and my vision began to blur. I looked back at my leg and willed it to stop hurting. In the glare of the moonlight, I could see the metal winking back at me.*

*Then something huge and powerful came striding towards me. It had a large black skull and meaty forearms. It made a series of deep grunting sounds and then appeared to grow in size. I peered at it and realised that whatever it was, wasn't growing in size but standing up on two muscular legs and spreading a pair of giant black wings. It then began to beat its chest with two solid fists and roar into the night.*

*"Get back, you filthy wolves. She's mine!"*

*I could hear the surrounding wolves begin to whine. Some were less brave than others and I heard them scampering away into the grass, but others stayed.*

*"She's ours!" one of the werewolves protested.*

*The beast looming before me swung a huge, powerful arm into the air as a warning and bellowed:*

*"Get away I tell you! She's mine!'*

*The last of the werewolves bounded away, and as they did, the creature roared after them:*

*"Back to the facility and remove any trace of what's gone on there!"*

*My mind swam in and out of consciousness and the pain from my leg devoured me. I then felt myself being roughly picked up and held tightly against a mass of course, wiry hair. Before the blackness finally consumed me I opened my eyes again and found myself peering into the face of a terrifying-looking Vampyrus.*

*I wanted to scream but the sound was drowned out by...*

...the door to the room slowly swung closed. I rolled onto my side expecting to find Potter, but he had crept away while I'd been asleep. I got out of bed and hurriedly put on my clothes and boots. I eased the door open an inch and peered through the gap to see Potter walking away down the corridor. Without making a sound, I slipped out and closed the door behind me.

Potter walked some way ahead and I pressed myself close to the wall where the shadows fell and followed silently behind him. He walked confidently and with purpose as if he knew exactly where he was going and what he was going to do once he got there. Was this the secret that he had spoken about? If so what was it? I intended to find out.

From the shadows, I watched as Potter climbed the stairs down to the wide, open area on the ground floor of the hangar. He stopped before the giant sliding doors as if waiting to meet someone. The doors were still slightly open and outside all I could see was the night sky and a crust of a moon. The snow looked as if it had stopped for the time being.

I tiptoed halfway down the stairs to a small landing, and crouching down, I tried to make myself as small as possible. I waited only a few minutes until a long stretch of a shadow fell across the hangar floor. I knew who that shadow belonged to; I had seen it before when spying on Murphy in that derelict farmhouse.

Seth appeared below me and approached Potter. At first they didn't speak, they just looked at one another. Potter spoke first, but I was too far away to hear what it was that he was saying. I wished that I had Kayla with me, but I sensed that I didn't have time to go searching for her now. Leaning forward, but not too much for fear of them seeing me, I strained to hear what they were saying to one another. Every so often, a snippet of their conversation would float back towards me but it wasn't enough to truly understand what they were talking about. Although they showed no emotion in their voices, I could see that the conversation had grown heated by the way they gestured at one another with their hands.

So, crawling on my hands and knees, I inched myself along the walkway above them, and stopped when I had reached a discreet place but could hear their voices.

"You can't stop me from going to The Hollows,' Seth said. "Eloisa and I are in as much danger as you and your friends."

"Well go and find somewhere else to hide," Potter snapped.

"There is no other place, the town has been sealed off!" Seth barked. "You know we can't escape from here."

"Not my problem," Potter replied. "Murdering scum like you doesn't deserve the protection of The Hollows."

"I didn't kill those women," Seth insisted. "It wasn't me who tortured them."

"You seem to be forgetting that I caught you at the crime scene of the twelfth victim," Potter hissed. "You were leaning over her body with blood all over your muzzle."

"Murphy wasn't convinced," Seth said, and smiled.

From my hiding place, I could see Potter tense as Seth said Murphy's name. Then, stepping closer to Seth, Potter said, "You might have fooled Murphy but you're not fooling me. You took advantage of a grieving man. Murphy had just lost his daughters, he wasn't thinking straight. If he had of been, he would've never come to you for help in the first place."

With that crazy look in his eyes and the sinister grin playing on his lips, Seth looked down at Potter and said, "Murphy believed me. He trusted me."

"Yeah, and look where it got him," Potter growled, going toe to toe with Seth. "You tricked him, led him to Phillips who ripped his heart out! I'm not as trusting as Murphy. Do you really think that I would've let Kiera go with you into The Hollows – a perverted serial killer who gets his kicks out of murdering children and women?"

"You don't have a choice, Potter," Seth sneered. "You can't stop me."

"No, it's you who doesn't have the choice," Potter said, unfastening the front of his shirt. "Leave now voluntarily and go find some other place to hide or you don't leave at all."

"Don't you threaten me…" Seth started, but then, without warning Potter reached out with breath-taking speed and reached for Seth's throat. Seth was just as quick and seized Potter's arm. Both of them stared blackly into each other's eyes.

"Only one of us can go forward," Potter told him.

"Then it shall be me," Seth said.

Realising that Seth wouldn't give in to his demands that easily, Potter broke his arm free and threw his arms out to his side. His back arched as he rolled his head back and his wings unfurled from his back. Seth wasted no time in dragging his claws across his own face as he ripped his flesh away and his wolf's head appeared from underneath. His baseball cap flew away, along with his long, flowing coat and jeans. As if reading each other's mind, both sprang into the air within a fraction of a second. Potter roared and Seth howled as they collided with one another. I flinched backwards as lengths of black wolf hair sprayed into the air as Potter ripped at Seth with his claws. The werewolf released a howl that was so deep, it sounded like thunder. With his lips rolling back, Seth lunged at Potter and buried his teeth into him. Both were equal in strength and speed and each tried to tear the other apart. Potter rolled back one of his muscular arms and drove his claw straight at the werewolf's colossal skull. There was a sickening crack of a sound and Seth shot backwards through the air.

"You cannot go forward from here," Potter warned him, racing through the air in a blur of black shadows.

"Why you and not me?" Seth barked, landing on all fours on the floor of the hangar.

"Because I know you're a killer and you betrayed Murphy," Potter boomed as he raced through the air towards Seth.

"If there is no reasoning with you, Potter, then you must die just like Murphy did,' Seth barked at the top of his voice. He then suddenly shot forward, raking at the air with his giant black paws.

Seth caught Potter, who stumbled backwards momentarily in

mid-air, but that was all the werewolf needed to come racing forward, his jaws open and teeth gnashing. Potter was just as quick, and ducking out of Seth's way, he dropped out of the air, rolled across the shiny surface of the hangar's floor, and sprang to his feet. Seth came at him again and they fought each other. They rolled over and over, a blur of black fur and wings. They struck out at each other with such speed and ferocity that they became a blur like the rotary blades of a helicopter in flight. The sounds of their claws ripping and teeth tearing echoed off the metal walls of the hangar as the two of them leapt, spun, and dived at each other.

Sparks flew up from beneath the werewolf's claws as he skirted across the floor of the hangar. The light from his eyes glittered and he came racing forward again. He thrust Potter backwards again and he flew through the air, smashing into the side wall of the hangar. Potter seemed to hover momentarily in mid-air, then rocketed back towards the ground, leaving the wall battered and bent out of shape.

Seth ducked and skidded around as Potter came screaming forward, lashing out at the wolf with his claws. They crashed into one another and more sparks flew into the air as they skidded down the length of the hangar.

"You can't win!" Seth howled.

"Neither can you!" Potter roared back.

"Then we both die!" Seth barked and pounced at Potter again.

Potter sprang into the air to meet him head on, his wings pointed like arrows behind him. Their arms whisked through the air as they sliced at each other. Blood sprayed from Potter's chest, and I slapped both hands over my mouth to stop myself from screaming. Their arms locked and they clashed heads as they tried to bite lumps from each other's faces. Both pushed fiercely against each other. But they were equally matched – and I feared that perhaps Seth had been right, both of them would die.

From my hiding place, I knelt and watched as Seth suddenly whipped his giant tail from behind him, lashing Potter across his back. There was a crunching sound, then Potter collapsed onto the floor. He reached out with his arms as Seth came forwards, brandishing his razor-like teeth and snarling. I stared at Potter and he looked beat. Slowly, he lowered his arms, his shoulders sloped and he dropped his head. I wanted to scream at him to get up, to fight back, but my throat was locked and I felt as if I was suffocating. Then, to my amazement, he dragged himself into a sitting position and crossed his legs in front of him. He tilted his head back as if exposing his neck for Seth to bite.

Seth seemed to wait several moments before coming forward again, as if he suspected a trap of some kind. Potter remained still, his head back, throat exposed. Seth finally sauntered forward, brandishing his teeth and snarling. Before I'd even had a chance to register what had happened, Potter had snatched hold of the werewolf's giant head and twisted it violently to the right sending Seth spinning through the air. Before Seth had a chance to react to what had happened, Potter launched himself off the ground and had him in a headlock. Seth tried to bark, but all that came out was a series of coughing sounds as Potter tightened his arms around the wolf's throat. Seth kicked out widely with his back legs, his claws making a scraping sound across the floor and his huge, fleshy tongue rolled from the corner of his mouth.

"You helped kill my friend Murphy and if I leave you alive, you'll kill Kiera, too," Potter growled into one of Seth's pointed ears.

Seth began to make a final struggle and he kicked out wildly with his paws, as Potter tightened his grip further.

The wolf made a panting sound, and his eyes started to close, and just when I thought that it was over, something huge and grey came leaping into the hangar through the gap in the open doors. Glancing down, I gasped at the sight of Nik standing over Potter as he gripped Seth on the floor.

"I killed those women," he yelped at Potter. "It was me you and your friends were chasing back then. I was the one who butchered and tortured all of those women, not Jack Seth!"

# Chapter Thirty-Seven

"What are you talking about?" Potter growled, refusing to release his grip on the dying werewolf. "Who in the hell are you?"

"My name's Nik Seth," he barked at Potter, "And it was me who committed those murders, not my father."

"I don't believe you!" Potter growled, as blood ran from the claw marks which now covered his body.

"It's true," Nik howled. "Jack Seth is my father. He discovered it was me who was killing those women. He tried to stop me, but I couldn't be stopped, not back then. He followed me one night as I picked up another woman from a bar and headed back to her apartment. We went to her room, and as she got undressed, I took my skin off and revealed my other self to her. She wanted to scream – God how she wanted to scream – I could see it in her eyes. But she looked into mine and I had her. She was transfixed by my stare and I could do anything I wanted to her, and believe me, I did. But my father knew that you were hunting me down and were close by that night. He reached me first and told me to go so he could be in my place when you, Murphy, and Luke came crashing through the door. My father took the blame for those killings, but I didn't go unpunished. He cursed me, leaving me captured in the wolf's form until I redeemed myself. He never wanted me to entice a woman away again, place her in a trance and then kill her. He knew, looking like a wolf, I'd never be able to trick another woman to go with me again."

"How do I know you're not lying?" Potter said, as Seth stopped twitching in his arms and fell still. "Any son of Jack Seth's has got to be lying scum."

"It's true," a voice said, and I looked down to see Eloisa walk across the hangar floor towards Potter. Her long, blond hair bounced beautifully about her shoulders and her eyes glimmered like crystals. "Jack took the blame for his son; he took his place in the cells down in The Hollows."

"So you're this wolf's mother?" Potter said.

"I'm not his mother," Eloisa smiled with her perfectly formed lips. "Nik's mother died when he was just a baby. I am Jack's lover, that is all."

Potter stared into her eyes, then slowly released his grip on Jack. He stood, then looking down at the wolf, he rolled the giant beast away with his foot.

"Father," Nik howled, then licked Jack's face with his giant tongue. "Wake up, father. I've done good this time."

Seth made a gurgling sound in the back of his throat and lifted his head an inch off the floor. Nik licked his father's face again. "Father, wake up, please," he said. "I want you to see that I've done good for you."

Seth's mighty flanks began to heave up and down as he started to draw air through his snout. Potter stood and looked down at the wolf, then at Eloisa. Then, Seth was getting up, staggering onto all fours. He sniffed the air and looked at his son.

"What are you doing here, boy?" Seth woofed.

"I came to save you," Nik barked softly.

"I told you I never wanted to lay eyes on you again," Seth said. Now get out of my sight." Then looking at Potter with his yellow eyes, he added, "It looks like your friend, Murphy, was right about me all along."

Without saying a word, Potter walked directly towards Eloisa. She smiled at him and her eyes twinkled. Potter's face looked grim and his eyes a dull black. Then, so quick if I'd blinked I would have missed it, Potter shot his arm out and thrust his claw into Eloisa's chest. It all happened so fast that Eloisa still had that smile on her face as Potter ripped out her heart. She looked at him as if to say something, but all that came out of her mouth was a thick jet of black blood. Eloisa fell forward, crashing face first onto the floor of the hangar.

With her heart still beating in his fist, Potter walked back to Seth. Holding the heart out in front of Seth's huge face, he said to the wolf, "You might not have murdered those women, but you helped take the heart of somebody I loved." Then, dropping Eloisa's heart on the floor in front of Seth's giant paws, Potter looked into the wolf's eyes and said, "I guess that makes us just about even."

I couldn't believe what I had just seen and those words from Ravenwood's message swam sickeningly in the front of my mind. *"... Elias Munn plunged his fist into her chest and tore her heart out..."*

185

"No!" I screamed over the edge of the walkway. "Potter, what have you just done?"

No sooner had those words left my mouth, Isidor and Kayla came running down the stairs above me. "What's happening?" Kayla called out.

Potter glanced over his shoulder and saw me standing on the walkway above him. Within an instant, he had flown up to join me.

"What did you just do?" I gasped.

He looked into my eyes and said, "You asked me last night if I had feelings. Murphy was my friend – like a father to me – and I loved him. Do you really think that I'd let his death go unpunished?"

"But you just ripped her heart out," I said still in shook at what I'd just witnessed.

"And they took Murphy's," he said flatly.

I looked into his eyes and they looked dead and heartless. "You're scaring me," I told him, blinking away the tears that were standing in my eyes.

Coming closer, Potter said, "Now go straight to The Hollows and wait for me. I'll come back with Luke, I promise." Then leaning in, he kissed me on the cheek and at the same time, he whispered in my ear, "It's not me you have to be scared of, sweet-cheeks."

He turned away, leapt over the edge of the stairs and landed on the ground in front of Seth. Leaning forward, he said something to the werewolf, then strode purposefully between the gap in the hangar doors and out into the dawn.

I looked over my shoulder at Kayla and said, "Did you hear what he said to Jack Seth?"

Kayla looked at me and nodded.

"What did he say?" I snapped at her.

"If Seth harmed as much as one single hair on your head while he was gone in search of Luke, he would rip his heart out with his teeth and…" Kayla stopped.

"And what?" I demanded.

"Potter said that he would eat Jack Seth's heart," Kayla shuddered.

# Chapter Thirty-Eight

With my head spinning, I made my way down the stairs to the ground floor, Kayla and Isidor close behind me. Eloisa's body lay to one side, and a thick pool of blood trailed from beneath her. I looked away. Seth was twisting and contorting from a werewolf back into human form. His limbs almost seemed to stretch as if made from putty and his head looked as if it was being sucked in on itself. When he had completed his metamorphosis, he looked down at his son.

"You're not welcome here," he hissed.

"But I saved your life," Nik yelped like a lost puppy.

"And took countless others," Seth said.

"So have you," Nik suddenly snarled. "You have murdered hundreds."

"Not for many years," Seth shouted back. "I've been trying to redeem myself – to lift the Lycanthrope curse."

"You seem to have a funny way of showing it," Isidor suddenly cut in.

"And what's that supposed to mean, boy?" Seth turned on him.

"Betraying Murphy like you did beneath the mountains," Isidor said standing firm against the serial killer. "He was our friend and he trusted you."

Glancing over at Eloisa spread face down on the floor, Seth said, "And it looks like I've paid for that too."

Nik came forward, his giant tail swishing behind him. "But I have changed, father," he said. "It's not only your life that I've saved. I helped Kiera escape from her cage and her friends, too."

"It's true," I said to Seth. "Your son helped me – I think we helped each other in some strange way. We were both fighting our cravings for human flesh together. Nik could have killed me at any time, believe me, he had plenty of opportunities. But he didn't. Instead of killing me, he helped me and my friends. And even when I'd escaped, he kept watch over me and guarded me. I think it's time you lifted the curse."

"Don't tell me what I should and shouldn't do with my son!" Seth roared and spittle flew from his lips. He then came towards me, his eyes spinning in his sunken eye sockets like two burning planets.

Before he could reach me, Kayla had stepped into his path. "I so wouldn't do that if I were you," she hissed. "I heard what Potter said to you before he left. So *back-off*, wolf man!"

"Potter doesn't scare me," Seth smiled grimly.

"Oh, no?" Isidor said, coming to stand next to his sister. "It certainly smelt like Potter scared you. You don't just talk shit – you smell of it!"

Seth looked at Isidor, and for the briefest of moments I thought that his eyes were going to pop from those sunken sockets. Without giving him the chance to reply, Kayla quickly added, "So as far as I can see, Jack Seth, you have two choices. You can either crawl back under whichever rock you came out from, or you can keep your freaking face shut, get in line, and follow Kiera into The Hollows." Then, in a spray of shadows, she was hovering in the air just inches from his emaciated face. "Because I promise you, one more threat – just one more – and you won't have to wait for Potter to come back and eat your heart out, I'll hit you so freaking hard that it will explode out of your arse!"

Without saying anything, Seth smiled and turned to walk away. I couldn't believe the change in Kayla and Isidor. Maybe Potter had been right after all; perhaps what they needed was to toughen up. However harsh he had been to them, it had changed them. For the better? I didn't know. But they both seemed ready to confront whatever lay ahead for us.

Nik bounded after his father, and almost seeming to yap at his heels, he said, "Please, father, lift the curse."

"No! Not ever!" Seth roared at him. "I took the blame for you – I've done what any father would do for their son, but now you are on your own."

"But it isn't just your life that I've saved," Nik barked. "I've come with some news – news that could end all of this today."

Hearing this, I went to Nik, and said, "What news? What are you talking about?"

"The invisible man," he started, "the one who's behind all of this has made a mistake. He's visiting a site not too far away from here. He wants to oversee the site the Vampyrus are building to stage their attack against the humans."

Isidor and Kayla came rushing over, and Seth stopped dead in his tracks and looked back at his son.

"How do you know this?" I asked him.

Looking at his father than back at me, he said, "I tortured two of the Vampyrus that had come to prepare the way for him. I'm sorry father, but it was the only way. I had to kill them."

Seth grunted and looked at his son. "Go on, what else do you know?"

"Not much," Nik said. "Only that he is coming above ground. I know where he is going to be, so this is our chance to take him and end this today."

"Where is this site?" I asked him.

"About two miles from here," Nik said. "It's set between two mountains."

"We should wait for Potter to return," I said.

"It will be too late by then," Nik said, looking at me. "We only have one shot at this."

"I don't know…" I started.

"If no one is going to rip my throat out for speaking," Seth said and glanced at Kayla, "I think Nik is right. We should go now and end this. Look on the bright side, once this is all over, you'll never have to see me or my kind again."

"I hate to agree with him," Isidor said, "But I think he's right. We should go – it might be the only chance we ever have of defeating this invisible man."

"Elias Munn," I said.

"Who?" Kayla asked.

"That's his real name," I said looking at them. "That's what this invisible man is really called. Whether he still goes by that name now, I don't know – but his true name is Elias Munn."

"How do you know that?" Kayla asked me.

"Ravenwood wrote it in that message he left for me," I explained.

"What else did he say?" Isidor said.

"I'll tell you another time," I said. Changing the subject, I looked at Nik, "How long will it take to get to this place between the mountains? Remember, there's a storm blowing out there and we're vulnerable in the open from Vampyrus attacks during daylight."

"We don't have to travel above ground," Nik woofed.

"How come?" Kayla asked him.

"There's a tunnel that leads right from this facility to the site," he barked. Then turning to Seth, he added, "See, father, I haven't let you down this time."

"We'll see," Seth almost seem to sneer.

On hearing Nik mention the tunnel, I remembered the diagrams I'd seen on the computer disc. There had been a tunnel leading away from the facility but it didn't show where it ended. Looking back at the opening, I hoped that perhaps I might see Potter heading out across the fields, but all I could see was snow. Potter told me to go straight to The Hollows, but he hadn't known about Elias Munn making a visit to a site that was only two miles from here. If Potter were here, he wouldn't have wasted the opportunity to attack Munn while he was vulnerable.

Looking at the others, I said, "Okay, what are we waiting for? Let's get moving."

# Chapter Thirty-Nine

The entrance to the tunnel lay hidden under a mountain of rubble in the basement beneath the hangar. There was a ladder that led down into utter darkness, which didn't pose a problem to me, but the others wouldn't have been able to see their own hand in front of their faces. Isidor found some torches in a workshop at the rear of the hangar and shared them out.

Holding onto the ladder, I climbed down into the hole. At the bottom, just like Nik had said, was a tunnel. It was high enough for us to stand up in, although Seth had to walk stooped forward so as not to strike his head against the roof.

Torchlight splashed across the walls of the tunnel as we followed it. The sound of water dripping could be heard all around us, as well as the noise of rats scurrying around at our feet. We hadn't gone far when Nik snatched one of the rats between his jaws and swallowed it. My skin crawled at the sound of the rat's bones crunching and snapping between Nik's mighty jaws.

After some time, I could just make out a pinprick of white in the distance. Speeding up, we rushed on, knowing that the end of the tunnel was now in sight. We found another set of ladders, and switching off our torches, we started to climb. We found ourselves at the edge of a tree line. Hiding amongst the trees, I could see a large, open area spread between the feet of two mountains. The area was uncovered and searchlights flooded the ground beneath the darkening sky. Snow fell all about us.

Kayla yanked my arm and we squatted by the base of a large tree. "What now?" she asked.

Peering into the distance, I could see some rocks jutting from the uneven ground. "Let's make our way over to those rocks. It will give us cover while we take a closer look."

The snow was falling so heavily, I hoped it would offer us some camouflage as we made our way across the open ground to the rocks.

"Are you ready?" I asked the others as I looked back at them. Even though we were sheltered by trees, flurries of snow had still managed to cover them, and they sat looking at me, shivering. Seth had his baseball cap pulled low over his eyes, and its beak was covered white. Nik's fur was silver-white and it was hard to distinguish what was his coat and what was snow.

Facing front again, I said, "C'mon, let's go."

With the wind screaming all around us and our clothes pulled tight, we hunkered down and made our way across the bleak, open area towards the rocks. It seemed to take forever, and by the time we had reached our new hiding place, my hands were numb and almost purple in colour. I couldn't remember ever feeling so cold and I couldn't stop my teeth from chattering. The clouds above us were black and they lumbered across the sky shedding their snow and turning the day into night.

We peeked over the lip of the rock and stared in disbelief at what lay in the valley set between the mountains. There were hundreds of vampires shuffling back and forth. Not only could we see vampires, but to our shock, we could also see row upon row of humans and a handful of Vampyrus keeping watch over them. From our hiding place, we could see a gigantic crater in the ground at the centre of the valley. All around this huge hole were trucks, which trundled back and forth full of stone, rock, and earth. I could see humans – some as young as about ten – were manacled at the feet and joined together in a huge chain-gang. They looked pale, undernourished, and exhausted. I wondered how long it had been since they had last eaten or rested.

For as far as I could see, there were rows of people tied together with heavy chains, digging mindlessly at the rock that surrounded the crater. I watched as some of the people collapsed to the ground, too weary to stand up again. Seeing this, a Vampyrus would step from the side, yank the human from the ground, and toss it to the vampires to feed on.

"Looks like they've got somebody else to do the dirty work," Isidor said bitterly.

Kayla made a move away from our hiding place, and I yanked at her arm.

"Don't, Kayla, you'll be seen!" I whispered.

"I just want to get a better look, that's all," She complained. There was a line of military-type trucks parked nearby. "Okay, we'll move closer, but be careful," I warned.

We headed towards the trucks. We virtually crawled along on our bellies, and, on reaching one of the trucks, we rolled underneath it. From here, we were so close now, that I could see the feet of the vampires passing us by.

With my heart racing in my chest like a trip hammer, I peeked from beneath the truck. There were chains hanging from some sort of pulley, which was fixed high above the centre of the crater. Attached to these chains were large metal bathtubs. One end of these chains disappeared down into the hole and the others were fed via the pulley to a large metal wheel that was being turned slowly by a group of mindless-looking humans. I could see the wheel they were forcing around was very heavy. Even though ten of them had been employed to turn it, their eyes were nearly bursting from their skulls under the strain of pushing it.

As they turned the wheel, more of the metal bathtubs were fed down into the hole while others rose from it. These were full of more rocks and earth. When they reached the surface they tilted upwards, emptied and went back around again. The pile of rocks were then shovelled up by the humans and loaded into the back of the trucks. The vehicles then made their way to the rear of the crater, where they disappeared into the night and the falling snow.

"See, I was right," Nik whispered, as he lay squashed under the truck, his snout resting on his paws. "They're digging a hole in the earth so deep and wide that the Vampyrus can flood the country in minutes."

"I don't believe it!" Isidor said.

"Your eyes aren't deceiving you, boy," Seth breathed. "Although, even I didn't believe that they would go this far."

Then before I knew what was happening, Kayla was squirming out from beneath the truck.

"Kayla! Where are you going?" I hissed as quietly as I could.

"To rescue these people!"

"But that's not why we came..." But she was gone. "Why me?" I asked myself with a sense of despair. Potter had had a bigger influence on her than I'd first thought. But he wasn't here now to pick up the pieces. I lay there for a moment more, contemplating what I should do next. I couldn't let Kayla go on her own. So, I rolled out from beneath the truck and went after her. I crept around one of the army vehicles to find Kayla peeking over the top of the bonnet. I sneaked up behind her and looked over her shoulder. She immediately turned and shoved me in the chest.

"There's a vampire coming! Get down!" she breathed.

We crouched beside one of the vehicle's colossal wheels and I prayed the vampire would walk by without discovering us. I closed my eyes and waited for a cold, bony hand to fall on my shoulder. But it never came. As soon as the vampire had passed by, Kayla was back on her feet again. She weaved her way through the vehicles and piles of rocks until we were only a few feet away from the massive wheel, which was being continuously turned by those people. We came to rest against a large rock, which protruded from the ground like a gigantic tooth.

"Kayla, I know you want to help these people, but this is crazy," I whispered.

"I'll think of something," she said, looking over the rock at the people. I looked back and could see that the others were still hiding beneath the truck.

"Kayla, we don't even know how *we're* gonna get outta here, let alone rescue a load of half-starved people!"

But Kayla made no reply. She was on her feet again and scurrying over the rocks. I crouched down, and moving like a crab, I scuttled over to the wheel. Kayla reached one of the people, an emaciated looking boy of about thirteen and gently took hold of his arm.

"Hey," she whispered at the boy.

He didn't respond. He kept his head down and continued to mindlessly push the wheel round and round.

"You want to get out of here, don't you?" Kayla almost seemed to plead with him.

I found it upsetting to watch Kayla desperately try and get a response from this boy. Kayla shook the boy again and said, "Please! My friends and I could rescue you!"

Moving closer to Kayla, I placed my hand gently on her shoulder, and said, "Kayla, he can't hear you. Look at him, whatever they've done to him, he's not like a normal person anymore…he's a shell."

Kayla pushed my hand away and said, "I want to help these people."

"But Kayla…" Before I could finish, the boy spoke, ever so faintly, but he had said something.

"What did you say?" Kayla asked.

"Help me," he said.

Hearing his cry for help, Kayla bent down and picked up a rock, which filled her whole fist. She brought it up above her head and I could see she intended to try and break the chains which held the boy prisoner. Kayla swung her arm down and I thrust my arm out, grabbing hold of her wrist before the stone crashed into the metal chain. Kayla looked at me and tried to break her arm free.

"No Kayla!" I warned her.

"Get off me!" She hissed, her eyes fixed on mine. "I'm setting this boy free."

"Now's not the right time…"

"Let go!" and again she tried to wrestle her arm free from my grip.

"Kayla, if you try and rescue the boy now, you will alert the Vampyrus, and none of us will ever get out of here. Let's just do what we came for, find this Elias Munn and then come back and rescue him…we can come back and rescue them all!" I pleaded with her.

Before Kayla could respond, my arm was gripped from behind. I wheeled round to see a Vampyrus, just inches from me.

"Who said you could stop working?" it screeched. Looking down at our legs and seeing they weren't manacled, he screamed at the top of his voice, "Intruders! Intruders!"

I looked quickly about and could see that the other Vampyrus, who were standing within earshot, had stopped what they were doing and were looking at us. Kayla brought the rock she was holding down onto the top of the Vampyrus' head. I heard a sickening thud as it collapsed onto the ground, where it lay twitching.

"I'll come back for you, I promise!" Kayla told the boy. Then Kayla turned to me and said, "Here we go again!" and a part of me wondered if she was looking forward to slaying some vampires and Vampyrus.

Kayla darted away from the wheel and ran alongside the empty tubs, which were beginning their ascent back to the top of the pulley. As she drew level to one of them, she jumped in. Kayla looked back at me and shouted, "I thought you wanted to get out of here!"

Glancing over my shoulder, I saw a group of vampires running towards me, their eyes burning red and their fangs drooling. Not needing any encouragement, I turned and ran as fast as I could towards the tub that Kayla had jumped in. But it had started to rise and move away from the ledge of the crater.

Kayla lent out of the tub and shouted, "C'mon Kiera, run!" I drew level with it and took hold of Kayla's hand, which she dangled over the edge. She wrapped her fingers tightly around my wrist and yanked me up into the tub. Looking over the rim as we began to rise, I could see the vampires jumping into the tubs that were close behind us, desperate to sink their teeth into us. I pointed down at them and shouted, "They're coming!"

In the distance I heard sirens begin to wail, and I suspected the Vampyrus were alerting Elias Munn to the mayhem, which was now unfolding around the crater. The tub behind us was about six feet away and although it couldn't get any closer, the four vampires that had managed to clamber into it were now desperately trying to reach for us. They waved their arms about frantically and snatched at the side of the tub that Kayla and I were in.

"Hungry!" they moaned.

One of the vampires managed to take hold and put all of his weight on that end. The tub began to tilt down, forcing us to slide towards the awaiting arms of the vampire. It clawed at my legs and managed to take hold of my feet. The vampire tugged fiercely at me and I began to slide from the tub. I looked back at Kayla and she'd managed to take hold of the other end, stopping herself from falling towards the vampires like I had done.

"Get the fuck off me!" I shouted as the vampire continued to pull at me and I slipped further towards it. I looked down through the gap between the two tubs and screamed. Although we were only about twenty feet from the rocky ground around the crater, I was now suspended above it, and it spiralled away below me. It looked so deep and black, that it could have almost reached the Earth's core. I couldn't even see the bottom, only darkness. All around the walls of the abyss there was scaffolding, which housed even more humans, digging and chipping away at the walls. Realising that if I should fall I would certainly die, I began to frantically kick out at the vampire, who was pulling me from the tub. I then felt Kayla take hold of my arms and begin to yank me back towards her. It was like a bizarre game of 'tug of war' that they were playing, and I was the rope.

"Kayla, pull!" I screamed.

"I am!" she shouted back over the wail of the sirens and the shrieks from the vampires.

I lashed out again with my feet and struck the vampire straight in the face. Its head rolled back, and then snapped forward again. It was grotesque-looking, and had a badly stitched scar running from the bridge of its nose and right over the crown of its head. It looked as if someone had tried to stitch the vampire's head back together. Kicking widely, I managed to break myself free. Kayla hoisted me back into the metal tub and I collapsed onto the floor of it.

"Get up, Kiera, there's no time for rest," she shouted.

I looked up and she was pointing at another vampire that was now making its way across the chain that linked the tubs together.

*Don't they ever give up?* I asked myself.

The vampire managed to take hold of our tub and it began to climb aboard.

It screamed at us, spit and drool splashing our faces. I pushed it backwards, but the vampire managed to take a hold of the edge of the tub and pull itself in. It loomed up and came towards us. As it did, the tub began to roll dangerously from side to side, like a small boat on a rough sea. Then an idea came to me.

"Kayla, hold on!" I yelled, as I took hold of the side of the tub and began to rock it from side to side.

The vampire began to wobble and I rocked the tub even harder and faster. I looked over my shoulder and saw Kayla gripping the side of the tub, her knuckles glowing white through her skin. Seeing that Kayla was safe, I rocked the tub back and forth as hard as I could. The vampire began to lurch from side to side, as it fought desperately to maintain its balance. I pushed the side of the tub again and again, and even though the night was bitterly cold and snow swirled all around us, sweat ran from my brow and into my eyes.

I watched the vampire stagger violently to the left, so I kicked out at it with my feet, almost spilling it over. The vampire flapped its arms wildly, then disappeared over the edge of the tub. I watched it spin and turn through the air as it fell into the crater. Over and over it spun. The vampire seemed to fall forever, the crater was so deep. Before it had even smashed into the bottom, it had disappeared from my view and into the darkness. Then, I heard the sound of screaming. Looking back, I could see that two of the Vampyrus had swooped through the air and were now trying to yank Kayla from the tub. Scrambling forward, I tried to reach for her. With a *booming* sound, the night felt like it was being torn apart as Isidor raced through the sky towards his sister. With his crossbow drawn, Isidor fired off a flurry of bolts, harpooning the Vampyrus through the head. Within seconds, they were spinning lifelessly away down into the abyss. Isidor winked at his sister and was gone again, chasing down more Vampyrus that had sprang into the air.

We had reached the highest point of the pulley and were now making our descent. The remaining vampires in the tub behind lent out and tore at the air hysterically. One of them stood up, as if getting ready to jump the six foot gap that separated us.

I looked down and could see we were now about ten feet away from the ground. Throwing a quick look over my shoulder, I could see the vampire was just about to leap at us. I turned to look at Kayla, who was now standing in the tub, with her wings out. Wrapping her arms around my waist, she shouted, "Jump!"

Together we leapt from the tub and soared through the air. We hit the ground softly.

"Why didn't you do that before?" I asked her.

"Kicking vampire butt was way more fun," she grinned at me.

Potter had a lot to answer for.

Within an instant, Kayla was heading back towards the trucks, which we had earlier used as cover. I sped after her. Sticking her head beneath the truck, she said to Seth and Nik, "I wouldn't lie under there if I were you!"

"Why not?" Seth snapped.

"Because, I'm going to be moving it!" Kayla said as she climbed up the side of the truck, yanked open the door to the drivers cab and climbed in behind the wheel.

"What's with the sirens?" Nik howled, and covered his ears with his paws.

"I think Kayla blew our cover," I said, as the truck's engine rumbled into life. Snatching a spade and pickaxe from two of the mindless humans who were digging away at the rocks, I looked at Isidor as he landed beside me and said, "Get in the truck!"

Nik shot out from his hiding place and Seth followed. Over his shoulder I could see a crowd of vampires racing towards us at an incredible speed.

"Look behind you!" I shouted.

Nik spun around, his giant tail almost whipping me across the face. Seth looked back, and seeing the approaching vampires, he tore the flesh from his body in a series of quick movements. Within moments, he was no longer the emaciated figure that towered over me, but a giant wolf that bounded into the air and sunk his colossal jaws into the nearest vampire he could find. Turning back to the truck, I stopped and my heart leapt into my throat. On the other side of the crater, I could see another truck. Climbing into the back of it was my mother, Phillips, and Sparky. But there was another. This person's head was covered with a long, flowing hood which hid their face.

"Elias Munn!" I breathed. Throwing the pickaxe and spade into the drivers cab, I climbed in.

"Do you know how to drive one of these things?'" I asked Kayla, as she sat behind the steering wheel.

"No! Why, do you?" she asked.

"Why did you climb in here if you don't know how to drive?" Isidor yelled at her.

"How hard can it be?" Kayla asked, as she yanked at the gear stick and stamped on the pedals with her feet.

The truck lurched forward and I slammed into the windscreen, smashing my head against the glass.

"You're gonna kills us!" I roared.

"Hang on!" Kayla shouted, as she pressed her foot hard against the accelerator and we sped forward.

"Kayla, when Potter told you to toughen up a bit, I don't think he meant to get yourself killed!" I yelled at her over the roar of the truck's engine.

"Where are we going?" Isidor shouted.

"After that truck!" I hollered, pointing through the windscreen at the vehicle I'd seen Elias Munn climb into.
Kayla swung the truck violently around and started to race towards a large gate that had been erected on this side of the crater. She pulled and twisted the gear stick and the truck shook and shuddered as it made agonising grinding noises.

On seeing us approach, the two Vampyrus guarding the exit began to slide the gate closed, shutting off our escape. Kayla pushed down harder on the accelerator and we sped towards the diminishing gap.

As we drew closer, the two Vampyrus let the truck with Elias Munn inside slip through, then raced to shut the gate. The gap now seemed too narrow for the truck to squeeze through.

"Kayla, we're not gonna make it!" Isidor shouted.

But on we sped.

"Kayla, stop the truck!" I yelled.

Faster and faster we went towards the closing gap.

"Kayla....!" Isidor roared and threw his hands over his eyes.

With an ear-piercing sound of scraping metal and a flurry of sparks, we tore through the opening and out into the night. I looked over at Kayla in disbelief, only to find her chuckling to herself.

"You're insane!" Isidor shouted and we began to laugh along with her.

# Chapter Forty

We raced through the night, the windscreen wipers squeaking as they swept away the snow. The back end of the truck swung out as we skidded on the frozen road beneath us. The taillights of the truck in front of us glowed like two hot coals. The searchlights were sweeping frantically backwards and forwards. The siren was screaming and I couldn't ever recall feeling so alive. Then I heard the sound of thumping coming from the rear of the truck. There was a hatch in the cab that slid open so you could see into the cargo hold. I snapped it open, and a corpse-white hand shot from the back of the truck and clawed at my face.

"We've got vampires!" I shouted at Kayla, who seemed oblivious to the hand that was waving wildly about at us through the open hatch. Isidor ducked out of its way and screamed. Kayla glanced at it quickly, taking her eyes off the road and the truck lurched sideways, then righted itself.

I rammed the hatch closed against the vampire's wrist. An agonising scream followed, then the hand withdrew back into the darkness. With the hatch closed and fastened, I turned in my seat and as I did, something reflected back at me from the wing mirror. Staring into it, I could see a vampire hanging from the side of the truck. It was inching its way towards the cab.

"Kayla, there's a vampire hanging onto the side of the truck – and it's coming towards us!" I yelled over the roar of the engine and the wailing of the sirens.

"Hang on!" Kayla shouted, yanking the steering wheel from left to right, sending the vehicle swerving violently across the road.

I turned to look in the wing mirror, praying that Kayla's erratic driving had thrown the vampire free. But to my horror, it was already at the passenger window and reaching in at me.

It screamed, only inches away from my face. I could see its waxy lips rolled back, revealing a set of yellow-brown fangs which protruded from its crimson gums.

Reaching down between my legs, I snatched up the spade I'd grabbed during my escape. Holding it firmly with both hands, I began to repeatedly hit the vampire with it.

It screamed over and over again as I bashed it over the head.

The truck continued to lurch from side to side, as Kayla wrestled with its steering. We continued to speed along the road. I hit the vampire again and again until it lost its footing. It swung like a kite from the side of the truck as it desperately held on. Then, from over my shoulder appeared the tip of Isidor's crossbow. The vampire's head snapped backwards as a stake slammed into the fleshy skin between its eyes.

It screeched one last time and disappeared from beside me and under the wheels of the truck. The vehicle shook as its wheels rolled over it.

I sat back in my seat and then all three of us screamed at the top of our voices. From out of nowhere, a vampire swung down from the roof of the cab and spread itself across the windscreen. Like the others, its face was hideous, a patchwork of purple and blue veins. The vampire looked at the three of us with its burning eyes and grinned. Its tongue then slithered from between its lips as the vampire licked the windscreen in one long, drawn-out movement.

"That's so gross," Kayla shouted and slammed on the breaks.

The truck lurched forward, catapulting the vampire from the front of the vehicle and into the night. Kayla then threw the vehicle forward again as she hammered on the accelerator with her foot. The truck zoomed forward across the rough, uneven ground as we chased down the truck with Elias Munn inside. I knew that my mother was in there too, and the thought of seeing her again scared me. But I had to tell myself that she wasn't my mother anymore. Just like those half-breeds in the facility, she was just a rough sculpture of the woman she used to be. Then ahead, I saw two giant granite rocks sticking out of the ground. I doubted that Kayla had seen them. The truck ahead swerved around them, almost tipping up on two wheels to do so.

Kayla raced towards them, refusing to slow down.

"Kayla we won't make it! Kayla, stop the truck!" Isidor roared.

Kayla sat rigidly behind the steering wheel, her eyes fixed on the rocks ahead and her foot pressed firmly on the accelerator.

"Kayla, stop!" I hollered. The rocks loomed up before us and got closer and closer with every passing second.

Just as I thought we were going to smash straight into them,

Isidor leaned over and yanked on the steering wheel, causing the rear of the truck to spin out. Then everything was upside down and I was being crushed against the roof of the cab as the truck flipped over and rolled across the ground.

Everything seemed to swim hazily past my eyes, as I shook my throbbing head. I looked up and could see the passenger door of the cab above me. Then there was the sound of moaning. At first, I couldn't place where it was coming from. Gradually, I realised it was Isidor who was groaning, he was crushed beneath me.

I hoisted myself up, using the back of the seat and the dashboard for leverage. Leaning down, I took hold of Isidor's arm and pulled at him.

"Isidor, we've got to get moving!" I shouted, my voice full of urgency. I looked up through the windscreen that was now facing me vertically and I could see a line of vampires running towards the truck. Glancing around the cab, I searched for Kayla but couldn't see her anywhere. I pulled at Isidor again. "Get up!" I roared.

Isidor groaned and opened his eyes. I grabbed hold of the spade and pickaxe, and pushed my feet against the dashboard. Manoeuvring myself out of the passenger door window, I leapt off the side of the truck and rolled into the snow. It was then a strong smell of petrol forced its way into my nostrils. Realising that it must be leaking from the vehicle, I turned to look for Isidor. He poked his head from the side window.

"Hurry!" I screamed at him, fearing that the truck was going to explode at any moment.

Isidor tried to force his way through the window. "I'm stuck, Kiera!"

From above me, something swooped out of the sky so fast that it was just a blur. Then Isidor was being lifted out of the truck, as Kayla soared up into the sky with him in her arms. I watched as Kayla released Isidor, and then spreading his own wings, they both swooped back towards the ground.

"Is it me, or can you smell petrol?" I asked, as they landed beside me.

"Yeah, I can smell it too!" Isidor said pointing his nose into the air.

"Then run!" I shouted, sprinting away through the snow.

I ran as hard and as fast as I could, the searchlights now tracking my every step in their white glare. Suddenly, I heard a tremendous cracking noise, as if the sky were being torn apart. I was lifted off my feet and thrown forward in a blast of seething heat, as the truck erupted into a ball of orange and red flames behind me.

I hit the ground hard and landed on my back. Kayla and Isidor swooped above the flames that licked from the truck, which was now a raging pile of burning, twisted metal. I put my arm up to shield my eyes from the bright glow of the flames and blistering heat radiating from them. Several of the vampires that been running towards us were now charging up and down hysterically, flames licking their clothes, consuming them. But there were more of them, and they were racing straight towards us.

Getting to my feet, I could see that I had nowhere to run. The vampires were nearly upon me and I could see the taillights of the other truck disappearing into the distance. Bracing myself for their onslaught, I thrust my hand into my coat pocket and let the tips of my fingers caress Murphy's crucifix.

*Good old Jim Murphy*, I smiled to myself and pulled out the crucifix. I held it out before me, and the approaching vampires appeared to falter. It wasn't much, but it was something and it gave me some extra time. Then the vampires were flying through the air. The night became filled with the sound of howling as Jack Seth and Nik bounded through them. With their gigantic paws, they knocked the vampires aside like scarecrows in a gale. They snarled and bit at anything that came too close to them, ripping limbs from the vampires as they went.

I didn't think I'd ever feel so grateful to see Jack Seth. More vampires appeared from behind me, and I spun round, brandishing the crucifix before me. The vampires seemed to cower, throwing their hands across their faces as the Lycanthrope took their chance. They raced forward, jaws open wide, tongues lolling out. Bounding through the air, they sliced through the vampires with their claws. From above, Isidor and Kayla swept through the sky and I could see that both of them had writhing vampires in their claws. With a quick flick of their wrists, they had torn the vampires in half, chucking their remains into the night. Then they were off again, searching out more vampires. Walking backwards, keeping the vampires in view, I tried to edge my way nearer to Seth and Nik who were busily devouring their latest victims. Blood covered their snouts and ropey bits of flesh hung from their whiskers. Then, as if from nowhere, a vampire sprang through the air and landed on Nik's back. He howled in pain as the vampire sunk its teeth into his throat. Blood jetted from Nik's neck and his yellow eyes rolled in their sockets. But however hard Nik tried to shake the vampire free, it held fast with its fangs. With the crucifix clenched in my fist, I raced forward, and just like at the police station, I had travelled several hundred yards in the blink of an eye.

Leaping through the air, I pressed the crucifix into the vampire's forehead and at once it released its jaws from around Nik's throat. The vampire screeched and held its face in its hands as it began to crumble away between its fingers. Turning, I could see Nik, lying in the snow which was now red from the blood that pumped from his neck.

"Nik!" I screamed, racing towards him.

Dropping to my knees, I pressed my hand to Nik's throat, but his blood just pumped over my fingers. I knew that he was bleeding to death. His tongue jutted from between his jaws and he made a panting sound. Rolling his eyes so as to look at me, Nik said, "I tried to make amends, Kiera. I really tried…"

"Shhh," I told him, and stroked the fur along his flank.

"Tell my father that I'm sorry…" he started but stopped as something strange began to happen. As Nik lay dying in the snow, his body began to change shape, and the thick silver hair that covered his body began to fall away. I watched his head twist as his long snout disappeared, leaving behind the face of a young boy. Just like he had described himself to me in the zoo, his hair was blonde and he had the face of a cherub. I stroked the bare skin that now covered his back, and like his father, he was long and incredibly thin. His ribcage and spine could be clearly seen through his skin. With the tips of my fingers, I brushed his fair hair from his brow.

Looking at me, he forced a smile and said, "At last Kiera, I'm free." Then he closed his eyes and fell still.

From behind me, I heard a deafening roar. I looked back to see Jack Seth rising up on his hind legs. He howled into the night as if

in agonising pain. "What have they done to my son!" he howled.
Then dropping once more onto all fours he bounded over to Nik's
lifeless body. He licked his son's face and yelped. "My son," he
howled again. "My precious son – look what they've done to you!
Oh my God, Nikolaou, they've killed you."

I watched this unexpected display of grief from Seth as once again,
he licked his son's human face with his long, pink tongue. "I'm so
sorry, son," he seemed to whimper like a dog that had been beaten
too many times. "I would have lifted the curse. I was proud of
what you did to save me, but my heart was too full of hate to show
it." Then rising again on his back legs, he howled so loudly that I
thought my eardrums would burst. "What have they done to my
precious boy!"

Dropping to the ground, he sent up a shower of snow, and
came towards me. "Where is this Elias Munn?" he growled so
deeply that his voice sounded like thunder.

"He went that way," I said, pointing in the direction that I had
last seen the truck heading.

Without saying another word, Seth bounded away into the
night.

"Wait for me!" I roared and raced after him. My feet crunched
through the snow, and I worked my arms like pistons beside me. I
stared ahead, and concentrated on catching the truck with Elias
Munn inside, the man who had caused so much pain. I thought of
my mother sitting with him and my heart ached for her – it ached
for my father, too. I had promised him that I would find her – and
even though I had, I'd lost her. Blood surged through my veins,
and with my heart pounding in my chest, I pushed on, faster, faster,
faster! My legs became a blur beneath me as I ploughed through
the snow, sending up a wake behind me. Then ahead, I could see
the taillights of the truck in the distance, their red glow shining
back at me. I saw something else, racing along beside the truck – it
was Seth. I thrust myself forward, my feet now almost seeming to
skim across the surface of the snow.

Ahead, I could see Seth racing along beside the truck as he
slammed his giant skull into the side of it. The truck lurched over,
its wheels raising up off the ground. He struck it again and the
truck almost skidded out of control. Faster and faster I went and
with every heartbeat I got closer and closer. It was as if my feet

were no longer touching the ground but treading air. I looked down and gasped, my feet really were no longer on the ground, but about seven feet above it. I looked back over my shoulder to see two shimmering wings protruding from my back. They stretched out on either side of me, black and sparkling as if showered with glitter. At the tip of each wing were those bony black fingers and they clutched at the air as if pulling me forward. I discovered that if I tilted my head up and placed my arms by my sides, I soared upwards. Looking down, I could see the truck snaking its way through the snow below me. Seth continued to race along beside it, smashing and crashing his great body into it.

On either side of me I felt a rush of air. I looked right and could see Isidor soaring beside me. I looked left and could see Kayla.

"You look beautiful, Kiera!" she yelled over the roar of the rushing wind and driving snow. "Awesome!"

I didn't know how I looked or felt, but to be able to race through the sky was a rush and I could feel adrenaline thundering through my body. I lowered my head and immediately began to lose altitude.

"Let's go and finish this!" Isidor bellowed at me. Then, with a grim look of determination on his face, he rocketed down towards the truck.

"See you later, alligator!" Kayla smiled as she banked left, then soared downwards.

"In a while, crocodile!" I yelled, racing after her.

With my wings rippling on either side of me like two giant sails, I raced back towards the ground. I swooped above the truck, and as I did, I saw Phillips and my mum soar out of the back and up into the sky. I watched my mother go, and half of me wanted to go after her. Kayla must have sensed my feelings, as she shouted over at me, "I've got her." Then Kayla was gone in pursuit of her. Isidor back-flipped through the air, and with a swift nod of his head in my direction, he soared after Phillips. Tucking my arms into my side, I aimed myself at the truck and dived towards it. When I was only feet away, a werewolf leapt from the rear of the truck and bounded away across the snow covered fields. I watched as Seth wasted no time in charging after Sparky.

That just left me and Elias Munn, who was still in the truck.

Drawing a lungful of ice cold air, I shot towards the back of the truck. With my hands stretched out before me, I grabbed the roof and climbed inside. It was dark, but looking through the darkness, I could see a figure huddled in the corner. He sat, bent forward, on a bench that ran the length of the cargo hold. His face was covered with a hood he had thrown over his head.

With my heart beating so fast in my chest I thought it might just explode, I approached Elias Munn. I stood before him. Slowly, he raised his head so as to look at me.

He pulled back the hood and said, "Hello, Kiera."

*"Doctor Hunt?"* I gasped as I staggered backwards, my heart almost breaking as I looked upon his face.

# Wolf House
## (Kiera Hudson Series One)
## Book 4.5
## Available Now

## More books by Tim O'Rourke

Vampire Shift (Kiera Hudson Series 1) Book 1
Vampire Wake (Kiera Hudson Series 1) Book 2
Vampire Hunt (Kiera Hudson Series 1) Book 3
Vampire Breed (Kiera Hudson Series 1) Book 4
Wolf House (Kiera Hudson Series 1) Book 4.5
Vampire Hollows (Kiera Hudson Series 1) Book 5
Dead Flesh (Kiera Hudson Series 2) Book 1
Dead Night (Kiera Hudson Series 2) Book 1.5
Dead Angels (Kiera Hudson Series 2) Book 2
Dead Statues (Kiera Hudson Series 2) Book 3
Dead Seth (Kiera Hudson Series 2) Book 4
Dead Wolf (Kiera Hudson Series 2) Book 5
Dead Water (Kiera Hudson Series 2) Book 6
Witch (A Sydney Hart Novel)
Black Hill Farm (Book 1)
Black Hill Farm: Andy's Diary (Book 2)
Doorways (Doorways Trilogy Book 1)
The League of Doorways (Doorways Trilogy Book 2)
Moonlight (Moon Trilogy) Book 1
Moonbeam (Moon Trilogy) Book 2
Vampire Seeker (Samantha Carter Series) Book 1

Printed in Great Britain
by Amazon.co.uk, Ltd.,
Marston Gate.